CW00727395

SO SHALL YOU REAP

A Selection of Recent Titles by Audrey Willsher

CANDLE IN THE WIND
THE SAVAGE TIDE
INHERIT THE EARTH*

* *available from Severn House*

SO SHALL YOU REAP

Book Two of A Leicestershire Chronicle

Audrey Willsher

This first world edition published in Great Britain 1997 by
SEVERN HOUSE PUBLISHERS LTD of
9–15 High Street, Sutton, Surrey SM1 1DF.
First published in the USA 1997 by
SEVERN HOUSE PUBLISHERS INC., of
595 Madison Avenue, New York, NY 10022.

British Library Cataloguing in Publication Data

Willsher, Audrey
So shall you reap
1. Domestic fiction
I. Title
823.9′14 [F]

ISBN 0-7278-5134-9

Typeset by Palimpsest Book Production Limited,
Polmont, Stirlingshire, Scotland.
Printed and bound in Great Britain by
Creative Print and Design Ltd., Ebbw Vale, Wales.

To Pam, Eileen, Mary and Monica with love

Chapter One

When, at three days old, her daughter Judith had opened her eyes and scowled at her, Charlotte Bennett wasn't surprised. In fact the resentment was mutual. What with sickness, swollen ankles, the pearly whiteness of her legs disfigured by a criss-cross of engorged purple veins, her social life curtailed, the whole nine months of pregnancy had been a misery. Then had come a long, exhausting labour, after which the doctor offered the opinion to Harry that it would be better if there were no more children.

Charlotte had heard these words with a sense of relief. "Thank heavens," she'd murmured, collapsing back on the pillows. Perhaps now there would be no more of 'that business'. Because, although she'd since heard that some women actually enjoyed it, the first night of her marriage had so shocked and disgusted her delicate sensibilities, Charlotte had wept in bewildered terror then demanded to be taken home to her father.

In spite of her distaste for such things, however, and the doctor's warnings, Harry's uncontrollable urges had resulted less than a year later in the birth of Olivia, who was now trailing some way behind Judith and Harry as they strode towards Charlotte across the sunlit lawn.

She's got the gait of a farm labourer, and she smells like one, thought Charlotte, wrinkling her nose in distaste as Judith threw herself down on the grass.

"We gave the horses their heads and had a good gallop this morning, didn't we Jude?" Dropping down beside his fourteen-year-old daughter, Harry ruffled her hair fondly.

"Mmm," Judith murmured and lay back and squinted up through the spiky branches of the Cedar of Lebanon that shaded them all.

"Must you call her Jude?" Charlotte asked in a peevish tone, then almost in the same breath, added, "And do you have to sprawl on the ground in such an unladylike manner, Judith? Sit up in a chair."

Judith, who knew there was little she could do that would please her mother, didn't budge. Instead she stretched her arms above her head, elongating even more her rangy, narrow-hipped body, over which Charlotte cast a despairing eye daily for signs of approaching womanhood. "I'm hot after the ride, let me get my breath back first, Mama," she answered a shade defiantly.

Her mother said nothing but gazed at her with cold eyes. Charlotte was seated in a wicker chair and at her elbow there was a table set with glasses and an earthenware pitcher Judith knew contained cold lemonade. She was dying for a drink but her head was now propped comfortably on her father's stomach and she couldn't find the the energy to move. She knew better, though, than ask her mother to pour a glass in her present mood.

By now a cross, panting Olivia had reached the small group and was helping herself to a drink.

"Pour one for me, too, Livvy, there's a dear," said Judith and lazily extended an arm.

"No. You're an absolute beast, you never wait for me, so get your own," Olivia snapped, then won her mother's instant approval by sitting down in one of the chairs and decorously arranging her riding habit about her.

"You shouldn't be such a slowcoach," Judith retorted.

"If I sat astride a horse like some common gipsy girl perhaps I wouldn't be. Not that I would ever want to be seen behaving in such an improper manner."

Charlotte's lips tightened into anger. "Judith . . . are you telling me . . . ?

Her daughter gave a nonchalant shrug. "Papa said I could. Anyway, I don't like riding side-saddle, it's for milksops."

"What you like or do not like is beside the point. Have you no sense of propriety?" Not sure who exasperated her the more, her husband or her daughter, she added sharply, "And you should know better too, Harry. In fact sometimes I think you are determined to turn her into a hoyden."

"Nonsense, my dear. She sits on a horse better than anyone I know. It's just a pity she isn't a boy for she'd have made a bally fine dragoon. Anyway, what's the harm at her age and on our own land. She will have restrictions put on her soon enough. Let her enjoy herself while she's still able to."

"It's hopeless talking to you."

Sensing a confrontation, Harry removed his daughter's head from his stomach and stood up. He had no taste for arguments, particularly with his wife, for they often developed into silences that could last for days.

"I must go and bathe and change. I leave for London this afternoon."

"You're always going to London, Papa," Judith wailed and scrambled to her feet as well.

"I am a Member of Parliament, pet, and therefore my attendance is required at the House from time to time. And we've got Reform rearing its head again. I need to be there to vote."

"For it or against it?" his wife asked.

"For it, my dear, naturally. The country's in such a state of strife we must be for it."

"Every stockinger and farm labourer will have the vote before long then heaven knows what will happen to us."

"If the franchise is extended, very little I should imagine. And certainly less than if we let things continue as they are. No, I doubt if anything will disturb our way of life."

Harry gazed around him with satisfaction, at the smooth green lawn sloping to a lake with its floating island of lily pads, then up to the house, Fern Hill. A wisteria, as old as the house itself, grew across its entire frontage, and today flowers hung from it like bunches of purple grapes. Situated some miles north of Halby and on the edge of the village of Stanton Parva, Fern Hill had been given to Charlotte and himself by his father-in-law on their marriage fifteen years before. It was as solidly built as a yeoman farmer, and he loved it dearly.

Was it worth the sacrifices he'd made? Realistically, Harry knew one couldn't have everything and by and large he considered himself fortunate, particularly on a golden June morning like this. His life, divided between being a country squire and his duties as a Member of Parliament, ran smoothly enough. And he had the girls, although, alas, no son, at least not a legitimate one. He'd gone into marriage with his eyes open and for purely mercenary reasons, he admitted that. The price though, had been a union that was empty and sterile. For Charlotte lovemaking was such an act of martyrdom, he hadn't touched her since Olivia was born.

He remembered still, with a sense of shame the years couldn't obliterate, that night Olivia was conceived.

In spite of the final, emotional meeting with Matilda

on the evening of the harvest home supper; her stricken response to his explanation that as the widow of his uncle, he was unable by law to marry her, then her emphatic denial that Adam was his son, he didn't really believe that she'd carry out her threat and set the dogs on him if he ever set foot on her land again. No one could switch off their feelings like that. He knew she loved him, knew that his sexual hold over her had been total. So, increasingly frustrated by his wife's coldness, a couple of months after Judith's birth, and confident that with time to think about it, Matilda would be just as eager to re-establish their old relationship, he'd ridden over to Trent Hall.

But she'd changed. Matilda was no longer the willing, infatuated young girl he'd seduced with such ridiculous ease. She was the one in control now, he the one who pleaded and poured out declarations of love. But if his words gave her some satisfaction, her features gave no hint of it and her face remained distant and unforgiving.

"I told you never to come here again, Harry, and I meant it. You took me for granted once too often. Thankfully you'll never be able to hurt me again. My feelings for you are quite dead." She pulled the bellrope by the fireplace. "See Mr Bennett out, Hodge."

He'd allowed himself to anticipate their reunion by indulging in memories of past amorous pleasures with her. And her iciness, instead of cooling his ardour, had made her twice as desirable so that he'd ridden home in a state of pent up sexual frustration and anger. Striding into the house he'd thought to himself, Matilda might reject me but by God I'll see to it Charlotte doesn't. It was her duty as a wife. As always, though, when he approached her, she shrank from him as if he were the devil incarnate. But that night he was having none of it. Deaf to her pleas he'd ripped her nightgown from neck to hem and taken her by force, smothering her screams with his hand. His shame afterwards had been total. The bruises on her body such a terrible reproach that when Olivia was born it was several weeks before he could bring himself to look at her. Neither had he made any objection when Charlotte moved out of their bedroom, and from then on he'd found consolation elsewhere, usually in London. For although Harry was a little heavier than in his youth, his jawline less well defined and his dark hair flecked with grey, the looking glass confirmed that the years had dealt kindly with him. With his charm still intact, Harry, at forty-three, was in the enviable position of being able to have the pick of almost any woman he chose.

He saw Matilda rarely, but if they did happen to meet at a social function she was aloof but polite, giving no hint of the pleasures they'd once shared in each others arms. Once he'd dared to ask after Adam and she'd replied, "He's growing into a fine young boy," then before he could question her further, she had turned to talk to someone else.

Over the years he'd watched with amazement, and some envy, as she took the depleted, debt-ridden estate his uncle had left her and turned it into a thriving concern. Now she was one of the most prosperous landowners in Leicestershire, someone to be reckoned with. Although he imagined that with her diamond-hard beauty, she must, once she was out of debt, have had plenty of offers, Matilda had never re-married. Harry often wondered why. Did she, in spite of what she said, still love him, or was it because she was reluctant to lose her independence? Perhaps she was waiting for someone to come along who could offer her a title.

He wouldn't put it past her. From hosier's daughter to a Lady – Matilda would relish that.

"Papa, I'm asking you a question, answer me." Judith was shaking his arm vigorously.

"What is it my love?" Still thinking of Matilda, Harry gazed at his daughter with an absent-minded expression.

"When will you be back from London?"

Remembering a fellow MP's wife, a delicious, plump creature who'd invited him to call on her next time he was in town, Harry did a swift calculation. "In about two weeks," he replied, thinking cynically to himself that her seduction probably wouldn't take half that time.

"As long as that?"

They were now walking towards the house together and putting an arm round his daughter, he pulled her to him. "Yes, sweetheart, as long as that. It's my job."

His daughter scowled up at him and to placate her he said, "Look, why don't we look for another pony for you when I get back, perhaps something a bit bigger. Toffee is getting a bit long in the tooth, she ought to be put out to grass. We'll go over to Halby. I know a Miss Dobbs who has stables there and we could see what she's got. Would you like that?"

The scowl vanished. "Oh Papa, I do love you." Grabbing her father's hand, Judith smothered it in kisses. She hated it when he went away and left her with Mama and her illnesses, eternal complaints and disapproval.

"But keep it under your hat. Not a word to your mother until I get back. And I want you to be nice to Olivia. If I hear of any unpleasantness, I'll have to think again about that new pony. Is that understood?"

Judith nodded her head vigorously.

"Off with you then, back to your mama and Olivia while I get changed and packed."

"Promise you won't go without saying goodbye."

"As if I would."

Judith let go of his hand reluctantly, ran a short way down the lawn, then to her mother's outraged disgust, she did three triumphant cartwheels in quick succession, while her father looked on with an indulgent smile.

It wasn't that she disliked her sister. No, mostly she loved Olivia, it was just that she sensed they were different. Although still several months off fourteen, Olivia had taken to preening herself in front of the looking glass and giggling when even the spottiest of youths hove into view. Her breasts were swelling too while Judith's remained as flat as Lincolnshire. Not that she wanted bosoms, Judith told herself as she slipped out of bed, they struck her as being the most awful nuisance.

When her father was away, and without her mother's knowledge, Judith often slept in his bed, forcing herself to stay awake, then creeping into his room when she was certain the house was quiet. The masculine smell of cigars, shaving soap and leather made up in some way for him not being there. Padding around the room now she examined souvenirs of Harry's army days, a badge, a spent bullet, castanets from Spain. She idly opened a drawer and fingered one of his silk shirts then on an impulse went over to his wardrobe and after rummaging around in its interior for some moments, drew out from the back an army jacket. In the drawing room there was a portrait of her father, painted when he was a dragoon and wearing the same jacket. Except that the blue had faded, the brass buttons were dull and the gold lacing tarnished. Removing her nightgown she slipped on a silk shirt then the jacket and went and stood in front of the the cheval glass. Scraping back her hair, Judith studied her thin white legs and homely features dispassionately. It was no good, no matter how hard she tried, she would never look like Papa. How handsome he must have been, how brave when he fought against Napoleon, she thought, rubbing her cheek along the coarse material of the sleeve. Although it was too large for her, wearing the jacket eased the loneliness of her father's absence. Dare she keep it on, she wondered. Go riding in it? Judith glanced at the clock. Seven. Certainly Mother wouldn't be up. She always breakfasted in bed and rarely rose before ten. Olivia was a different matter but if she kept quiet as a mouse, she might be able to slip out of the house and be away before she woke.

Judith smoothed out the pillow and linen sheets, pulled up the cover on the bed and quietly opened the door. After a quick glance up and down the hall to check that there was no servant around to see her in her half dressed state, she scampered back to her own room two doors down. She stepped hastily into a skirt and was still tucking the shirt into the waistband as she walked into the stable yard.

Toffee, her mare, was already saddled and when she saw her, Judith turned with a frown to Ned, the stable lad. "I thought I told you last night I didn't want the side saddle."

"Them's my instructions, Miss Judith."

"Who from?"

"The mistress. Miss Judith rides side-saddle or not at all. Them wa' her very words."

Her father she could twist round her little finger, but not Mama. Mama, Judith had realised long ago, didn't really care for her. It had hurt her as a child, later it had puzzled her. Now she had grown a skin of indifference over her pain and, like her father, avoided confrontation, dreading, like him, the recriminating silences that always ensued.

"Oh, very well." Scowling at the blameless Ned, she moved over with Toffee to the mounting block. She had adjusted her legs to the pommels and stirrup and was moving off, when Olivia came running into the yard, calling plaintively, "Wait for me, Jude, please."

"Damn and blast her!" She didn't realise she'd given voice to her annoyance until she saw Ned's rather reproving look, and this irritated her even more. Ignoring her sister's plea, she went to move off, then in time remembered her father's warning. No new horse. That could be the penalty for any unkindness to Olivia, because Papa could be surprisingly stern if promises were broken. Curbing her impatience, Judith pulled in her mare's reins, stared into the middle distance, and waited for Olivia to mount Lady Jane.

But Olivia found it served her better to ignore Judith's moods. And at least they passed quickly, which was more than could be said of their mother's. Besides, her attention had been caught by the odd assortment of garments Judith was wearing and as they moved out of the yard she studied her sister in silence for a few moments, giggled then asked, "What on earth have you got on, Jude?

"None of your business."

"It's Papa's army jacket, isn't it?"

"Why ask if you know?"

"You do look a sight and it's miles too big for you," Olivia said with sisterly honesty.

"Breathe a word to Mama and I shall never speak to you again. And if you're ashamed to be seen with me, you know what you can do. Turn round and go back. I'd prefer my own company anyway."

Judith moved off at a canter, but Olivia, who with her father's dark hair and blue eyes, was well on her way to being a beauty, disregarded the rebuff and continued to keep pace with her sister, giving her occasional sideways glances and wondering why she dressed so strangely. Eccentric, that's what Jude was, she decided. This was a word only recently added to her vocabulary and it pleased Olivia that she at last had a chance to use it. But she still couldn't understand why her sister spurned anything pretty and seemed often to deliberately set out to make herself look plainer than she actually was. Then there was this fondness for riding astride like a man, bareback even sometimes, showing her legs and driving Mama almost to apoplexy.

Olivia wanted to chat, but Judith refused to be drawn into conversation so they rode on in silence, until they reached a rough area of common. Here Judith could give Toffee her head and she was away.

Olivia made no attempt to keep up with her. If that's what she wants, let her go, she thought crossly. Although Olivia was a competent horsewoman she knew she was no match for her sister, who could outride almost anyone. And she had no wish to end up smelling of sweat and the stable yard, like Jude often did.

Although it was set to be another hot day, the air was still cool. Dew was cupped in the pink flowers of the blackberry bush, old man's beard twined its way along the hedgerows and Olivia could hear the the insistent rat-tat-tat of a woodpecker.

In her hurry Jude's missing all this, Olivia thought and shading her eyes, scanned the horizon for her sister. If they didn't want to be in hot water with Cook, they really should be turning back for breakfast. However, except for some young rabbits chasing each other joyously, the flat, scrubby common was devoid of life. In the distance the countryside became more undulating and a few oak trees were scattered along the skyline. Deciding not to wait for her sister, Olivia was just about to turn for home when she saw her move out from the shadow of some trees. Without pausing Toffee began to pick her way down a sheep track. At the same time Olivia became aware of two more figures on horseback, some way to the left of Judith. But she had no chance to wonder who they might be, because Toffee had reached the bottom of the track and a sudden movement in the gorse, the glimpse of a red brush perhaps, startled the mare, who shied suddenly. Caught off guard, Judith toppled backwards and landed heavily on the ground, with a yell that carried across the quiet morning fields.

Her sister had been thrown from too many horses for this to trouble Olivia, and she waited for her to do what she normally did, leap to her feet, brush herself down and remount immediately. Instead Judith lay very still.

"Dear Lord, what's she done?" Pushing her heel into Lady Jane, Olivia urged her into a gallop. By the time she reached the scene of the accident, the two strangers were already there and well in control of the situation, the boy trying to calm a still nervous Toffee, the girl solicitously attending to Judith, whose head was now resting on her lap.

It frightened Olivia to see Judith, usually so rumbustious and healthy, lying pale and still. Paying no attention to the other two she bent and took her sister's small rough hand. Rubbing it between her palms, she said in a voice that wasn't far from tears, "Judith, Judith, are you all right?"

"I think perhaps she's just a little stunned," said the girl in a voice that was meant to reassure, continuing with, "see, she's coming round," when Judith's eyelids began to flutter.

The young man, having calmed Toffee and tied her to a fence post, now joined them and as Olivia stood up he said, "You know this young lady then?"

"She's my sister. And we should be getting back." Now that she could see there was little wrong with Judith, a sisterly irritation began to surface. They were going to be most dreadfully late and Cook would report their inconsiderate ways back to Mama.

"She really ought to rest for a while," said the boy. His tone was polite but firm.

"There isn't time."

"Of course I can't stop you but I think it would be irresponsible to move her too quickly."

A trifle put out by his tone, Olivia studied him properly for the first time, saw a young man grown to almost six foot and just waiting to fill out; found herself staring into eyes that were blue like her own.

While they were sizing each other up, Judith stirred, became aware of gentle hands stroking her forehead and opened her eyes. Someone with the sweetest of smiles was gazing down at her. Dazzled by a halo of golden ringlets she blinked and knew she'd died, gone to heaven and was looking into the face of an angel.

Chapter Two

Chewing anxiously on her lip, Matilda stood at the window watching for Adam and Clare's return. She had some rather astounding news to relay to her niece and she still wasn't sure how she could word it to lessen the shock. In spite of his promises, there had been no communication from her brother George since he'd slunk away from her house in fear of his life more than fifteen years since. Her father had made extensive enquiries but, as a decade of silence came and went, Matilda came to assume that George must be dead. But now the prodigal son had returned to the fold, to be greeted with moist-eyed joy by her mother, who'd come rushing up with the news this morning, so early, Matilda was hardly awake.

Esther Pedley was plumper, her hair white, but the years hadn't dampened her Christian conviction that though it might take some finding, there was good in everyone, even her son, George. Having moved with unaccustomed speed from Thatcher's Mount to Trent Hall, she was panting from her exertions when she was shown into Matilda's bedchamber by the maidservant.

Her expression was radiant, though and she stood with her hand on her chest until she'd regained her breath then burst out, "The most amazing news, darling!"

"Wouldn't it have kept an hour or so, Mama? It is

rather early," answered Matilda, who was sitting up in bed and about to help herself from a tray set with a silver chocolate pot and transparent shavings of bread and butter. Shortly after Francis's death, Mrs Sawyer had departed to a better life as well, and Matilda now had Mrs White, an excellent, well-trained cook.

"You won't think so when you hear what I have to tell you." Mrs Pedley dropped with a gasp onto the bed, her weight nearly sending the contents of the tray flying. "I've prayed so often for this day, and finally the good Lord heard me." She placed the palms of her hands together and lifted her eyes piously to the ceiling.

"Prayed for what, Mama?" Matilda sipped her chocolate with growing impatience.

"Your brother's return."

"George?" Matilda spluttered, nearly choking on the hot drink. She put down her cup. "Are you telling me he's come home?"

"Yes, isn't it wonderful? He arrived by chaise from Leicester last night."

"Well I never." Matilda shook her head in disbelief then getting down to practicalities added, "Who's he running away from this time, his debtors?"

"Darling!" Esther Pedley's tone was reproachful.

"Well, I can't think of any other reason why he should return to the bosom of his family. It certainly can't be out of love for us." Matilda put the tray on a bedside table and flung back the bedclothes. "I suppose I'd better get dressed. What's my dear brother like now?"

"Oh, a little heavier," answered Mrs Pedley tactfully.

"Did he go to America?"

"It appears he didn't manage to get any further than London."

"And he couldn't even bother to scribble a few lines

to set your mind at rest and let you know he was still alive. How typical." Matilda snorted in disgust.

"I do think he's turned over a new leaf and he's very keen to see Clare. He didn't know he had a daughter."

"He hasn't actually made any attempt to find out, has he?"

"Try and be a little charitable darling, life hasn't been easy for him."

"Do you think it's been easy for me, Mama? I didn't get all this sitting on my derrière. I also had a child to raise, but I accepted my responsibilities and got on with it."

"I know, and you've done amazingly well." Mrs Pedley patted her daughter's hand placatingly. "But where is Clare? I was hoping to take her back with me."

"She's out riding with Adam. But telling the child her father has returned from the dead, so to speak, is going to be a tremendous shock. It's news that will have to be broken to her gently. You'd better leave it to me, Mama, then I'll bring her up to the house."

"If you don't mind, dear. George will probably sleep late anyway. The poor boy was absolutely exhausted when he arrived last night, so there's no hurry. And Matilda . . . try to sound a bit more pleased, if only for my sake." Esther Pedley entreated. "In spite of everything George is my son and, don't forget, your brother."

Matilda kissed her mother. "I'm very happy for you Mama and I'm sure he's a reformed character."

Her mother went then and while Ruth, her maid, dressed her hair, Matilda put these new worries aside briefly to study her reflection. Another year and she'd be forty, dreadful thought. Where had the years – her youth – gone? Into running the estate of course. Ruth was instructed to pull out any grey hairs she found and Matilda took trouble with her appearance and dressed fashionably. Never having had the opportunity to lead an indolent life, her muscles were taut, her figure trim, her mind sharp and her business sense as acute as any man's. Although Matilda had no intention of remarrying and losing control of all she'd worked for, men, thank heaven, still found her desirable. Over the years she'd had discreet liaisons with various gentlemen of the County, but although she could still experience a slight twinge of pain around the heart when she saw Harry, he'd taught her the folly of loving and her emotions were kept on a tight rein. This hadn't stopped her lovers expressing their appreciation with lavish gifts and she'd netted some fine pieces of jewellery, her little nest-egg as she liked to call it. Because one day she intended handing over the estate to Adam, and when she did, she would sell the jewellery and have a dower house designed and built to her own specification and taste.

"Is that to your satisfaction, Madam?" asked Ruth, giving a curl a final tweak with the comb.

"That will do nicely, Ruth." Matilda stood up and her maid helped her into her gown and buttoned it up at the back. As soon as she was dressed Matilda crossed to the window and Ruth began tidying the room.

"Come back later and do that," Matilda ordered.

"Right you are, Madam." With a brief curtsey, Ruth went, closing the door quietly and Matilda stood straining her eyes for her first sighting of her son and niece. How glad she was that they'd been honest with Clare about the circumstances of her birth. The scandal had given the gossips plenty to exercise their tongues on and it would have been impossible anyway to keep the truth from her in a small place like Halby. After Susan and Robert Levitt had died so tragically within two days of each other from the terrible fever that raged through the village, Clare gone to live with her other grandparents. Initially Joseph Pedley had sworn that no bastard child would darken his doorstep, particularly one who was most likely a simpleton like her mother. "The proper place for her is in the workhouse or lunatic asylum," he'd thundered in that charitable way of his.

But for once his wife had dug her heels in. "Simple or not, Clare is our granddaughter and entitled to our protection. George committed a terrible crime against Polly and I will not compound it with another. If you refuse to have her here then I will go and live with her in the cottage. She is a complete innocent and one way or another, I am determined to look after that child."

It was the first time in her life that Esther had dared to stand up to Joseph Pedley and he was astounded, and although he continued to bluster and fume, he knew he'd lost the argument. So at the age of two, Clare had moved from a humble cottage in the village to the relative comfort of Thatcher's Mount and taken the surname of Pedley. Just as at her birth she'd defied expectation and lived, so by some miracle, as she grew out of babyhood and began to talk and walk, it became apparent she was a normal healthy child. Sweet-natured too and so pretty she even, in time, melted her grandfather's flinty heart. Devoted to her cousin Adam, Clare moved easily between the two establishments of Thatcher's Mount and Trent Hall. Since children they'd been taught together, first by a governess and now a tutor, a Mr Christopher Harcourt, recently down from Oxford. Although they'd always been like brother and sister, Matilda was conscious that they were maturing into healthy young adults, and it worried her at times that their feelings for each other might develop into something more intense. Much as she loved Clare she didn't want Adam marrying his cousin. Polly's simple-mindedness had skipped a generation but there was no telling if it might re-emerge and she had no wish to be grandmother to children who weren't quite all there. Mr Harcourt was suggesting that he should be preparing Adam for university with extra lessons in Latin and Greek and although she would miss her son desperately, Matilda knew she had to start giving it serious thought. Adam needed to get away from Halby for a few years, sow his wild oats like any normal young man and see a bit of the world.

Although she still had no idea how she was going to break the news to Clare, as soon as Matilda saw Adam and her niece cantering across the field she ran down to greet them. They were talking animatedly as they crossed the stable yard and dismounted and when she saw her aunt, Clare, blond ringlets dancing, brown eyes alight, rushed over to Matilda, the words bubbling out of her in her eagerness to tell the story of their adventure that morning.

"Sorry we're late, Aunt Tilda, but we met this extraordinary girl who'd taken a tumble, and her si . . ."

But Matilda was so preoccupied she hardly heard the girl's chatter. "Clare, I think you ought to get home quickly."

"But we've got French this morning." Previously Clare had found conjugating French verbs extremely tedious, but that was before Mr Harcourt, whom she considered very handsome, had arrived at Trent Hall.

"It will have to keep. Something more important has cropped up. Something that concerns you directly."

"How mysterious! What is it?"

"Come inside for a moment." Matilda took her niece's arm and drew her towards the house.

"Do you want me to come as well?" called Adam, who'd been giving instructions to the stable lad.

"I'd prefer to speak to Clare on her own if you don't mind, dear. Anyway I expect you're hungry."

"You bet I am. Famished, in fact."

"You run along and have breakfast, darling. And explain to Mr Harcourt for me that Clare will be a little late."

"Oh all right." Looking mighty relieved, Adam vanished into the house.

"But I'm hungry too," complained Clare.

"Grandmama will give you breakfast, don't worry." While she spoke, she guided her niece up the steps and into her small office.

"Sit down dear."

"My, you do look serious Aunt Tilda," Clare said, laughing. "What is it all about?"

Matilda inhaled deeply and took the plunge. "There is someone to see you at Thatcher's Mount."

"To see me?" questioned Clare. Her sweet face looked puzzled as she thought who it might be. "Is it Jed and Rachel?" she asked, for apart from them she knew few people outside Halby.

Matilda, who was finding it harder than she'd imagined, shook her head.

"Who then?"

"This is going to be something of a shock for you, I fear." Matilda took her niece's hand in what she hoped was a reassuring gesture. "You know that Polly, your mother, died when you were born."

"Yes."

"You know too that your father was my brother, that he wronged Polly deeply and went away. Since that day no one has heard a word from him and in time we came to assume he was dead. Until this morning."

Matilda felt a tremor in Clare's fingers. "Wh you mean?"

"Well last night he turned up at Thatcher's Mount and is there waiting for you."

"Are you telling me I have a father?"

"You have indeed," Matilda replied and felt a father in Clare's life, especially someone like George, might prove something of a mixed blessing.

It was a great deal to take in and Clare stared back at her aunt with a bewildered expression. "I don't know what to say Aunt Tilda."

"I understand, and it's going to take some getting used to. But knowing George he might be gone again tomorrow for another fifteen years so you'd better go and make his acquaintance while you have the chance. By all accounts he's most anxious to see you."

"Supposing he doesn't like me?"

Matilda laughed. "What a ridiculous notion. How could he help but like you?"

"Must I go on my own?"

"Of course not. I shall come with you. Wait here while I go and get my bonnet."

Normally Clare was quite a chatterbox but this morning, walking along Blackthorn Lane to the house, she chewed on a blade of grass in a preoccupied manner. But then I feel uneasy myself, thought Matilda. Trust George to come back and upset the apple cart. No doubt he was on his uppers and on the scrounge. But he wouldn't get a penny from her and she doubted if Papa would feel too generous. In that optimistic way of hers, Mama seemed to think George had changed for the better, but Matilda doubted it. Trouble spread like a disease when her brother was around and he wouldn't be welcomed by the villagers, who had long memories and bore their grudges like a badge of honour.

"I hope your grandmama has some cold drinks prepared," said Matilda, stopping to fan herself and draw breath before pushing open the gate of Thatcher's Mount.

Clare didn't answer, for too many thoughts were buzzing around in her head. Halby was quiet so not much happened in her life, but in the space of a few short hours she'd met two interesting girls, who she'd love to be friends with and gone from being an orphan to having a father. A shadow hovered briefly in the window as they walked up the path, and, knowing she was being assessed by her father, Clare's cheeks flushed pink. Would she be up to the mark as a daughter? She didn't know because it wasn't something she'd ever had any practice at.

They went round the back and into the cool stone-flagged kitchen, where Prudence, the young maid-servant, was slicing cold ham onto plates for their breakfast, assisted by Mrs Pedley. "Ah, here you are my dear." She took her granddaughter's arm and felt a resistance, a nervous pulling back. But she was having none of it. "Come, your papa is in the drawing room and dying to see you."

George was standing facing the door when they entered, and what struck Matilda immediately was the size of her brother's girth. It had expanded threefold. A pale straggly moustache couldn't disguise his pendulous cheeks, or his several chins, so that there was something faintly ludicrous about the abundance of blond curls. He is two years younger than me and yet he looks at least fifty. The thought comforted Matilda.

"Hello, George." Matilda spoke as casually as if they'd parted only yesterday. Neither did she rush to embrace her long-lost brother, that would have been hypocritical.

"Hello, Matilda," he answered, his eyes moving past her to Clare. "So this is my little girl. Well, are you going to give your papa a kiss?" George held out his arms and Clare went to him and obediently kissed him on the cheek. Then he held her away from him and studied her with interest. Polly being a few pennies short of a shilling, he hadn't been sure what to expect, but, by gad, this child was a beauty. Took after him, obviously, although she had her mother's trusting brown eyes. It struck him that she could be a means of solving his financial problems too. If I took her to London, paraded her around a bit, I might have her wed within the year to some rich young buck, or an old one come to that. But she'd only go at a price, then *voilá*, his debts would be settled, his problems solved forever and Lord Slepe could go to the devil. His Lordship had accused him of cheating him at cards, then the damned fool of a man had demanded satisfaction. That had frightened the wits out of George, particularly since his Lordship was a renowned shot. Hence his hasty departure from London. Once the dust had settled, he would go back, though, for he had no intention of permanently exchanging the fleshly pleasures of London for dreary Halby. Of course, getting Clare to London wouldn't be without its complications, especially under the eagle eyes of Mama and Matilda. And even if he did persuade them, she would have to be chaperoned, so it would need careful planning.

"Shall we go in to breakfast then?" George heard his mother say.

"Of course, Mother." Taking Clare's hand, George drew it through his arm and patted it in a fatherly manner. "As long as my enchanting daughter can sit next to me."

George pulled a chair out for Clare, sat down beside

her and surveyed the repast with satisfaction. At least his mother hadn't lost her touch. The table was set out with home-cured ham and boiled eggs, curls of golden butter nestled on sprigs of green parsley, there was freshly baked bread and milk from the dairy as well as coffee and home-brewed beer.

Wasting no time, George tucked in. "Bit peckish don't you know," he said and piled his plate high with cold ham.

By the way she glanced shyly at George from time to time, it was obvious Clare was still coming to terms with having a father and Matilda wondered what she made of him. There must be questions she was dying to ask, although whether her father would give her a satisfactory answer was quite another matter.

Finally, Clare managed to overcome her nervousness and, turning to her father, asked, "How long are you staying, Pa . . . Papa?" She blushed prettily as she tried out the unfamiliar word.

George tore off a hunk of crusty bread and covered it with butter. "Well, I'm not in any hurry to move off." Not until the air had cooled in London at least.

"Oh I am glad, dear." Mrs Predley beamed fondly at her son and Matilda snorted.

"Did you say something, Matilda?" her mother enquired.

"Not a word."

"I sense my sister is thinking plenty, though. She could afford to be charitable as well. After all I've been down on my luck whereas the years have treated her kindly."

Matilda bristled. "Any success I've had is through sheer hard work, dear brother. Francis left me nothing but debts." Fearing she might lose her temper and spoil things for Clare, Matilda stood up. "Anyway, I'd better get back to Trent Hall. I have to go into Leicester on Wednesday to see the corn chandler and in the meantime I've some sums to do."

"May I come with you to Leicester, Aunt Matilda? asked Clare. "It's such ages since I visited town."

"Of course, my dear."

George leaned back in his chair. "I wouldn't mind a trip in myself, visit some of my old haunts y'know."

"Yes, why don't you all go?" suggested Mrs Pedley, "make a day out of it."

"That sounds a splendid idea to me," said George, lifting his tankard and downing the beer in one go.

"Promise me faithfully, Olivia, that you will not breathe a word to Mama about our adventure this morning," said Judith as the sisters trotted their horses home for breakfast. "If she finds out what happened she's quite likely to forbid us go out on our own again."

"And whose fault would that be?" Olivia snapped. "Anyway, for your information, I don't go telling tales."

"I know you don't," said Judith, anxious to placate her sister.

"I thought you were dead, you know," Olivia accused.

"Me! It would take more than a fall from Toffee to kill me," Judith scoffed.

"I'd like to know how you're going account for the great bump on your forehead. It's swollen to the size of an egg already."

"I'll say I hit it on a branch, don't worry."

Olivia shrugged. "Let's hope Mama believes you." Then turning to a vastly more interesting subject, she asked, "Who do you think that boy and girl were who helped us? He was very handsome, don't you think?"

"Yes, I suppose so," answered Judith who only had

the vaguest memory of what he looked like. But not the girl, she could remember every feature of her beautiful face; her soft cheeks, that sweet smile, the halo of curls. Still slightly dazed from her fall, Judith wafted off into a dream and imagined them running together through a field of corn, golden as the girl's hair. She must see her again. But what was her name? She had to know. In the meantime Angel, for that was how she thought of her, seemed a very fitting title.

Chapter Three

No peace for the wicked, thought Rachel. She gave a resigned sigh, turned over in bed, pulled a blanket over her ears and tried to blot out the all too familiar sounds of her sons, Simon and Benjamin, locked in mortal combat. However, the thumps and squeals of anguish were reaching a level she could no longer ignore. Exasperated, she pushed herself up into a sitting position and banged on the wall. "Will you two be quiet, please."

The commotion subsided, then after a pause, Simon, the elder of the two, called back meekly, "Yes, Mama." But Rachel guessed it wouldn't be long before hostilities were resumed and gazing down at Jed, she envied him his ability to sleep through any turmoil. There was one thing guaranteed to wake him though. With a secret smile, Rachel slipped down between the sheets and ran her hands lightly over her husband's body.

In an instant Jed's eyes were open. "Are you molesting me, woman?"

"I am at that," Rachel giggled and reaching out Jed pulled her into his arms. Nuzzling her neck, he slowly hoisted her nightgown.

Rachel responded with enthusiasm and, unable to hold their desire for each other in check a second longer, Jed was easing himself on top of his wife when the door slowly opened and a small voice pleaded, "Mama, Papa, may I come in with you?"

"Go away, child," Jed ordered.

But seven-year-old Benjamin knew his papa didn't mean it and they hardly had time to draw apart before their youngest son had scrambled up onto the bed and plonked himself down between them.

Jed groaned with frustration and closed his eyes. Leaning over his father, Ben prised open an eyelid and enquired innocently, "Why are you groaning, Papa?"

"Because it is Sunday morning, little fellow, and your Mama and me were hoping for an extra hour in bed."

"Well you still can," his son informed him, and with no sense of not being wanted, he put a further divide between his parents, by snuggling down between them and shoving his thumb in his mouth. Rachel gazed down at her youngest child, at the dark curling lashes, the button nose and plump cheeks and felt a great rush of tenderness. She found motherhood intensely satisfying and considered herself blessed to have three lovely children and a fine husband like Jed. Over her son's head she smiled at her husband and mouthed, "Later."

But the 'later' seemed set to recede even further when Simon burst into the room, closely followed by fourteen-year-old Emily bearing a tray of tea, which she placed on a side table.

But Emily, older and more thoughtful by nature, sensed that her parents wanted time to themselves. Leaning over, she lifted her squirming brother out of the bed and carried him from the room. "Mama and Papa want some peace," she said, when he began protesting loudly. "You too," she called to Simon who had ducked down on the other side of the bed.

Rachel laughed as the door closed. "Determined, that's our Emily. Leave it her, she'll always sort things out. Later it will be the world she's putting to right, just like her father."

"Well she might have my character but she's got your looks."

"Except for that determined chin," Rachel said, laughing.

"Yes, she'll be a great asset in the shop once she's finished her schooling."

Rachel poured the tea and handed a cup to her husband. "When will that be?"

"Business isn't bad so I think we can afford to let her stay on another year."

"She's a good scholar, she'll be pleased." Rachel drank her tea sitting on the edge of the bed, then went and poured water from a jug into a bowl before pulling off her nightgown.

For Jed it was an unending pleasure to watch Rachel prepare herself for the day, and he lay back with his arms behind his head. Although her figure was fuller, her breasts slightly less firm after three children, in his eyes, this didn't detract from her beauty. His desire for her still hot in his loins, he held out his arms. "Rachel, turn the key in the door and come here," he called quietly

Rachel smiled languidly, dried herself, locked the door and padded over to her husband. He reached out for her and she went to him and although Ben's plaintive voice could be heard on the other side of the door from time to time, their passion for each other was so strong it could even exclude their children.

Jed lay for a while after Rachel had gone to prepare breakfast and thought about his life. By and large he was very content. And how could it be otherwise with Rachel for a wife and the three healthy children she'd given him? The bookshop, while not making them rich, provided a reasonable living and although he hadn't abandoned his political activities, the years, plus the responsibilities of family life, had made him less hot-headed than in the past. He was aware of the dangers of seditious literature being found on the premises, was sensitive to Rachel's fears, knew it was her great terror that there might be a repetition of those months he'd spent in prison before their marriage. He had no wish to spend further time in jail either, but he suspected that, as a known trouble-maker, government agents kept an eye on him.

For the government was twitchy and only last year a revolt of desperate, starving agriculture labourers, wanting only a living wage, had been brutally suppressed. As an example to others who might be similarly inclined, nine men were hanged and over four hundred transported. But as far as Jed was concerned the real trouble lay with politicians determined to look after their own interests. A few enlightened Members of Parliament saw the dangers of a dissatisfied population, but a Bill for reform, put before the House in March, had been defeated by ignorant men without the sense to know that they might soon have a civil war on their hands.

But now the Bill was coming up for a second reading in the Commons and although he had no influence over the results, this time Jed intended to be there. It was cowardly, he knew, but he still hadn't plucked up courage to tell Rachel and he was off in a couple of days.

Jed tried to raise the subject several times during breakfast, but always one of the children piped up with some question or other and Rachel went off to church still not knowing his plans. Jed stood and watched his family's progress down High Cross Street with a fond eye; Ben holding his mother's hand, Emily quite the little lady, walking a few paces behind while Simon slouched along grumbling at the double indignity of having to wear his Sunday best and sit through a boring sermon. Jed, who viewed the church with the same disdain as he did the government, sympathised with his son. Nevertheless he was sensitive to Rachel's reasons for wanting to attend, so held his counsel. After her own harsh early years, it was all part of the security and respectability she yearned for, and which she was determined her children would have in abundance.

Sunday dinner was finished, Rachel was clearing the plates and Jed still hadn't got round to telling her.

"You're quiet, Jed," Rachel said, placing the cheese dish in front him. The children were fidgeting to leave the table and she let them go with the warning that they were not to play in the street, it being Sunday.

Jed cut a chunk of ripe Stilton, helped himself to a piece of bread and cleared his throat. "Rachel, I'm going down to London on Wednesday to meet up with a group of Radicals."

"Whatever for?" Rachel, who'd sat down, stood up again.

"A second Bill is being brought forward in Parliament. It must go through this time and I want to be there when it does."

"Oh Jed, I thought you'd put all this behind you!"

He clasped her hand. "This is important, Rachel. It's about democracy and surely you care about that?"

"I care more about you staying out of prison. And anything could happen in London. There's always trouble from the mob at these times. Supposing the military are called out? In one slash of a sword I could be a widow, the children fatherless."

Jed shook her hand and laughed. "That's looking a bit on the the black side, isn't it? If I swear I won't do anything foolish, and stay well away from trouble, will that reassure you?"

"Not really. But nothing I say is going to stop you, is it? Your mind is made up already."

Jed shrugged, unwilling to admit that it was.

"So who's going to run the shop, pray?"

"I had hoped you would?"

"On my own, with three children to look after as well? It seems I have to pay highly for your self-indulgence."

"Please, Rachel, don't be angry."

Rachel went and stood by the window. "I can't help it. Why do politics always have to come first? I sometimes wonder how much your family mean to you."

Jed went over to his wife and pulled her round to face him. "Everything, you know that. But wrongs have to be righted and surely you don't think things should continue as they are?"

"We manage to make a reasonable living and none of us go hungry," answered Rachel then immediately felt ashamed of her small-minded view of the world.

"It isn't just for us, it's for our children's children; all the generations that will follow after us."

Rachel admired Jed his ability to see everything in the long term. When she locked up the house at night all that concerned her was that her family were safe within its walls. It was about as much as she could cope with.

"When I get back we'll hire a waggon and take the children on a picnic to Bradgate Park, would you like that?"

"You don't have bribe me Jed, but you're to be away for no longer than a week, is that clear?"

Jed kissed her soundly. "You're a wonderful girl, Rachel."

"Oh yes." Rachel leaned back and smiled at him. "You might not think so when I tell you who's coming to tea."

"Go on, tell me."

"The Brewin girls."

Jed groaned. "Not all four of them at once, it's more than flesh and blood can stand." Rachel was very fond of the sisters but Jed quickly tired of their inconsequential chatter.

"Yes, and see that you're nice to them. We were talking after church. Lily has an admirer and she's dying to tell us about him."

"I bet the other three are green with envy, her being the youngest."

"A little bit of sisterly jealously would be natural, I suppose."

"Jack will be pleased, knowing there's a chance he might get a daughter off his hands. But if you don't mind I'll make myself scarce when they arrive, go and see to some accounts in the shop."

"Oh no you won't. I'm letting you go to London, so in return you can stay and help entertain them."

Jed gave her a martyred look. "Oh, all right."

"And now I must wash the pots, then make some scones and sandwiches – they'll be here at four o'clock."

It was rare for her and Jed to be parted, but whenever they were, Rachel could never rid herself of a sense of unease. She knew it was a hangover from those months he'd spent in prison before they were married and though he'd promised to stay clear of trouble in

London, she'd seen too many examples of Jed's reckless behaviour to be entirely reassured.

Fortunately there wasn't time to brood. Shopping, cooking and attending to the children all had to be fitted in between running the shop, which after all was what provided them with their bread and butter.

The day following Jed's departure the shop was particularly busy. Rachel closed for the dinner hour but when she came downstairs again at two o'clock and pulled up the blind a young, smartly dressed young woman was already hovering outside.

Rachel held open the door and the girl, a smile on her face, stepped over the threshold. "Hello, Rachel."

"Clare, good heavens, I didn't recognise you." Rachel stood back and studied Polly's daughter. "My, you've really grown up."

Clare, who'd found childhood tedious, looked pleased. "Do you think so?"

"Yes, a real young lady and a very pretty one at that. But what's brought you into Leicester in this heat?"

"I came with Aunt Tilda and Adam. They've gone off somewhere to talk business and I'm supposed to be looking at bonnets and gloves. But I decided I'd rather come and see you."

"You'd better not tell your aunt, we're not the best of friends."

"Grandmama won't mind me visiting you. Anyway I've got the most astonishing news." Clare was about to launch into her tale when a customer interrupted their tête à tête. He was immediately followed by a scholarly gentleman with a long list of books, some of which weren't in stock and had to be ordered. Clare stood glaring at the man's thin neck and willing him to go, but it was a good ten minutes before Rachel bid him good afternoon. "Well, tell me your news, then," she said at last.

"Guess who turned up in Halby the other night?"

Rachel, who was still writing out the order, dipped her pen in the inkpot. "I've no idea."

"Papa."

Shock immobilized Rachel and the ink dripped from her pen onto the paper and spread into huge spidery blobs. After a moment she turned her head slowly. "Do you mean George?"

"Yes, my papa. Imagine, after all these years! Isn't it exciting?"

Rachel, who'd hoped he was dead, didn't answer. Instead she started to write again, but her hand had developed such a tremor she had to put the pen down. "What brought him back to these parts?" Rachel was surprised how casual her question sounded when her thoughts were in turmoil.

Clare, who wasn't sure herself, shrugged. "To see me perhaps. He's been telling me all about London as well, the theatres, the fashions and he says he wants to take me down there and show me all the sights. Wouldn't that be just wonderful? Halby is so terribly dull." Clare clapped her hands in innocent delight and in that moment, her resemblance to her dead mother, Polly, was so strong, Rachel was overwhelmed by an awful dread.

She knew that George wouldn't have dared set foot in Halby while Susan and Robert were alive, but it must have slipped George's mind that Jed had also threatened to kill him, both for the harm he'd done to Polly and his attempted rape of her. Rachel doubted if Jed's hatred had been diluted much by time, so it was imperative that the news was kept from him, or a bloody encounter could ensue.

"So where is your father today?"

"At home. Both he and Grandmama intended coming with us but then decided it was too hot."

Her fear was irrational, Rachel knew that, because he would never dare come near the shop, but even knowing he was in the area had the power to chill her blood. "And what does your grandmama say to you going to London?"

Clare pulled a face. "She tells me I am far too young and if I do go, she will see she comes with me as my chaperone."

Rachel felt easier. Mrs Pedley was a sensible woman, a trifle doting where her children were concerned, but she would make sure her granddaughter came to no harm.

"I must go. I promised Aunt Tilda I would meet her outside The Bell Hotel at three o'clock, and I had better not be late. First, though, I must purchase a book. Recommend a novel, Rachel."

Rachel reached up to a shelf behind her. "What about *Ivanhoe*? I think you would enjoy that." She wrapped the novel, handed it to Clare and went to the door with her. Emily was dawdling along the street, swinging her school books and daydreaming as usual. Rachel waved to her daughter and called, "Come and say hello to Clare."

But Clare was waving to a young man a few yards behind Emily, and as he approached, Rachel was unnerved by his resemblance to Harry. Put him in a uniform and he would almost be his double, she thought, and wondered how Matilda explained their likeness away. Adam had caught up with Emily by the time they reached the shop and they stood for a moment, scrutinizing each other, with more interest than Rachel cared for.

Adam bowed courteously as he was introduced by Clare but he was obviously in a hurry. "I don't want to be rude, but I've been sent in search of you. Mama wants to be away."

Rachel leaned forward and kissed Clare affectionately. "Now promise me you won't leave it so long before you come and see us again."

"I promise."

Adam took his cousin's arm and led her off down the street. Standing watching them, Rachel wondered if he'd inherited his father's reprobate ways along with his looks.

"He's rather handsome, don't you think?" said Emily, who was observing Adam with a young girl's eye.

Rachel gave her daughter a sharp look. "It's character that counts, not looks."

"Well he might have a nice character too."

"Clare is kin but I wouldn't give you tuppence for the rest of that family. I skivvied for them and there's not a thing I don't know about Matilda and her brother. She's spoilt and self-willed, he's loathsome." Rachel was about to add, "And your father nearly killed George once," but changed her mind. Opening old wounds, stirring up old hatreds, served no purpose.

But anxiety continued to press in on her and before she went to bed, Rachel double-checked that every door was secured with locks and bolts; all windows closed in spite of the heat. But George had already cast his malign shadow and, waking early, Rachel sat drinking tea and silently berating Jed for leaving her unprotected when she needed him most.

Chapter Four

For several days after the accident, the sisters made a daily pilgrimage to the spot where Judith had been thrown, and here they hung around in the hope of seeing the young man and girl who'd so taken their fancy. Each time their hopes were dashed, though, and they would return home in a state of snappy discord.

They might have gone on putting themselves through this daily purgatory if Harry hadn't returned home bearing gifts: a hand-painted fan for Judith and an embroidered reticule for Olivia. And, with his tales of London, seeming to wave a magic wand that banished the gloom that hung over the house while he was away. Happily, their preoccupation with the mysterious young couple also faded from their thoughts.

Only at the dinner table did their father become serious and start discussing politics, a subject for which Judith cared little. A few evenings after his return she sat chewing in a bored fashion on a piece of meat, and only half listening as her mother asked, "What happened about this Bill you went down to London about, Harry?"

"It has to go to committee stage so we won't know definitely until October."

"But it looks set to go through?"

Harry shrugged. "Who can say? There are plenty of diehards in Parliament, but we remain hopeful."

Her parents didn't exactly go in for what Judith considered scintillating repartee, but she still knew better than to interrupt. Their father was inclined to take them to task for their lack of interest in politics, and she was anxious not to upset him tonight. The conversation between her parents soon dwindled to mere pleasantries but she had the sense to wait until the fruit came before putting the question she been dying to ask all evening to her father. "Now you are back, Papa, may we go and look at a pony? You promised to buy me one, remember."

"So I did. Tell you what, I'll send Ned with a message to Miss Dobbs and we'll ride over to Halby on Saturday."

Charlotte, who was bisecting a peach with a small silver fruit knife, looked up. "I assume Olivia is being allowed a pony, too. You cannot favour one girl above the other."

Harry smiled at his younger daughter. "Of course Olivia shall have one."

"Thank you, Papa, but I am perfectly happy with Lady Jane. If you don't mind though I'd like to come with you just the same."

The following Saturday, while Charlotte rested with a novel, Harry and his two daughters set off for Halby, Judith and Olivia in the gig, Harry riding behind. Judith, who had taken the reins, was wearing a comfortable but shabby riding habit. Olivia, in contrast, was dressed modishly in a pale lemon dress with such exaggerated puffed sleeves they took up most of the space in the gig. Under her bonnet, her glossy ringlets bobbed against her cheeks and although it was finery hardly appropriate for a visit to a stableyard, she delighted the eye of every passer-by.

"I don't know if I mentioned it, but Miss Dobbs also has a racing stud. She advertises under her manager's name for obvious reasons, and between them they've bred a few winners. But then she's always been an outstanding horsewoman. Still it does seem a surprising business for a vicar's daughter to be in, even so," Harry mused.

"She's not married is she Papa?" asked Judith.

"No, she isn't. Poor Jane, her looks always went against her."

"And her father, is he alive?"

"The Reverend Dobbs passed on some ten years ago."

"Then who is to support her?" Judith queried. "She can't starve and if I had to choose, I'd rather work with horses any day than act as governess to someone else's horrible brats."

"You are right there, my dear. Without adequate funds life is a struggle," Harry replied and wondered what his own circumstances might have been if he hadn't married Charlotte. Whatever the disadvantages, at least there was no chance of the coffers suddenly emptying, for Charlotte's father had been an extremely wealthy man. The cunning old devil had taken the precaution of tying a large part of it up in trust for Charlotte, as well as for the girls when they reached twenty-one, although not all of it. The old man had been realistic about his plain daughter's chances of matrimony and a carrot had needed to be dangled as an inducement.

As they drove into Halby and up Main Street, Harry moved out in front and called to Judith, "It's the gate just after the church."

A minute or so later they drove into the stableyard and a large, florid woman in an ill-fitting dress and man's jacket came out to greet them. "Harry, how nice to see you." Jane held out a work-roughened hand as Harry dismounted and he took it and gallantly pressed it to his lips.

"Lovely to see you too, Jane."

"So these are your daughters?" Jane smiled at the girls.

"This is my little tomboy, Judith," said Harry and affectionately patted his daughter's tousled mop.

"How do you do, Miss Dobbs," said Judith matter-of-factly as she jumped down from the gig and began prowling around the yard. She loved that stable smell of straw, leather, urine and manure. If only she could do something like this. But it was out of the question, she knew that. Her future was already mapped out: imprisonment in marriage and motherhood. The very idea made Judith want to vomit. Oh, how she envied Miss Dobbs.

"And that is Olivia," Harry went on with an indulgent laugh, as his younger daughter, who had no intention of spoiling her pretty dress, called plaintively, "Papa, help me down please."

Observing the sisters, Jane thought, chalk and cheese. One like Harry, one plain, poor girl. Knowing the anguish a lack of looks could cause, Jane felt an immediate sympathy with Judith.

"I shall go for a walk," Olivia announced and picked her way daintily out of the yard.

"Only Judith is going to relieve me of my money today," Harry explained. "Olivia is quite happy with the horse she has."

"What had you in mind, my dear?" asked Jane.

"Something a bit lively, Miss Dobbs. Toffee, my present pony, is getting long in the tooth."

"A thoroughbred mare would cost your papa ten

guineas, all others are three guineas. I've got four of my ladies up in the paddock, shall we go and have a look at them?" Jane suggested and led them up a short track to where several horses grazed. "Here girls," Jane called and the mares came trotting over, nuzzling her for the tit-bits Jane had hidden in various pockets.

"Wing was covered recently and is in foal, so you can't have her, but what about Star here?" said Jane indicating to a bay mare with a white blaze on her nose. "She's barren, poor lady, so I could let you have her for four guineas. I'm sure you'll enjoy riding her, she's frisky but good-natured."

The confident way in which Miss Dobbs bargained impressed Judith deeply. "What do you think, Jude? Would she suit you?" she heard her father say.

The mare's muzzle was soft on Judith's hand as she fed her a carrot and her heart was won. "Can I take her out and see how we get on together?"

"Of course. I'll get her saddled and Reuben, my manager, can come with you."

"I shall be quite all right on my own, Miss Dobbs, really."

"I think we'll do as Miss Dobbs suggests," Harry said in a voice Judith had learned not to argue with.

"As you say, Papa."

Reuben Smith was a large, coarse-featured man with a bit of the didikoi about him, Harry reckoned. He also addressed Jane in an overly familiar manner, and this put Harry's back up. Not a man he warmed to on first acquaintance.

It was apparent Jane valued him though, and her remarks confirmed it as they watched him ride out of the yard with Judith. "I don't know how I'd manage without Reuben. He's a genius with horses. It's because of him I've had some racing successes. One of my horses,

Sorcerer, recently beat a large field in the two-year-old stakes at Doncaster, then he did it again at York." Jane spoke with some pride.

"Where did you hire Reuben from?"

"He just turned up one day looking for work and I took him on."

"Was that wise?"

Jane gave him a sideways glance. "I know you think him rough and ready, most people do, but I trust him."

"I'm glad to hear it. Do you know anything of his background?"

"He's never spoken of it and I've never asked. I needed a man about the place. It's hard work for a woman on her own. I see he bathes regularly, so don't worry, he won't offend your nostrils. And I'd choose my life any day to poor old Grace's."

Harry had almost forgotten Jane had a sister. "How is Grace?"

"Perpetually pregnant and her husband's a clergyman in one of the poorest parishes in Leicester. My mares have a more comfortable existence than Grace. I try my best to help and I always have some of the children over in the summer to give her a break. Now," she said, becoming businesslike again, "shall we go into the house and settle our business over a glass of something? Reuben can then ride Star over to your place tomorrow."

Jane was about to turn away when Harry saw her glance over his shoulder. "Oh!" she exclaimed. Her already ruddy features went dark red with embarrassment and Harry knew it was Matilda.

Harry had half hoped he might bump into Matilda and he watched her now with a mixture of emotions as she crossed the yard towards them.

"Hello, Matilda."

She'd been staring intently at the cobbles, pretending she hadn't seen him, and she looked up with an expression of surprise. "Oh, hello, Harry."

In many ways, Harry decided, his uncle dying leaving Matilda in debt had done her a favour. Hardship had erased the girlish petulance and she was now a self-possessed, beautiful and extremely desirable woman. The disadvantage was that, whereas in her youth she'd been pliant and willing, now she was shot through with steel, at least as far as he was concerned. But he would woo her again, Harry decided, win her and gain access to her bed. Matilda had always participated enthusiastically in their lovemaking, risen to heights of inventiveness when locating places for their assignations. At this age, too, women were at their sexual peak, plus along the way she would have learned some new tricks.

Glad that his hacking jacket hid his rising excitement Harry turned to Jane who, confronted with this embarrassing social situation, began to babble. "Harry's here buying a horse for his daughter."

"Don't worry, Jane, I shan't be stopping."

"There is no need to hurry away on my account. If my presence offends you that much I shall go and look for my other daughter."

Harry had counted on making Matilda feel uncomfortable and he knew he'd succeeded when she hastened to add, "It has nothing to do with you. I just dropped by to invite Jane up to Thatcher's Mount this evening. Mama is having a small gathering for George and she'd like you to be there."

"George?" exclaimed Harry.

"Don't say it, you thought he was dead."

"No, but maybe in the Colonies."

"He's never been further than London."
"What's he been doing down there?"
"Gambling, living on his wits I assume. No doubt he'll return when the dust has settled on whatever scandal he flew from."
Matilda's tone was so contemptuous Jane was moved to rebuke her. "Tilda, he is your brother."
"Yes, but it's not something I boast about." Matilda thought for a moment. "You spend time in London, don't you Harry? And as a Member of Parliament, you must know some influential people."
"A few," Harry answered modestly.
"Perhaps you could make some enquiries. Find out why George departed in such a hurry."
Harry was about to say that, not being a gambling man, he didn't move in the same circles as her brother, when he realised she had just handed him the very opportunity he was looking for.
"I'll certainly ask around. There are quite a few heavy gamblers in the Commons, I might glean something from them."
"Thank you." The sound of hooves signalled Reuben and Judith's return. "We'll expect you tonight at eight o'clock then," Matilda said to her friend, then with a brief nod in Harry's direction, she turned and walked out of the yard.
With all three of them very much preoccupied with their own thoughts, there wasn't much in the way of conversation on the drive home. Judith's mind was focused on her new horse Star, which Reuben Smith had promised to bring tomorrow. An uncommunicative man, Reuben had only opened his mouth once all the time they were out and that was to offer the opinion that her father had made a sound choice in buying Star. She believed him too, for the mare felt

right and she saw herself on Star galloping over the Leicestershire countryside seeking out the mysterious girl who appeared to have vanished off the face of the earth.

Olivia, on the other hand, was bursting to tell Judith of her small adventure. How on her walk through the village she'd come across a cricket match being played. With nothing better to do, Olivia had paused to watch and immediately recognised the young man who was batting. Aware of how charming she looked, she moved round so that she was in his line of vision. But her beauty went unappreciated, because the young man never took his eye off the ball. With complete single-mindedness he whacked the ball hither and thither and had the fielders running all over the place. After twenty runs he still wasn't out and Olivia knew she'd have to be getting back to the stables. But even though he hadn't given her as much as a glance, she felt quite pleased with herself. She might not know his name, but she'd placed him geographically and that had to be a move in the right direction.

Harry's musings on the way home, were more carnal than his daughters'. He was realistic enough to know it would be no easy task winning back Matilda, but they were talking and she had appealed to him for help and he dared to allow himself a degree of optimism. Getting hold of information on George might take time, then he'd need to call on Matilda from time to time and courtesy would demand she offer him a drink. But it would be *slowly-slowly-catchee-monkey*. He would plan his campaign carefully, fan the old passions into life, wheedle his way back into her life and her bed. This time, though, Harry promised himself as he approached Fern Hill, he wouldn't make the mistake of misusing her.

* * *

Clare and Adam received their daily lessons in the library with Mr Harcourt. Adam, however, had gone with Matilda to a nearby farm on business, so Clare was on her own and she chafed at having to sit in a stuffy room translating text from French into English, while outside the sun shone. The windows were open and the scent of freshly mown hay wafted in, along with the voices of the mowing team as they scythed their way up and down the meadow. At this time of the year every available hand was needed and only two years since she and Adam would have been out in the fields with the village children, turning the hay, piling it onto wagons, helping to stack it, then when they'd finished, sliding down the ricks for the sheer youthful joy of it. But Adam would be master of the estate one day, and Aunt Tilda now considered it inappropriate for him to mix on familiar terms with the farm hands, while she had reached that age where young ladies were expected to act with some decorum.

Bored, Clare's attention moved from the world outside the window. Dipping her pen into the ink pot she aimlessly doodled in her exercise book and found she had written 'London'. Papa talked about that great city continually and she tried to envisage it: the busy streets, fashionably dressed crowds, theatres, pleasure gardens. Oh, how she longed for Papa to take her, but for all of his love of the place, he seemed in no hurry to leave Halby.

Clare heard the scratch of Mr Harcourt's pen and wondered if he was planning to give her more work. He had been their tutor for three months, was twenty-two, fair and slim with a dreaminess about his features which Clare found attractive. She coughed to gain his attention and when he looked up, she smiled winningly. "Could you help me please, Mr Harcourt, I'm not sure what this phrase means."

"Certainly, Miss Pedley." He moved over and stood behind her and when she pointed to the text, he leaned forward and his warm breath tickled her ear and caused a pleasurable tingling sensation to shoot through her body.

"What is it that you don't understand, Miss Pedley?"

"This." Clare knew she was being rather wicked, but it did relieve the boredom.

"*Je t'aime,*" the tutor read. "Why, it means *I love you,*" he went on, as yet unfamiliar with feminine wiles.

Clare turned and looked directly into his light hazel eyes. "Oh, does it?" She gave him a coquettish smile.

"Er . . . yes," the young man stammered. Totally out of his depth, his fair skin stained red with confusion. He hurried back to the safety of his desk where, for the rest of the lesson, he sat staring at a Latin primer, the words of which made no sense to him at all.

Chapter Five

Jed rose early, slipped out of bed, dressed and, without disturbing Rachel, crept from the bedroom. After a chunk of bread and cheese washed down with milk, he picked up his heavy coat and carpet-bag, hearing St Nicholas's clock striking the half hour as he strode down the High Street. Jed eased his pace. The mailcoach for London left at four o'clock so he was in good time and his place on the outside was already booked.

In comparison to the dark, silent streets, the yard of the Bell Hotel seemed to Jed like bedlam. Hooves clattered on cobblestones, steam rose from piles of dung and ostlers cursed as they hoisted heavy baggage and the mailbox onto the coach. Those travelling inside had already made themselves comfortable but Jed, only able afford the twelve and six outside fare, had to wait for the coach to move out of the yard. Finally everything was stowed away, the lamps lit and the coachman and guard took their seats. The coachman flicked his whip, the horses moved out of the inn-yard, paused to allow the outsiders to jump on, then rattled along Granby Street and up London Road. As they approached the tollgate the guard gave a warning blast on his posthorn and a yawning keeper staggered out to allow the Royal Mail to pass without hindrance.

Soon they were bowling along towards Market Harborough at such speed every bump and pothole jarred Jed's spine. He was also sitting next to a stout gentleman who took up more than his fair share of space. He had straw under his feet but the October air was raw and Jed, grateful for the comforter Rachel had knitted him, wound it more securely round his neck. Still, it won't be so bad when the sun comes up, Jed consoled himself and tried not to think of the miles still to be covered.

"Well, at least it's not raining," observed his fellow passenger, as the coach swayed dangerously and they had to cling on for dear life.

"That's true," Jed agreed, for churned up mud could delay a coach for hours.

"Barring accidents, broken harnesses or a robbery we should reach London by seven this evening," the man continued cheerfully, then pulling his collar around his ears, he appeared to nod off.

It was a marvel to Jed that anyone could sleep in such uncomfortable conditions and without falling off the coach. He must have dozed himself, though, because the guard's horn warning the posting house of their imminent arrival startled him out of his slumber. The sun had risen on a placid autumn landscape of burnt umber and gold, but Jed gave little attention the beauty of the day for, to his embarrassment, he found that his head was resting on his travelling companion's shoulder. Straightening up, he apologised profusely.

"Think nothing of it, sir," answered the gentleman and held out his hand. "Septimus Rodway, cabinet-maker, at your service."

"Jedidiah Fairfax, bookseller," Jed replied, shaking the proffered hand.

"Will you be taking breakfast when we stop?" enquired Mr Rodway.

"Most certainly," answered Jed, whose stomach by now ached for sustenance.

"Perhaps we could partake of it together," suggested the cabinet-maker and Jed, not wishing to appear churlish to such an amiable man, had no choice but to agree.

Steam rose from the tired horses' backs, and the coachman announced, "Half an hour stop 'ere." Jed and his new friend clambered down, stamped their feet to get some sensation back into them and gingerly eased their aching bones. Then Mr Rodway sniffed the air like a hound. "My, that smells good," he exclaimed, and the two men, propelled by the enticing smell of coffee and bacon, moved towards the inn, where a welcoming fire awaited them.

Because of his size, Jed had imagined his companion to be an older man. In the light, however, he could see that they were probably of a similar age. They took their places at a table and a serving-girl had just taken their orders when a voice said, "Morning, Fairfax."

Jed looked up but his face darkened when he saw who it was. "Morning, Bennett," he answered curtly, remembering jealously how Rachel had once been sweet on him.

"Would that be Mr Bennett the Member of Parliament?" asked Mr Rodway, and watched with interest as Harry joined some fellow passengers at a corner table.

"It is," answered Jed.

"He'll be going down for the Bill, no doubt. I wonder if he's for or against it?" pondered Septimus Rodway, then tucked into the enormous platter of rashers, kidneys and eggs the girl placed before him.

"He's a Whig so I presume he's for reform. And the Commons have passed it, it's just up to the Lords now.

Let's hope they see sense this time and allow it to go through, for the sake of the whole country."

Septimus, who had forkful of fried egg half-way to his mouth, paused. "Are you saying there will be civil disorder?" The yolk dripped onto his plate.

Not knowing what his new friend's politics were, Jed saw he had to be wary of making intemperate remarks. "Who knows. But maybe you should have delayed your trip to London."

"I have business there that can't be postponed. A wealthy gentleman has ordered some pieces of furniture and I am going down to discuss the design with him. It is a big opportunity for me, and might get my name known in London."

"A future Hepplewhite eh?" Jed laughed.

"Perhaps so," answered Septimus quite seriously and polished his plate clean with a slice of toast dripping with butter.

The sun, a crude orange splash like a child's painting, was descending below the sky-line when the coach drove into London, became tangled with the traffic and slowed to a snail's pace. The passengers began to grow impatient at the delay, for by now everyone was travel-weary and dirty. They finally reached the Star & Garter in Holborn half an hour late, although Harry Bennett wasted no time and was away first, Jed noticed. He tipped the coachman, then directed an ostler towards a private carriage waiting at a short distance. Jed caught a brief glimpse of a smiling female face before Harry climbed in and the vehicle drove off.

Septimus Rodway had also been observing this scene and his next remark amused Jed. "Surely Mr Bennett is a married man?"

"He is, but from what I know of him he's not the

sort of gentleman to allow a few marriage vows to get in the way of his pleasures."

Jed only had a small amount of luggage, which he quickly laid claim to, then he held out his hand. "Thank you for your company, Mr Rodway, and if you are ever passing my shop do drop in."

"I will certainly take you up on that offer. But where are you planning to stay while in London?" asked Septimus.

"I haven't made any arrangements, but here I assume."

An ostler attending to the passengers' baggage heard Jed's remark and looked up. "Sorry sir, there ain't a room to be 'ad. We've bin turning folks away all evening."

"Oh no!" Dog-tired, the last thing Jed wanted was to go hunting for a hostelry where the bedlinen was changed occasionally and he wouldn't get bitten alive by bedbugs.

"Listen, why don't you come with me?" suggested Mr Rodway. "I'm staying with my Aunt Dolly. She's a widow lady and keeps a lodging-house in Covent Garden. I'm sure she would find a bed for you."

"Wouldn't it be imposing?"

"Certainly not, it's her living."

"I would be grateful."

"Shall we be on our way then?" Septimus picked up his bag and Jed followed him out of the inn-yard and into High Holborn. After a short distance they turned into Drury Lane. Even with Sir Robert Peel's new police force it was a dodgy area in which to be walking at night, an opinion quickly confirmed when a gin-sodden drab fell out of a tavern door and stumbled against Jed. "Fancy a good time, love?" She leered toothlessly. Jed pushed her away in disgust, and as they walked on a stream of invective followed them down the street. From the opposite direction, and highly amused by this tableau, swaggered some cane-swishing young bucks, seeking out, Jed guessed, either a brothel or a molly-house, depending on their sexual preferences. Further down the road a carriage, bearing some noble lord's coat of arms, rumbled in the direction of the Theatre Royal.

"Bit of a mixed area, Covent Garden," commented Septimus as they passed a noisy, crowded coffee house.

He was right, London was brash and dangerous and Jed was wise enough to its wicked ways to know he had to watch his back all the time, for pick-pockets and garrotters were a constant hazard. Nevertheless he was exhilarated by the great city, loved the chance to engage in debate with fellow radicals such as Francis Place in his bookshop in the Charing Cross Road and was guiltily aware that he spent more time here than Rachel approved of.

"Here we are," said Septimus, and he ran up the steps of a house and pulled the bell. Jed stood back to get a better look at the three-storey dwelling and was reassured by its neat aspect. He doubted if he would be plagued by bedbugs tonight.

The door was opened by a girl of about twenty and of a similar build to Septimus. "Cousin Septimus, how nice to see you!" She leaned forward and kissed him affectionately.

"Hello, Constance dear." Septimus returned her kiss then turned and beckoned to Jed. "Con, an acquaintance of mine from Leicester, Mr Jedidiah Fairfax. I'm sure Aunt Dolly can find him a bed for the night, the poor fellow, like me, is done in."

With a look of distrust, Constance moved forward to get a better look at Jed, and he groaned inwardly. Oh Lord, she wasn't going to turn him away. She was carrying a candlestick and she held it high to enable her to study his features. She gave him a brief, critical appraisal then, liking what she saw, Constance smiled so widely her small eyes disappeared into her doughy features. "Don't stand on ceremony then, come in, come in." She beckoned them into the hall and closed the door.

Jed gave a sigh of relief. Saved. "Thank you most kindly Miss . . . ?"

"Sorry old chap, very remiss of me," Septimus apologised. "My lovely cousin, Miss Constance Drew."

"Pleased to meet you." She simpered then waddled up the hall. "Mama is in the kitchen, I hope you don't mind."

A large woman was carving a huge joint of sirloin while a downtrodden-looking skivvy washed pots and pans in the sink.

"Septimus!" The woman put down the carving knife and embraced her nephew.

This was obviously Aunt Dolly and Jed waited to be introduced and to wonder again if he would be welcome. But Mrs Drew was a businesswoman and unlikely to turn away trade, although she did explain that Jed and Septimus would have to share a double bed, every other room being taken.

"I think it's this business with the Bill. It's attracting troublemakers, come to rouse the mob if the Bill fails. You wouldn't be one of 'em, now would you, Mr Fairfax?"

"Aunt Dolly!" Septimus rebuked her.

"I've a right to know. I can't afford the authorities at me door."

"I'm a bookseller by trade, Mrs Drew, here on business and looking for some rare books for a customer." He wasn't lying, Jed told himself. Ostensibly that was why he was in London, that it coincided with the Bill was just his good fortune. "Three nights, if you could accommodate me, then I'll be gone."

Harry propped a pillow behind his head, stared down at Adele, the girl whose bed he had shared for the past few nights, and sighed as he remembered past pleasures. She was a right little minx, and the tricks she knew! How a girl of eighteen could be so skilled in the ways of lovemaking was beyond him. Sir Stafford Barker had been her protector since she was sixteen, that he knew, but he'd wager she'd been on the game longer than that, maybe even before the age of fourteen. He thought of his own two little innocents, protected and sexually unawakened, and felt a twinge of guilt at his own exploitation of Adele's young body. But, as she pointed out herself, she had to live. Sir Stafford, the lucky devil, had discovered a rich seam of coal on his land, and was now a man of considerable wealth, able to keep her in some style in this apartment in Piccadilly. Unfortunately, Adele had a passion for gambling, jewellery and gowns which even his generous allowance couldn't sustain.

So today, before Harry departed, he would leave money, discreetly of course, which she would lose at the gaming tables tonight instead of saving for when her looks deserted her.

Now, in sleep, she had the face of a Botticelli angel and Harry leaned over and kissed her naked breasts. But she didn't stir and he knew she would sleep until well past noon. Still, she was a valuable source for all the London scandals and he'd heard several snippets which would no doubt be of interest to Matilda. George, apparently, had been caught cheating at cards and Lord Slepe had demanded satisfaction.

Harry smiled to himself. No wonder that lump of lard had scuttled back to Halby. His Lordship was the best pistol shot in London. Or had been, for the noble lord's brain was rotting away with the pox and he was now in an advanced state of imbecility.

Well, at least he couldn't have been one of those idiotic Peers who'd thrown the country into turmoil by rejecting the Reform Bill yesterday, thought Harry and decided it was time to stir and get going. The windows were heavily draped with thick brocade to muffle traffic noise, but as he swung out of bed, Harry had become aware of the insistent sound of tramping feet. Quietly, so as not to disturb Adele, he moved to the window. Slipping between the curtains, he opened the long windows that led on to a small balcony. Below him, surging along Piccadilly was a vast, angry mob chanting: "The Bill, the Bill, nothing but the Bill." Harry had no doubt where they were heading, to Apsley House, the Duke of Wellington's residence. For His Grace wasn't the great war hero of Waterloo now, but one of the most reviled men in England for depriving manufacturing towns of a parliamentary representative and honest burgers of the right to vote. Harry had fought in several campaigns with Wellington and had admired his soldierly courage. Somehow, though, over this Bill, the Duke's intelligence had deserted him, and it was apparent he was about to reap the consequences of his folly.

Harry now noticed two men on horseback moving against the crowd down Piccadilly. To get a better look, he leaned forward and heard a voice below shout, "There goes the Marquis of Londonderry, let's get 'im for a start!"

It was both arrogant and foolhardy for a member of the Lords to move amongst such a volatile crowd, and as the news spread they began to hoot and jeer. Then a stone was hurled. It missed him, but the idea quickly caught on. Shouting "Reform", the crowd moved in and began pelting him with soft balls of horse dung. His fine clothes ruined and apoplectic with rage, the Marquis stopped his horse and pulled out a brace of pistols. At the sight of the firearms the crowd went quiet and in the silence Londonderry's aristocratic voice rang out. "I solemnly declare that I will shoot the next person who molests me, right between the eyes."

Intimidated by the threat, the mob gave way enough for the Marquis and his companion to move off. But their mood had grown even more menacing, and he hadn't gone far before more missiles were hurled. This time one struck Londonderry with such force on the temple, blood flowed. He swayed and looked about to fall from his horse. The crowd pushed in on the two men and it became apparent to Harry that their lives were now at risk. If he didn't intercede quickly, they were both likely to be torn to pieces. Only then did Harry realize he was stark naked. Fortunately at that instant, some Hussars pushed their way through and their presence, and their sabres, were enough to calm the crowd. Somehow tragedy was avoided and the Marquis was assisted into a hackney coach and driven off under escort. As the crowd parted, Harry saw Jed Fairfax. He might have guessed it, the man was a real troublemaker and always in the thick of it. Probably it was him who was responsible for the Marquis's injury. Careless of him to leave a beautiful wife behind too, he mused. And Rachel was unfinished business, so maybe one day, on the pretext of buying a book, he would pay her a call.

The crowd was breaking up now and as Harry moved back into the stuffy, darkened bedroom he realised he was sweating from tension but shivering too. If it was like this here in London, what might the situation be back in Leicestershire, where he'd left his wife and children unprotected?

Moved by a sense of urgency, Harry dressed. A pity he had to leave the delectable Adele, he thought, as he stuffed a roll of notes under her pillow. Still, there would be other times and if trouble was brewing in the Midlands, that was where his duty lay. Whether he would find a seat on a coach was, of course, quite another matter.

Chapter Six

What with the more radical newspapers appearing with borders of black mourning, muffled bells being tolled, 'for the death of the bill', then at the posting-houses listening to rumours of outbreaks of violence in some of the larger towns, Harry was in a fever of anxiety on the journey home. For the life of him he couldn't stop visualising what he'd always predicted if the Bill failed; Leicester in the hands of a revolutionary mob and the tumbrels rolling.

To his surprise and relief there was no evidence of any disturbances when the coach drove into town. Although there were a few more constables about than was usual, a reassuring calm prevailed; houses were shuttered, the streets empty. Of course rumours always expanded in the telling, Harry reminded himself, so perhaps today's grim testimonies were merely the consequence of over-fertile imaginations.

Harry relaxed. His family was in no danger, but he was dog-tired, so it seemed sensible to put up at the Bell for the night and continue for home in the morning. Detailing the Boots to take his bags to his room, he went through to the dining-room to order supper.

Someone hailed him from across the room and, recognising the man as a neighbouring landowner by the name of John Smith, Harry strolled over for a chat. "Quieter here than I expected," he remarked.

His neighbour leaned back and hooked a piece of gristle from between his teeth. "Which is more than can be said for Nottingham and Derby. But then they've always been contentious blighters."

Harry shifted uneasily. "Why, what's happened there?"

"As soon as the news of the defeat of the Bill arrived in Nottingham, the mob armed themselves with crowbars and smashed the windows of every anti-reformer they could find. If that isn't enough, I heard this evening that those stupid buggers in Derby have broken into a House of Correction and released all the prisoners. Think what that means. Villains and cut-throats swarming all over the countryside. Take my advice, Bennett, keep your family in the house with the doors and windows barred day and night and always have a pistol by your bed."

"Good God," Harry exclaimed. "I'd heard rumours, but I thought it was all right in these parts."

"No fear, there are some real vicious specimens out there baying for blood."

Scenes of carnage such as he'd witnessed in battle flashed before Harry's eyes and he saw his daughters lying raped and murdered. Engulfed by the most awful dread, he turned and strode out of the dining-room, calling over his shoulder as he went, "Sorry, old chap, but I must get home immediately." In the yard he shouted for an ostler and ordered a horse to be saddled. Leaving his bags to be brought on by carrier cart, Harry set off for Fern Hill.

His horse was fresh and cantered along at a steady pace, covering the miles with ease. An occasional glimmer of light told Harry that there was a village and people and a hostelry not too far distant. With his taut nerves it was the sort of reassurance he needed, because low clouds distorted shapes and when the branch of a tree caught on his jacket it almost startled him out of his wits. You're an ex-soldier so stop behaving like a nervous virgin, Harry berated himself. He cast his mind back to Adele and remembered the unsavoury details she'd given him on George. He had the excuse he needed to call on Matilda now and maybe out of gratitude she would invite him to linger a while. Harry's thoughts had just begun to meander down amorous byways, when he felt a backbreaking jolt and the reins were wrenched from his hands. "What the devil . . . ?" But Harry didn't finish, the horse whinnied in fright, reared and he was hurled backwards onto the road.

His body twisted awkwardly and he hit the ground hard and face down. Momentarily stunned, he came round to find an evil smelling bundle of rags sitting astride him and the gritty taste of damp soil between his teeth. His wrists were tied behind his back and out of the corner of his eye, Harry was aware of a raised cudgel.

"Don't move, or else!" a voice warned.

God damn it! Just what he should have been on his guard against, an escaped convict. There might be others lurking the the hedgerows, too. Harry cursed his own stupidity at allowing his attention to wander and for riding about unarmed when the country was in ferment.

Bony fingers gripped the back of his neck and the scarecrow leaned closer, huffing his foul breath into Harry's face. "Hand over yer money, or I'll make dogs' meat of you."

"Take . . . take whatever there is," Harry stammered. "You . . . you'll find a purse of sovereigns in my jacket pocket." But money or not, Harry knew there wasn't a chance in hell of his life being spared. The convict was desperate and on the run, he was about to be bludgeoned to death and his brains splattered all over the highway. In a gentleman's clothes and with a horse, the felon would soon be miles away from the scene of the crime.

"Where the bloody 'ell is it?" the man demanded, and dug around fruitlessly in various pockets.

The fog of terror cleared in Harry's brain. "Right side," he lied.

Greed made the felon careless and in his haste to get his hands on the gold coins, he let go of the cudgel. Harry heard it clatter to the ground and took his chance. A deep fury, plus a desire to see the sun rise on another day helped and, mustering all his strength, he gave an almighty heave. Caught unawares the man went flying. Harry rolled over, shook loose the hastily tied rope and he and the man scrambled to their feet together. But Harry had a quick soldier's mind and his fist came out and smacked the felon straight in the face. The man gave a yell of pain and nursing his bloody nose, staggered off up the road. Grabbing the cudgel, Harry made after him with murder in his heart. His own legs had very little strength in them and he feared the convict had got away until he heard his rasping breath. Harry saw him then, leaning against a tree and before the man had time to dodge, Harry swung the cudgel high, taking aim at his skull.

The man fell like a skittle, and without stopping to find out whether he was dead or alive, Harry rolled him into the ditch with the toe of his boot then slung the cudgel over the hedge. This done, he found his horse, which was grazing nearby, remounted, and rode on home.

But he had trouble thinking straight, and his hands shook so violently he could scarcely grip the reins. Slowly it dawned on Harry that behind him lay a man he'd probably killed. He'd taken many a life in the due process of war, but this was murder. In self-defence, though, Harry told himself, struggling to justify his deed, and the man was a desperate criminal. In fact his swift action had probably saved several other lives. And who could possibly connect him with the death of a tramp? Who would even care? Gradually his guilt eased and he spurred his horse into a gallop, more anxious than ever to reach home.

When Harry at last rode into Stanton Parva, he was perturbed to see a group of silent, sullen youths lounging outside the King's Arms obviously looking for trouble for they carried large staves. As he passed, they began that familiar chant, "The Bill, the Bill and nothing but the Bill."

Harry knew there was no point in stopping to reason with them or to remind them he wasn't an anti-reformer. With passions running high, that would be a minor detail to hot-headed young men, particularly if they decided to attack the house.

Fern Hill stood on high ground above the village, and the first glimpse of light drawing him in to its cosy familiarity, was a truly blessed sight. At first he thought the voices were in his head and that his recent violent encounter with the tramp must have made him slightly deranged. But as he cleared the drive, he was startled to see his wife, along with his daughters and the servants, standing on the terrace. They all appeared to be in a state of some agitation and were waving their arms like windmills.

Judith noticed him first and as he dismounted, she came running to greet him.

"What on earth are you all doing out here at this time of night? Don't you know it's both stupid and dangerous?" Harry's voice was harsh with an accumulation of anger and fear.

"Oh Papa, do look, over there," Judith cried.

Harry turned. To the north of them there was a great glow in the sky, like some heavenly visitation. "Hell's teeth, what is it?" he exclaimed, although he could already guess the answer.

"Nottingham Castle," answered Judith, in great distress. "They say the mob have set fire to it."

"All of you, inside the house at once," Harry barked. "Bolt every door and window and bring me my pistols," he ordered a servant. "Tonight, I fear, the world has truly gone mad."

Right through the remainder of the year and well into the spring Judith and Olivia chafed against the restrictions put on them by both parents. After an outbreak of cholera and several deaths, Charlotte forbade them to visit Leicester and their papa, who had always been the most tolerant and indulgent of fathers, made it clear that under no circumstances whatsoever, were they to go out riding unless accompanied by him. Complaining about it, Judith discovered, was a waste of breath.

"It's for your own safety. I was set upon and nearly murdered, and I'm a man, so what chance do you imagine two girls on their own would have?" asked Harry.

But Judith and Olivia refused to see the possible dangers, to them it just meant that their freedom was curtailed. But Harry knew that dangerous men still roamed the countryside and although the Hussars had been brought in to several towns to maintain order, it was an edgy peace, likely to erupt into violence again at the slightest provocation.

"Teach me to use a pistol then, Papa," suggested Judith.

"It would do no harm, I suppose, for both you girls to be able to protect yourselves." Taken with the idea,

Harry added, "In fact I'll start giving you lessons tomorrow."

Learning to shoot wasn't to Olivia's taste, she hated the noise and soon gave up. Judith, however, was more persistent and it wasn't long before she was an accomplished marksman. Pity she wasn't a boy, Harry reflected watching her hit a bull's-eye. She could have done so much. But he still felt darn proud of his daughter's abilities and on her fifteenth birthday he presented her with a brace of pistols. "And don't be frightened to use them if you are attacked," he advised her as he rose from the breakfast table.

"Where are you going, Papa?"

"To Loughborough."

"Can I come with you?"

"And me too," echoed Olivia, who woke every morning praying that she might be granted the opportunity to see the handsome young man who invaded her dreams most nights.

"Another time perhaps," answered Harry, for he was actually planning to call on Matilda.

"But why?" wailed Olivia. "I shall die if I have to stay cooped up in this house."

"I doubt it. Anyway I've got see my political agent. Far too boring for you and I'm not sure how long it will take."

"Will you be here for dinner?" asked Charlotte, who wasn't fooled by Harry's excuses. It was her bet he was off after some popsy. He had sex on the brain. "If you aren't going to be in, I must tell Cook."

Harry thought. Would Matilda invite him to dine, then perhaps linger over a brandy? "Assume I won't be back, my dear," he answered, taking the optimistic view that, with all the trouble he'd gone to over George, Matilda would want to show her gratitude.

But his confidence proved misplaced. For while Matilda wasn't exactly cold, there was no unbending, no intimation that in a small corner of her heart she still cared for him. In fact, she made sure he didn't put a foot past her office, and by way of refreshment all he was offered was small beer. However he did enjoy her full attention while he related the details of George's scandalous lifestyle, and the reasons for his hasty retreat from London.

"There's no telling how long he'll be staying in Halby then?"

"According to my source, Lord Slepe's days are numbered. And being a Peer of the Realm, his death will no doubt be announced in the obituary column of the *Times*."

"George will be gone as soon as he reads it, he hates the country. My great worry is Clare. He keeps promising her a visit to London."

"Can't you prevent it?"

"She is his daughter. Besides, Clare can talk of nothing else. She's little more than a child in many ways, and totally innocent of the ways of the world. Supposing he introduces her to some of his disreputable friends?"

"You could go with her," Harry suggested and thought how he might show her the sights.

"I don't like leaving the estate for long. It might have to be Mama, who, against the evidence of her own eyes, still feels there is some good in George."

"You are imagining the worst. Surely even George wouldn't do anything to compromise Clare?"

"I wish I shared your confidence. Thank you anyway for the information, Harry, although I guessed it would be something to do with his seedy friends." Matilda stood up. "Now I must get on. I have business to discuss with my estate manager in a half hour and there are still papers to be signed."

And with that Harry was coolly dismissed.

Although through the rest of the country thousands perished that winter in the cholera epidemic, perhaps because of the health precautions that were taken, the disease passed lightly over Leicester and there were few deaths. However, the girls' social life was still severely curtailed. Out of fear of infection, families in the County stopped giving parties and dances, even at Christmas, and Leicester remained out of bounds. Life was dull beyond measure.

It was a close run thing, but in June 1832 the Reform Bill finally passed through Parliament, became law, and as Harry commented to his wife, perhaps saved the country from a bloody revolution. There was bell-ringing and banquets and it was such a significant episode in the country's history, the sisters were certain their father would ease the restrictions imposed on them during the past months. However, his own brush with death remained fresh in Harry's mind and he wouldn't budge.

"It's like being in chains," Olivia sobbed with a stamp of her feet.

"But loving chains, darling. Can't you see it's because I care about my two little girls. And there are still men wandering the countryside who would happily murder for a pair of shoes. Be patient."

Olivia, seeing she had no choice, sulked and took out her annoyance on the elderly tutor who came in to teach them twice a week.

Another year was to pass before Harry felt secure enough to loosen the fetters, then he astonished his daughters one evening with an announcement.

Harry enjoyed a cigar after dinner but Charlotte always complained about the smoke so, to save argument, he usually took a turn round the garden. This evening with a daughter on either arm, he felt well content with life and pausing, he cast his eyes over the landscape."

"Lovely here, isn't it?"

"No it's not, it's boring," Olivia snapped.

Harry puffed his cigar and looked thoughtful. "You're fifteen soon aren't you, Olivia?"

"Yes. Can I have a party, please, Papa?"

"What about something better, a trip to London for you both?"

Olivia stopped and stared up at her father with a deeply serious expression. "Please don't be joking."

"Now, would I joke about such an important matter?"

"When, when, when shall we go?" Olivia chanted, leaping up and down in excitement. Then she hugged her father. "Oh Papa, I do love you."

"Will we go to theatres?" asked Judith.

"We'll do whatever my girls wish, but first we must have a word with your mother and arrange a date."

Charlotte was reading and she looked up with a frown of annoyance when her daughters galloped in with their news. After taking a sip of tea, she replaced the cup in the saucer then said, "I trust you are not including me in this trip of yours, Harry."

"Well, I had hoped we would go as a family, Charlotte."

"I do find London quite exhausting, particularly in the summer heat. If you don't mind, I'd prefer to stay here."

"As you wish." Harry wasn't going to pretend he would miss his wife's company. She would probably put a damper on the occasion and he did so want his daughters' first visit to London to be rather special.

Chapter Seven

Harry had secured lodgings for them in Dover Street just off Piccadilly and immediately Judith and Olivia arrived, they fell into bed exhausted after the longest journey they had ever taken in their young lives. They slept heavily but were awakened by the unfamiliar noise of London traffic. Impatient to see the sights, they didn't want to waste time eating breakfast. But Harry insisted and when they finally set off in the open carriage waiting outside for them, it was a fine warm day.

"Drive up Regent Street, along Oxford Street and through Hyde Park," Harry instructed the coachman, and at his command the horses moved off. The girls' bottoms barely touched the seat as they twisted this way and that in their eagerness to absorb every new experience. Brash and noisy it might be with street vendors, ballad singers and great crowds competing for space, but what Olivia couldn't get over were all the luxurious goods displayed in modern plate glass windows. Eventually, quite overcome with all the finery, she pleaded, "Oh Papa, may we stop and look inside the shops?"

"Tomorrow, Livvy dear. You have a whole ten days remember. We shall be going to the theatre and for it you shall both have new gowns."

This quietened Olivia and she sat planning what

style she would have, until they drove into Hyde Park where, it seemed to Judith, that the whole of London society was displaying its fine feathers. Rotten Row was packed. Extravagantly attired ladies accompanied by small black pages waved in the grand manner, reckless young bloods showed off by driving their phaetons so fast they were in danger of overturning.

Harry was hailed from every direction and when a young creature, hardly older than herself called, "Hello, Harry," Judith asked curiously, "Who is that, Papa?" For it struck her that the young woman, with her over-pink cheeks, was a trifle on the common side.

"Just an acquaintance," answered Harry, acknowledging another young woman in an open landau. She nodded graciously as she passed, while the gentleman with her raised his hat and called, "Afternoon, Bennett."

"Is that another one of your acquaintances?"

"Yes she is," answered Harry, remembering fondly how for several years Margaret had been a very intimate acquaintance indeed.

But many of the pleasantries and greetings struck a false note with Judith and she wasn't too unhappy when her father ordered the coachman to drive down Constitution Hill and past the Palace. "We might catch a glimpse of King William and Queen Adelaide," he said, clasping both girls' hands and feeling some of their excitement generating itself to him.

They were a trifle disappointed not to see the royal couple, but they drove on along the Mall, into the Strand and Fleet Street until they came to St Paul's. Even after this there was still more their father wanted to show them and they returned home tired out. "How dull and provincial Leicester is in comparison to London," Olivia declared later, as they prepared for bed, and gave a heart-felt sigh. She paused in tying up her hair with curl-papers and turned to face her sister. "Don't you just wish you could live here permanently, Jude?"

"Not really. It's fine for a week or two. But I should miss Star most dreadfully and my morning rides on her."

"What about Mama?" Olivia giggled.

"Let's say I'd miss her as much as she did me," answered Judith, then knowing it was wrong to love a horse more than one's own mother, she knelt and prayed to God for forgiveness.

The following morning Harry took them to choose the material and the patterns for their new gowns. Judith had little interest in clothes and she quickly decided on a light grey material and insisted on as plain a style as possible. Olivia, however, poured over fashion plates, lengths of material and patterns. After much indecision she finally chose a lovely musk rose silk and a dress pattern which had enormous sleeves. Extremely fashionable, of course, but in Judith's opinion, years too old for her. If their father had any misgivings about the style, he didn't say so. But then, what was the point, thought Judith. With her fully developed figure, Olivia could easily pass for seventeen or eighteen.

With an obsequious smile the proprietress showed them out, assuring Harry that the dresses would be ready within four days. A little later, when they were sitting fortifying themselves with hot chocolate and small cakes, the girls discovered Harry had another treat up his sleeve for them.

"We've got an invitation tonight to a party. It's from a fellow Member of Parliament, Sir Basil Collins and his wife, and only a street away from our rooms. His wife particularly wants to meet you both, so best bib and tuckers on, I want you to make a favourable impression," said Harry, remembering two sons of almost marriageable age.

Although Sir Basil Collins was over sixty, his wife, Lady Sylvia, had still to reach her fortieth year. Consequently she often found herself in need of diversion and that was when she would call on Harry. And he was more than willing to oblige, for she was a comely creature with a sharp wit. Sylvia also enjoyed shocking the stuffier elements of society. This made her parties highly enjoyable because she gathered about her musicians, writers and painters, slightly disreputable characters who were unlikely to be made welcome in other London drawing-rooms. It was also said – a rumour Sylvia never troubled to deny – that in her youth, she had been one of Byron's many mistresses.

"Now you are not to tell Mama I brought you here. She would probably consider it highly irregular," Harry warned his daughters as a footman opened the door to them and they were led through a black and white tiled hall into an elegantly furnished drawing-room with long windows that opened onto a small garden. The evening air was balmy, candles flickered in Chinese lanterns and the scent of lilies and roses had lured many of the guests outside.

"Harry! How lovely!" Lady Sylvia exclaimed when she saw them, and as they approached, she lifted a languid hand for him to kiss. Behind her stood two sullen-looking young men. "So these are your little gels?" she drawled. "Now, which one is Olivia?"

"Me, Lady Sylvia," Olivia simpered and gave a small curtsey.

"And the image of you, Harry, if I might say so."

Judith, who'd been hanging back was dragged forward by her father. "And this is Judith."

"Hello Judith." Lady Sylvia struggled to find something flattering to say about Harry's elder daughter but failed. She wasn't an unkind woman, though, so taking Judith by the hand she drew her towards the two young men. "My hulking great sons, Max and Gregory will entertain you. Max, get the gels some fruit cup," she ordered, then leaving the four young people to their own devices, she threaded her arm through Harry's. "Now you come and meet Mr Turner. A great artist, but I must confess I find his studies of light a trifle obscure."

Max returned with the fruit cup, went beetroot red when Olivia thanked him, while Gregory gazed mutely at the distant wall. Realising there was going to be little in the way of scintillating conversation, Olivia was about to seek more adult company in the garden when she was distracted by more guests arriving.

A large-girthed gentleman accompanied by a young man and young woman was ushered in and for a second Olivia's heart seemed to stop beating. Sir Basil guided the older man to a table where a card game was in progress then as he brought the other couple to join them, Olivia felt grateful that she was wearing one of her favourite dresses. The colour was flattering and it was cut to emphasise her slim waist. She looked lovely and knew it.

"Max and Gregory you already know, and coming from Leicestershire you're probably acquainted with these two young ladies as well." Sir Basil smiled at the sisters but for the life of him he couldn't remember their names. So, to spare himself further embarrassment, he moved quickly back amongst his cronies, leaving his sons to sort out the introductions.

Judith, her eyes fixed on Clare, moved forward. "We have met, do you remember, when I fell off my horse?" Although the girl's features would remain engraved in her mind forever, she wasn't confident that she'd made the same lasting impression.

"Of course we remember." Clare smiled and Judith was dazzled all over again by her beauty. "But we still don't know your names."

"I'm Judith Bennett and this is my sister, Olivia.

"It seems we share a name. I'm Adam Bennett," said the young man, "and this is my cousin, Miss Clare Pedley."

"Perhaps we are kin."

"Papa will know, shall I ask him?" said Clare.

"Not now, he looks busy," Adam replied with a glance at George. Following his gaze, Clare decided that it probably would be unwise to interrupt her father, now seated at the card table and wearing the fixed, intent expression of the true gambler.

"How long are you in London for?" asked Olivia.

Clare made a face. "Only until tomorrow I'm afraid. Grandmama, who came down with us, has been taken ill so we have to return to Halby."

"What a pity."

"But that doesn't stop us enjoying ourselves tonight, does it?" said Adam. "*On with the dance, let joy be unconfined, no sleep till morn, when youth and pleasure meet to chase the glowing hours with flying feet.*"

Max looked impressed. "By gad, that's clever of you old chap."

"Not me, Byron I'm afraid," Adam confessed, moving the group away from the card-playing adults towards a piano in an adjacent room. "Who wants to play?"

"I'll have a go," said Max, sat down, opened a book of music and began to play a waltz tune. Meanwhile Gregory rolled back the Turkish carpet.

"Would you care to dance, Miss Pedley?" he asked Clare with a slight bow, then led her on to the floor, his shyness evaporating as he swung her round and round the room.

Adam watched for a moment then turned to Olivia. "Perhaps you'd do me the honour."

Olivia smiled and moved into his arms. Max's playing was almost demonic and his fingers flew over the keys. Trying to stay in time with the music, Adam whirled Olivia around the room, faster and faster until the world reeled. Then with a sudden crash of discordant notes, Max stopped. "Someone else's turn now. I want to dance," he said in a petulant tone and stood up.

At the absurdity of his behaviour, Olivia and Adam collapsed onto chairs and burst into hysterical laughter.

Harry had moved back into the drawing-room to get himself a cigar and was lighting it up when he heard their laughter. Good, he thought to himself, the girls seem to be enjoying themselves with Sylvia's boys. There might be a match there for one of them, or even both, in three or four years' time. It would definitely be a leg-up socially. Sir Basil had a place in Derbyshire where Harry was sometimes invited to shoot, and earlier that evening he'd also given him an investment tip. "Forget canals, forget coaches, in a few years they'll be obsolete. Railways are the coming thing and it's where you should be putting your money, Bennett, take my word for it."

Mulling over this advice, Harry puffed on his cigar. He was about to go and see what the young folk were up to, when Sylvia came up behind him and spoke quietly in his ear. "Supper will be served in half an hour, in the meantime I'm going up to my room to rest. Care to join me?"

Harry looked about him. "Where's Basil?"

"Busy winning, he won't budge. Follow in a couple of minutes."

So it was, that Harry, ever the opportunist, by the merest chance, missed seeing Olivia and Adam together. And perhaps it was as well, because Olivia's body movements, the way she leaned towards Adam and gazed into his eyes, would have chilled his heart and brought his past whizzing back to haunt him.

Harry also missed George. Because a short while later, in a foul mood and having lost a considerable sum of money to Sir Basil, he went storming out of the house, with Adam and Clare trailing disconsolately behind him.

Chapter Eight

Septimus was a likeable man and during their few days together in London, he and Jed had struck up something of a friendship. So, once back home, Septimus often found himself in the vicinity of the bookshop, particularly around tea time. For Rachel had a lovely way with pressed tongue and he never tired of her gingerbread and scones. Rachel in turn, found him an affable, if somewhat awkward man and initially it was hard for her to connect him with the fine pieces of furniture he designed and sold at very good prices in London. However, when she discovered that, along with a thriving business, he was also a bachelor, she started to think about the four Brewin girls and hear wedding bells. He was no Adonis but what were looks against the solid virtues of thrift and endeavour? Rachel asked herself, and decided to give fate a shove.

When she had a plan Rachel wasn't one to waste time. She knew the simple answer would be to invite them all round to tea or for a game of cards, but that would look too obvious, and suddenly she hit on the idea of a picnic. Pleased with herself, that evening she said casually to Jed, "The weather's so hot, why don't we give the children a treat and take them to Bradgate Park on Sunday? We could have a picnic."

"Why not? It'll do us all good to get out into the country for the day."

"If I asked Septimus do you think he'd come?"

"You know Septimus, if there's food, he'll be there, particularly if you've cooked it."

Rachel held a glass she was drying up to the light and examined it intently. "I thought I might invite along Lily, Rose, Primrose and Marigold as well."

Jed laughed. "The penny's dropped. There's a bit of matchmaking going on here, isn't there?"

Rachel bristled slightly. "Well, there's no harm in trying. A man in Septimus's position needs a wife and the girls are desperate for husbands. Except for Lily, they haven't had much luck with men."

"Well they are plain, poor girls. Jack must wonder sometimes if he'll ever get them off his hands."

"If you took the trouble to study your friend, you'd see he's no oil painting either. Why are men are so stupid? Why can they never see beyond a pretty face? I helped bring them up and they are decent, respectable girls."

"I know that, Rachel. But don't be too disappointed if your scheme doesn't work out. They might all hate each other on sight."

"I'll make a bet with you. Septimus will be married to one of those girls within the year."

Seeing the determined glint in Rachel's eye, Jed didn't doubt it for a minute. "What's the stake?"

"A day at the races and a new dress."

"Who'll look after the shop?"

"Emily. Haven't you noticed, she's really rather good at the business."

"You're on," Jed laughed, then leaned over and kissed his wife with great affection.

Once Septimus and the sisters had accepted her invitation, Rachel set about organising the day with the precision of a general preparing for battle. She hired a wagon large enough to accommodate eleven people, spent all Saturday cooking meats, pies and cakes then finally, before falling exhausted into bed, she prayed that the weather would remain fine. The rest, she decided, she would have to leave to Cupid.

When she rose the following morning, Rachel was perturbed to see that the streets were wet from an overnight shower. All through breakfast she peered at the sky with anxious eyes and it wasn't until she was filling the hamper that streaks of blue began to push the cloud away.

But an earthquake couldn't have curbed Ben and Simon's excitement. Even their father's stern warning to behave went unheard, and as soon as the cart arrived, they scrambled up on it, and began throwing themselves about like whirling dervishes.

"Get down," Rachel snapped, "and help Emily with the hampers and rugs. That way we might get away on time."

Amidst all this chaos the sisters arrived. Rachel had invited Lily's sweetheart, Charlie, along as well, in the fond hope that it would make her motives look less blatantly obvious. For how Septimus would react to the company of four young ladies, three of whom were unattached, was anyone's guess.

Lily, the best looking and youngest sister, was busy being proprietorial. "Help me up into the wagon please, Charlie. Sit here beside me, Charlie." She patted the seat with a feline smile while the air throbbed with her sisters' envy. Lily had what the other three so ardently desired: an admirer, and it had rather gone to her head. Although Charlie hadn't actually asked for her hand yet, according to Lily it was a question of weeks rather than months before he went down on his knees.

Although their father's business had expanded and he was doing quite well, he still complained of the burden of four girls. But it was unlikely he would tempt any young man with the promise of a generous dowry, and Marigold, now only a couple of years off thirty, was having to confront the painful knowledge that her chances of finding a husband were slipping away.

The sad thing was, Marigold would make an excellent wife and mother, although Rachel suspected she'd have her job cut out today nudging Septimus into thinking along similar lines.

This gentleman, as yet innocent of Rachel's schemes, blundered into the group late, out of breath and wiping his sweating forehead.

"Sorry, Rachel, Mother had one of her turns."

Rachel, who suspected that Mother was the main reason why Septimus remained unwed, managed to sound concerned.

"She's all right now, I hope."

"Yes, Agatha, my sister, is keeping an eye on her." Septimus straightened his hat, adjusted his neckcloth, turned and found himself being scrutinised by four pairs of eyes. Watching him closely, Rachel saw his expression take on such a hunted look, for a moment she feared he would make a bolt for it.

But Jed placed a reassuring arm round his friend's shoulder and quickly made the introductions. Then everyone squeezed into the wagon. The enforced intimacy broke down most of the reserve and the party set off in high spirits.

As the horse ambled along, Jed joked good naturedly with the girls, but Septimus affected a deep interest in the local flora and fauna, which prevented him from joining in the banter.

Eventually Primrose, growing bold, enquired, "And what is your line of business Mr Rodway?"

Septimus cleared his throat nervously. "I'm . . . I'm a cabinet maker by trade."

"Do you mean a carpenter, old chap?" asked Charlie, who was a clerk with Pickfords and considered himself a rather superior sort of fellow.

"No, he doesn't," Jed replied on his friend's behalf. "As he said, he's a cabinet maker, and an extremely talented one at that."

Primrose, who now regretted not wearing her best dress, gave him her most winsome smile. During the rest of the journey, she managed to wheedle out of him his age – thirty-five – and that he lived with his mother and sister in New Walk.

Marigold, absorbing all this information, thought how she'd give anything to live in a nice modern house instead of their father's dank, dark place in Butt Close Lane. And Mr Rodway was unmarried and in a good line of business. So there and then, she decided to concentrate on these more positive aspects and ignore his three chins, receding hairline and a waistcoat stretched to bursting point over his stomach. A glance at Primrose's animated features, however, told her she was going to have stiff competition.

The good weather had coaxed many families out, all of them, it seemed to Rachel, heading for Bradgate. At one point the road became so clogged, traffic came to a halt, then Simon and Benjamin grew restless and began to whine that they were thirsty. Septimus on the other hand was beginning to relax and enjoy himself. He'd never in his life had the complete attention of three young ladies who treated his most trite remarks as pearls of wisdom and laughed merrily at his clumsy attempts at humour. In fact Primrose was so overcome with mirth she was moved to exclaim, "Oh, Mr Rodway, you are such a wit."

By the time they reached Bradgate, Septimus had become quite puffed up with pride, particularly when Lily, deciding that Septimus was maybe a better bet than Charlie, began to practise her charms on him as well. Rachel exchanged glances with Jed and he winked back at her. It was working out better than she could have hoped.

"Come back and pick us up at four," Jed instructed the driver when they eventually turned into Bradgate Park, and Septimus and Charlie had helped the girls, twittering like birds, down from the wagon. Gathering up blankets, hampers, drink, cricket bats and stumps between them, the party set off in search of a picnic spot. The boys insisted it had to be by the stream, Rachel wanted a place that was shaded and where they wouldn't be tripping over other families. It was quite a trek, but they eventually found a spot that seemed to satisfy everybody, until some young louts, who'd obviously drunk too much ale, started making spectacles of themselves by pushing each other into the water. But even they couldn't spoil Rachel's pleasure in the park. There was so much history here. For this had been Lady Jane Grey's home and Rachel could visualise her, a carefree young girl riding amongst the bracken and oaks, startling shy deer and unaware of the tragic fate that awaited her. A pawn to ambitious men and beheaded in the Tower only nine days after becoming Queen. Such a clever girl too – Rachel looked across at her daughter, as usual with her head buried in a book – and hardly older than Emily.

Rachel shivered. Perhaps being poor and unnoticed was the best way to be. "Come and help me unpack the hamper please, Emily," she called. She surprised her daughter by giving her a quick kiss, then spread out a blue and white check tablecloth.

Primrose and Marigold were busy vying for Septimus's attention but it was a few hours since he'd breakfasted and he was distracted by the slices of ham and beef Rachel was laying out on plates. His eyes followed her as she produced more delicacies from the hamper: pickled eggs, pork pies, several huge gooseberry tarts, thick yellow cream, deeply veined Stilton cheese and crusty bread. In an almost orgasmic state of ecstasy, Septimus's eyes glazed and his mouth fell open.

Not missing a trick, Marigold pressed him to try the ham, Primrose the beef.

"Oh . . . oh . . . thank you so much, and a slice of the pork pie . . . and while you're there a spoonful of horseradish . . . oh and a pickled egg if you'd be so kind."

Leaning back against the tree, Septimus tucked in. To tell the truth he found women rather daunting, and away from work he found solace in food. As he told himself, you knew where you were with food, and the same couldn't be said for women. At home, Agatha and the maid did the cooking between them, but it was dire: greasy stews, joints cooked to a cinder, hard pastry. Rachel, however, was another matter.

"Jed you're a lucky fellow, do you know that? Rachel's an inspired cook."

"I don't need reminding, I know old chap."

Pleased at the compliment, Rachel smiled. "I was well taught, by Jed's cousin, Susan, God rest her soul. Anyway, can you find room for a slice of gooseberry tart?"

"I might just manage to squeeze a piece down," Septimus replied and burped discreetly behind his hand. The gooseberry tart was heaven, the pastry crisp and golden. The thick cream counteracted any acidity and it slid down. Septimus finished and gave a blissful sigh. "If I could find a girl who could turn out a spread like this, Rachel, I might even consider marrying her."

Taking note, Marigold, who loathed cooking, decided she would start taking lessons from her step-mother tomorrow. Primrose, who was a fair cook, and so several points ahead in the contest, smiled at Septimus and with knife poised enquired, "Stilton, Mr Rodway?"

"Well, perhaps a soupçon, thank you Miss Brewin." It was a bit of a struggle getting the cheese down, but he managed to find a corner for it in his engorged gut, where it settled quietly. Septimus was a happy man. He closed his eyes and was about to nod off, when he was shaken roughly by young Simon.

"You can't go to sleep, Mr Rodway, we're gonna have a game of cricket."

"Oh no," groaned Septimus, and saw that Jed was banging in the stumps.

"Oh yes, Mr Rodway," laughed Primrose, and she and Marigold between them, pulled him to his feet, although not without a struggle.

Septimus had the rather humiliating experience of being bowled out by Lily after only two runs. Hoping no more exertions would be expected of him that day, he retired to the shade of a tree. Charlie made ten runs, but the game was soon over and then Marigold had a bright idea.

"Why don't we all walk up to Old John?"

"Yeah," roared Simon and Ben in unison and went rushing off.

"I'll stay and look after things, but the rest of you go," Septimus offered.

"I wouldn't hear of it," replied Jed. "You go with the others, Rachel and me will stay here."

Old John was a folly set on a hill and it was quite a steep climb to reach it. The others were all slim and agile, and they raced on. But Septimus's weight held him back and he struggled after them, breathing nasally and sounding like Puffing Billy. He now rather regretted over-indulging, for his dyspepsia was giving him gyp and he was in dire need of something to relieve the discomfort.

Charlie being a bit of a show-off reached Old John first. "Come on Mr Rodway, best foot forward," he ordered. Septimus knew this remark was made with the intention of showing him up in front of the young ladies, but he was past caring and when he finally reached the top, he sank down on a piece of rock and mopped his forehead.

"Isn't this a delightful view, Mr Rodway?" said Lily, sitting down beside him.

"Ind . . . eed it is . . . dear lady," gasped Septimus, trying to draw breath.

"Race you back," shouted Ben then galloped off with everyone else, except Lily, following close behind.

"Where do they get their energy?" groaned Septimus and struggled to his feet.

"Don't hurry, Mr Rodway, take your time," said Lily solicitously and wondered what it would be like sharing a bed with such a fat man.

On the way home they halted at an ale house for a drink. Once they were rolling along towards Leicester again Jed, his tonsils well lubricated by ale, started to sing John Barleycorn. Rachel and the girls were soon accompanying him but it took a nudge in the ribs from Lily, and a, "Come on, Mr Rodway," before Septimus could bring himself to join in.

Slowly the sky darkened and the creatures of the night took over. An owl shrieked, bats dipped and dived, and glow worms dusted the hedge rows. Perhaps it was the purity of the girls' voices, or maybe because it was coming up to midsummer's eve, but to Rachel it seemed there was a touch of magic in the air. The spell didn't break until the wagon was trundling along High Cross Street when Ben and Simon, who'd been asleep, awoke and started to bicker.

"Did you enjoy your day, Septimus?" Rachel asked, as he bent to peck her cheek and thank her.

"Do you know," he answered, sounding almost surprised, "I think it's been one of the best days of my life."

"Well, which girl do you think will get him?" Rachel asked Jed later on in bed.

"Marigold," Jed murmured sleepily.

"My money's on Primrose."

In fact, as it turned out, both of them were wrong.

Chapter Nine

On the journey home, Judith and Olivia talked of nothing but their stay in London, reliving in their youthful chatter each new experience, while Harry, pleased to have been able to make his girls happy, listened with an indulgent smile. Even after long, weary hours confined to a coach their enthusiasm remained undimmed and when they reached Fern Hill they hardly bothered to stop and wash off the dust, before rushing downstairs to their mother's small sitting-room.

Harry, who'd just made the required courtesy call on his wife, closed the door, put his finger to his lips and warned, "Now remember, some things are best kept between the three of us, especially if you want another trip to town, and we don't want Mama upset, do we?"

His daughters shook their heads vigorously, enjoying the idea of a shared secret with their father.

"In you go then." He patted them through the door and Olivia rushed to embrace her mother. "Have you missed us, Mama?"

Charlotte closed her book and appeared to deliberate on her daughter's question. "Of course my dear," she answered at last and reached up and stroked Olivia's cheek.

"And we've missed you too, haven't we Judith?"

"Oh yes," Judith lied and landed a dutiful kiss somewhere in the region of her mother's nose.

Charlotte patted the chaise longue. "Well come and tell me all about it."

Accepting her mother's invitation, Olivia sat down and plunged into a description of their holiday, in her excitement the words tumbling out in half-formed sentences. "Oh you should have seen the fashions in Hyde Park, Mama . . . we rode through there almost every day . . . and you've never seen such handsome young men . . . and we just missed seeing the King and Queen . . . and . . ."

"Then there was this actress," Judith went on, while Olivia paused to draw breath. "She was ever so old but when we saw her at the theatre she was painted and patched and done up to look about sixteen, except that when she sang she sounded like a frog." Here Judith did such a good imitation of the unfortunate lady, her sister had a fit of the giggles.

But Charlotte seemed neither entertained nor amused by her daughters' adventures and after less than ten minutes, she stopped them in mid-flow and pressed her fingers to her temples. "Girls, girls, please, your chatter is giving me a headache."

Judith's face grew dark. "Don't you want to hear any more?"

"Perhaps tomorrow," answered Charlotte, and picked up a book.

"You're not a bit interested in what we did, you never are," Judith accused and stomped out.

"Shut the door quietly," Charlotte called after her, adding to Olivia, "your sister is going to have one of her sulks I suppose, tiresome girl."

"What do you expect, Mama?" Olivia retorted and making sure she gave the door an extra loud slam, she went after her sister. She found Judith staring at her reflection in a mirror, her face was white and she looked on the verge of tears.

"Mama doesn't like me, you know. She never has."
"Don't be silly, Jude, you're her daughter. All mothers love their children, it would be unnatural for them not to."
"All I can say is, Mama's not natural then. I've known how she feels about me right from being a little girl."
Although she was aware that her mother looked more favourably on her than Judith, in the past Olivia had put it down to her sister's refusal to toe the line, and her sometimes rather hoydenish behaviour and strange way of dressing. Now she wasn't so sure.
"I think you're reading too much into it."
"Have it your way. I'm going out for a ride, I need to let off steam. Coming?"

"I enjoyed being London, but I'm happy to be home," said Judith. "It's so smoky and noisy compared with here."
Shaded by a willow, the girls lay on their stomachs staring into a stream where tiny black fish darted to and fro. A couple of feet away their horses cropped at the grass, a heat haze hung over the countryside and there was a faint murmur of nature going about its business; water gurgling over pebbles, the shrill warning of swallows swooping for insects, the industrious buzz of bees as, weighed down with sacs of pollen, they flew off to placate their queen.
"There's a lot more happening in London. Shops, theatres, parties, dances," answered Olivia, who had loved the clamour and constant movement of the city and was already pining to return. She stared morosely at fields of corn devoid of human life and blending into an empty horizon. How boring it was, she gave a deep, heartfelt sigh and speculated on Max. He was pretty boring too, but beggars couldn't be choosers and

he had promised to come and see her as soon as the hunting season started. Although he wasn't half as handsome as Adam, Papa had mentioned in passing that any girl fortunate enough to snare Max would one day find herself mistress of a rather fine establishment in Derbyshire.

"But what could be more lovely than the countryside at this time of the year." Judith's anger at her mother had abated and chewing on a piece of grass, she rolled on to her back and gazed up at the sky. Suddenly she stood up and began pulling off her drawers and boots.

Olivia watched in astonishment. "What on earth are you doing?" She was used to Judith's odd behaviour, this was carrying things a bit far.

"I'm going to cool off." A branch which had partially split from the trunk of the willow lay across the stream and, arms outstretched like a tightrope walker, Judith edged her way along it until she reached the middle of the stream. Here she sat down, hoisted her skirts above her knees and dangled her feet in the water.

"Judith, really!" exclaimed Olivia.

"What's wrong?"

"Don't act all innocent. Supposing someone comes? And what if it gets back to Mama?"

"No one will. Anyway, who cares?" Judith answered defiantly. "Come on, don't be such a spoilsport, it's lovely."

Although Olivia was conventional by nature she often envied Judith's indifference to other people's opinion. And thinking about it who, apart from a few cows, was there to see them anyway? And it was hot, and the water did look inviting. With a recklessness that was alien to her, Olivia kicked off her boots, draped her drawers over a branch, and wobbled cautiously to the centre of the stream. She dropped down beside Judith with an air of triumph then, freed from restricting undergarments, they plunged their feet into the water with childish glee. Kicking up great fountains of water, they threw back their heads and watched droplets of pure crystal spin high as the trees, catch the sun's rays and fall like strings of rainbow-coloured beads.

The sisters' laughter grew more abandoned, their clothes damper. The curl fell out of their hair, but for once Olivia wasn't bothered how she looked. A field away two riders heard the hilarity and, driven by curiosity, they spurred their horses on to investigate. But neither girl was aware they had company until a voice called, "Hello, may we join you?"

"Heavens!" Olivia exclaimed. Realising that her image of a impeccably dressed young lady was rather in tatters, she quickly pushed down her skirt, although she knew Adam had probably caught a glimpse of her bare legs. Then she noticed her drawers, dangling hardly an inch from Adam's nose and the blood gushed up her neck and stained her cheeks poppy red.

But Adam seemed to take the line of ladies' undergarments in his stride. "Is there room for us?" he repeated.

"Yes, come and join the fun," Judith invited, who was too entranced by Clare's blond ringlets to trouble to adjust her clothes.

Adam yanked off his riding boots and as he balanced himself along the branch, Olivia was transfixed by his hard-muscled calves. Hunkering down between the sisters he turned and beckoned to his cousin, who was hovering on the river bank. "What are you waiting for, Clare?"

This remark implied that she was scared, so Clare, who would have followed her cousin into hell if he'd suggested it, disrobed without further ado.

"Here, let me help you." Judith stood up and slyly encircled Clare's waist, so slender she felt sure the slightest pressure would crack her ribcage. Her cheek was invitingly close too, and Judith, her head spinning with half-understood emotions, longed to plant a kiss on its peachy softness.

"Shove along," Adam ordered, when they were all seated, taking charge like men were inclined to.

Judith obliged by squeezing up tight against Clare.

"Right, let's test our weight." Linking hands, they swung up and down on the branch, gingerly at first but then gaining confidence, with increased abandon.

"*Bobby Shaftoe's gone to sea . . .*" Adam sang as they bounced up and down. "*Silver buckles on his knee . . .*" the girls joined in. "*When he comes home he'll marry me, Bonny Bobby Shaftoe,*" they finished harmoniously and to great gales of laughter. But all this exuberance was too much for the branch. Unable to support such boisterous activity, it gave up the ghost, broke asunder from the trunk and pitched all four of them face forward into the river.

They surfaced spluttering, flailing their arms and trying to struggle to their feet. Adam was soon up but the girls were hampered by the weight of their wet skirts.

"Help us, Adam," Clare ordered but instead of going to their assistance he studied them with some amusement, then with the brutal honesty of the young, said, "The three of you look like drowned rats."

"Beast!" Clare retaliated and managed to raise herself and pursue her cousin as he scrambled up the river bank. Olivia and Judith were now close behind her and grabbing Adam's legs, between them they dragged him back down the bank and into the water.

* * *

Whenever Christopher Harcourt had time off from his teaching duties he liked to walk in the country and refresh his soul. He was a young man sick with love, but denied the right to declare it by his situation. Only in poetry could he reveal his true passion, so with the world to himself, Christopher declaimed in resonant tones and searched for a word that rhymed with beloved. It was hard, summoning up the muse, took all his concentration so Christopher paid little attention to where the path led, until female screams startled him out of his reverie. He stopped and his arms, which he was inclined to wave about when in full poetic flight, fell to his sides. Should he go on? It could be a country lad having his way with a maid and he had no wish either to trip over them or spoil their pleasure. On the other hand it could be a young woman in some sort of distress and needing help.

Although the shrieks came from quite nearby Christopher approached with a certain caution. The scene that met his eyes, however, was way beyond anything he could have imagined. For there was the object of his desire in the middle of the stream, disporting herself with two other girls like some common hoyden, and laughing immoderately. Her face was streaked with mud and she looked more like a savage, than a well brought-up young lady. Her wet clothes clung suggestively to her body and this so agitated Christopher he hardly knew where to look. Then to cap it all, he brushed against three pairs of drawers dangling from a branch of a tree and his skin caught fire. Hot and agitated but not wanting to be accused of spying, Christopher cleared his throat loudly. He expected some reaction from Clare; a slight shame, at least, instead when she saw him she waved gaily.

"Hello, Mr Harcourt."

"Good afternoon, Miss Clare." Christopher hoped he looked mature and stern, in the way expected of a tutor.

"The branch broke," Adam explained, "and we all fell in."

"So I see."

"I expect we look a bit of a mess," Adam suggested.

"That would be an understatement."

"You must promise not to snitch on us, because Mother would have a fit."

"It's not my habit to tell tales," Christopher answered coldly, wondering what Adam took him for. "But she'll find out for herself when you get home I should imagine."

"She's gone into Leicester and won't be home until late."

"Yes, of course."

Christopher waited, expecting to be introduced to the other two young ladies. But he could sense his presence was breaking up their fun and that they didn't want him there. Feeling lonely and excluded, he bid them good day and walked on. But the muse had fled and he was quite unable to think of one line of verse, let alone a word that rhymed with beloved.

Adam and the girls waited until he'd disappeared round a bend in the river, then giggling like wayward children they scrambled up the bank and threw themselves down on the grass.

"Who was that?" asked Judith.

"Our tutor, Mr Christopher Harcourt," answered Clare.

"I think he was a bit shocked by our behaviour."

"I'm not surprised, he blushes every time Clare asks him a question," Adam replied.

"No he doesn't you beast." Clare leaned over and good-naturedly clipped her cousin.

"Do you think he will blab to your mother?"

"No, he's a good egg really. He's giving me extra tuition for Cambridge."

Olivia sat up with a look of dismay on her face. "Are you going away?"

"Eventually. My mother has decided I need to see something of the world, meet new people, broaden my horizons before I take over the estate."

She was going to lose Adam. Although the sky was a throbbing blue, it was as if a cloud had appeared and obscured the sun. It had been a glorious afternoon, but for Olivia, all light and joy had suddenly gone out of the day.

Chapter Ten

Rachel was wrong about it taking a year. It actually took Lily a little longer – and considerable guile and cunning – to get Septimus to St Margaret's Church, where she vowed to love, honour and obey him. Jack Brewin gave his youngest daughter away with an expression of profound relief and Rachel, knowing him well enough, could guess his thoughts; one down, three more to go.

Even the plainest girl looks beautiful on her wedding day and Lily in cream lace was no exception. After the nuptials the bride, with an air of deep solemnity, laid her wedding posy on her mother's grave while behind her, Marigold sniffed noisily into her handkerchief and resolved to throw herself from Bow Bridge at the first opportunity. How could Lily do this to her? Steal Septimus away from her when she already had Charlie.

Rachel, watching Marigold and feeling in some way responsible, longed to do do something alleviate her distress. Marigold had no natural right to Septimus, she knew that, but it was the determined and unscrupulous way in which Lily had set out to win the big innocent that had shocked Rachel.

Charlie coped surprisingly well with his loss and had since turned his attentions to Rose, but Marigold was inconsolable. Rachel had nursed a vague hope that Septimus might have some eligible cousins, but looking around the church during the wedding ceremony, she saw no young men of promise who were unattached and of the right age.

Jack Brewin, on the other hand, had fallen on his feet with his second wife, the former Mrs Spence, and the house in Butt Close Lane, once so sparse and bleak, was now welcoming and warm. She refused to put up with her spouse's penny-pinching ways and had insisted on laying on a decent wedding breakfast for the guests, many of whom had travelled long distances to give the young couple a send off. So tempting was the fare, in fact, that when the wedding party reached the house, Septimus took one look at the spread, and rubbed his hands in anticipation. "By jove, that all looks delicious, Mrs Brewin," he beamed, then abandoning his new wife, he galloped over to the table, piled his plate high with food and began wolfing it down.

Mrs Rodway senior and her daughter Agatha had done all they could to discourage Septimus from marrying Lily, and were of the opinion that he had chosen a wife way beneath him socially. Today, though, with their relatives in noisy evidence, this was a fiction proving hard for them to maintain. Although his mother would have liked it otherwise, Septimus sprang from good artisan stock; carpenters, wheelwrights and blacksmiths, jocular, fresh-faced men with robust country ways, who were not inclined to mind their p's and q's and had a liking for strong ale. Wearing their best bonnets and with tongues wagging nineteen to the dozen, their lady wives sat and drank tea. The men, however, never moved more than a foot from the ale barrel, and as the contents went down the laughter became louder, the jokes broader.

"Coom 'ere m' lad," Septimus's uncle, Amos, called to him. "Seeing ye haven't got yer arms round yer lovely bride, take this." He thrust a tankard at Septimus, raised his own, and with a smirk said, "May all yer troubles be little 'uns." He drank deeply, wiped his hand across his whiskers, belched, then declared, "By 'eck that wa' good." Noticing his nephew had made no attempt to follow his example, Uncle Amos gave him a nudge. "Sup up lad, you're goin' ter need all your energy tonight. Yer mam will be looking for you to do yer duty, won't you Beatrice?" He loved to goad his sister-in-law, a starchy madam who'd got way above herself, considering where she came from.

Beatrice gave him a venomous look and refused to answer, while Septimus, suspecting certain duties were going to be demanded of him tonight in the bedchamber, supressed his anxieties by cramming more food into his mouth.

Lily, on the other hand, was loving the attention. After all, a bit of ribbing was only to be expected on your wedding day. She knew what everyone said behind her back; that she was a cold-hearted madam who'd stolen Septimus off Marigold, but she didn't care. All was fair in love and war, and she'd got what she felt she deserved; a man of some means. When she left here, she would go to her beautiful new home, its rooms furnished with fine pieces designed by Septimus. She'd already engaged a girl to work in the house and answer the door. Only one thing troubled her, and that was what happened when the bedroom door closed. Still, everything had its price, she reflected, so she would deal with that when she came to it. The main thing was that as Mrs Septimus Rodway she had status. The courtship hadn't always gone smoothly and Septimus had been a somewhat reluctant lover, so it was hard not to feel a sense of triumph at getting him to the altar. As an act of gratitude, Lily moved to her husband's side. She was reaching up to kiss his fat cheek, when she noticed, with a spurt of pleasure, Marigold, handkerchief pressed to her eyes, rush outside closely followed by Rachel and Emily.

Soon after the wedding Jed, being a man of his word, bought Rachel a new dress and bonnet and off they went to the races, leaving Emily in charge of the bookshop. Jed voiced doubts about leaving his daughter on her own for a whole day, and he was still giving her instructions as she pushed him out of the door. "Papa, I've been helping in the shop, one way or another since I was six, and I know what I'm doing. I won't give the wrong change, I promise."

"And no credit either," her father warned.

Emily ground her teeth with frustration. "Doesn't Mama look lovely in her new bonnet?"

Jed glanced at his wife. "Yes, she does, but don't change the subject Emily."

"She is quite sensible, Jed," Rachel interjected, for she could see this conversation continuing indefinitely.

"Thank you, Mama." Emily leaned over and kissed her mother. "Now go and enjoy yourselves, and I promise I won't bankrupt the business. And just you make sure you don't you lose it all on the horses, either."

Although the racecourse was only at the top of the London Road, it was one of the social events of the year, so her father had hired a trap and Emily stood waiting for it to turn into the High Street. She'd worked in the shop full-time since leaving school but, until today, always under her parents' guidance. Neither brother showed much interest in literature, Ben wanted to be a sailor, Simon an engineer. She, on the other hand, loved books, their smell, the texture of fine calf and reading was her greatest pleasure. Emily was inclined to be rather disdainful of girls who had no other thought in their silly heads but boys and marriage. She knew people would think it strange if she told them, but her ambition was to live among books for the rest of her life and when her parents could no longer manage, take over the running of the shop.

The trap reached the end of the road, her mother blew her a kiss, Emily returned it then went back inside. For a day she could pretend the shop was hers.

The circulating library they ran was particularly popular with young women in the town, who were in and out changing books all morning. Emily knew most of them and since there was to be a Ball at the Assembly Rooms at the end of race week, there was a great deal of discussion about dresses and possible partners.

"Will you be going?" asked Minnie Holmes, a girl whom Emily had known at school.

Emily shook her head.

"Is it your parents? Won't they let you go?"

"I haven't even asked them. I'm not particularly interested, that's all." Emily's answer was true enough, although her main reason for not attending was lack of a partner.

Minnie hid her astonishment that anyone should wish to forego such pleasures and went on to discuss an almost equally popular topic, Lily's wedding. "I hope I never get so desperate that I'd consider marrying anyone as fat as Septimus Rod—" she was confiding across the counter, when the bride herself walked through the door.

Minnie went pink, mumbled, "Oh, hello, Lily," picked up her library books and fled.

Trying hard to look unconcerned, Lily sat down and pulled off her gloves a finger at a time. "She was talking about me, wasn't she?"

"Eh . . . aah," Emily stumbled, for she wasn't good at lying.

Lily tilted her chin defiantly. "You don't have to answer, dear. Anyway, I don't care. It's jealousy that's all."

"I'm sure it is," answered Emily, although remembering the hours she and her mother had spent trying to comfort a distraught Marigold, she felt Lily was getting a justly deserved dose of her own medicine.

"I'm quite parched after the walk up here, any chance of a drink, Em?"

"I'll make some tea. Call me if I get a customer."

"How's marriage then?" Emily felt bound to ask when she returned with tea and slices of fruit loaf.

"Marvellous," Lily simpered although if it hadn't been for Emily's youth, she might have been tempted to confide in her. Because during the weeks in which they'd been wed, Septimus hadn't budged from his side of the bed and she suspected something was amiss. From childhood she and her sisters had debated endlessly on where babies came from and Lily was positive that more than a kiss was required of a husband to produce one. But that, and a "Goodnight dear," was as much as Septimus seemed able to manage before he was snoring contentedly into the pillow. As an ex-midwife, her stepmother would be the person to ask but she didn't dare, in case her sisters discovered her humiliating secret. So she spent her nights in ignorant misery and tried to count her blessings, for Septimus was a good soul, and generous, and hardly seemed to mind what she ordered from the dressmaker and milliner. Then of course there was her house, her pride and joy, which she wanted to show off to everyone. But although her father and stepmother had called, none of her sisters, in spite of numerous invitations, had set foot over the threshold. This she put down to simple envy.

Lily sipped her tea then, although it hadn't been her intention, she said, "Actually that's why I've come, Emily, to ask you to tea tomorrow."

"That's kind of you Lily." Emily had heard enough about the house to be curious to see it. "What time?"

"About three o'clock, then we can have a nice long chat."

While Emily was exchanging Lily's books, the bell over the door announced another customer. "I'll be with you in a moment, sir," Emily called to show he wasn't being neglected.

"Please, there's no hurry," the young man replied and went and stood by the bookshelves which were stacked to the ceiling with titles on almost every subject under the sun.

Lily departed with a final, "I'll see you at three o'clock tomorrow, then. The address is 6, Orchard Street by the way. Don't be late, will you?"

"I won't, I promise," Emily reassured her then immediately went over to deal with her new customer. "May I help you?" She smiled professionally.

The young man produced a sheet of paper and handed it to her. "Have you any of these books in stock, please?"

Emily looked down the list. "Most of them, but not all, although of course we can order them."

"How long would it take? You see I'm going up to Cambridge soon, so I'm a bit pushed for time."

Emily did wonder, if it was so urgent, why he hadn't ordered the books earlier. "It might take a week."

Adam, who found himself rather taken with Emily's dimples and dark eyes said, "You don't remember me do you?"

"I see so many faces," Emily apologised.

"I'm Adam Bennett, Clare's cousin. She came to see your mother and I met her here. It was some time ago, while you were still a schoolgirl. You've grown up a bit since then, of course."

Emily might have considered this remark rather personal, if she hadn't been even more conscious of his blue, dark-fringed eyes scanning her face. Her body grew warm under his scrutiny, but for the life of her, she couldn't move. They stood for several seconds like that, eyes locked, her heart knocking erratically against her ribcage and feeling quite light-headed as if succumbing to some sickness. Having had no practice, Emily was beyond understanding what was happening to her, and in a panic she reached out and grabbed several books from the shelf and moved round behind the counter. "Shall I wrap them for you?"

Adam smiled. "It's kind of you, but they're not actually on my list."

Emily looked at the titles on the spine, saw that they were romantic novels, blushed and shoved them under the counter. "Sorry." She snatched up the piece of paper. "If you would take a seat, Mr Bennett, I'll get the books you want."

Quickly she scaled the ladder, feeling safe amongst the rarely disturbed cobwebby tomes.

"Be careful," Adam warned half rising from his seat when her foot appeared to slip on a rung. "Wouldn't it be better if I did that?"

"I'm quite used to this, thank you, Mr Bennett, I'm up and down several times a day." Emily, from her lofty position, was in control of her emotions again and able to stare down at him with a studied coolness.

So Adam sat down and instead enjoyed the occasional tantalizing glimpse of petticoats, ribbons and slim ankles.

"If you'd oblige me by taking these, Mr Bennett." By Emily's cool tone Adam knew he'd been caught ogling. Ashamed, he leapt up, relieved her of several leather-bound books and placed them on the counter.

"Here, let me help you." Adam held out his hand to assist her down the last few rungs of the ladder.

To show her independence, Emily refused the outstretched hand and jumped. But she landed awkwardly, which somehow enabled Adam to slide his arm round her waist.

It was at this silent, exquisite moment that an old Jewish pedlar with a long beard came in selling quill pens. In a second Emily had unwound herself from Adam's embrace and a discussion ensued on the sort of quills she preferred, pinions or flags. In the end she bought some of each and the old fellow left, expressing his gratitude volubly. Avoiding Adam's glance, Emily bound up the books he was purchasing with string and handed them to him. "That will be four shillings please, Mr Bennett," she said formally.

Adam handed her the money and their fingers touched briefly. Emily snatched her hand away as if she'd touched hot metal and with a galloping heart wrote out the receipt.

"When may I call back for the other books, Miss Fairfax?"

"In about a week, Mr Bennett," she replied as Simon and Ben came charging into the shop like young bulls.

"Where's our dinner, Em, we're starving," they shouted and rushed on up the stairs.

Emily laughed and went to the door with Adam. "As you see, I've got two hungry brothers to feed, so I'll have to close."

"Good day to you Miss Fairfax." Adam raised his hat. Outside he gave her a further smile and small salute before strolling off down the street. As she pulled down the blind on the door, Emily craned her neck to catch a final glimpse of him. A whole week until their next meeting. It seemed like an eternity.

Emily wasn't completely taken by surprise to find that her first customer when she re-opened was Adam. "I'd forgotten that I'd promised to take Clare and my mother back a couple of novels," he lied. "What would you recommend?"

He searched her face as if he might find the answer there but Emily, who during the dinner hour had given herself a good talking to, struggled to resist him. "Many people seem to enjoy the novels of Miss Jane Austen. There are several there on the shelf."

"Show me where."

"Look under 'A'." As long as the counter was between them, she was in control.

"Isn't helping a customer part of the service?"

Emily moved over to the shelves, pulled down several books and handed them to Adam.

"Can you meet me later? Please say yes," he murmured as a husband and wife and several noisy children entered the shop.

She stared at him in panic. "Oh no, I couldn't."

Adam's face fell. "I'll go then."

"I think it might be a good idea." Emily had never been courted before and her young emotions were in turmoil. For along with the sweetness and excitement of sexual awakening was a fear that her parents might return at any moment, and without a doubt, the last person they would welcome as a suitor was Adam Bennett.

Chapter Eleven

Jed and Rachel returned from the races looking pleased as punch and richer by five pounds.

"It was a stroke of luck really. We saw Miss Jane Dobbs there, took her advice on a horse, put some money on it and it won!" Jed tossed a florin towards his daughter. "That's for looking after the shop."

"Who's Miss Dobbs?" asked Emily reaching out to catch the coin.

"Her father was the parson at St Philip's in Halby. Now she makes her living running a stud. I must say I admire her, it can't be easy for a woman on her own."

"She was telling me she couldn't manage without that man who was with her, Reuben I think she called him. A rough looking character, I thought," observed Rachel. "Frankly I wouldn't trust him an inch."

Jed gave his wife a look of mild rebuke. "You shouldn't judge a book by its cover, Rachel."

"Perhaps not," answered Rachel and went over to the mirror, asking while she untied the strings of her bonnet, "So how was your day, Em?"

Until today Emily had been unsparing in her contempt for girls who declared themselves in love with the first man who showed even a mild interest. But here she was, behaving no differently. Except that hers was no fickle attachment, this was a love she wanted to share with her parents – the world. Except that seeing who it was, she thought that would be unwise.

"Well?" her mother enquired, when she didn't answer.

"Quite good. Clare's cousin, Adam," she couldn't resist it, she had to say his name, feel it on her lips, "came in. He's going up to Cambridge soon so he placed quite a large order."

"Anyone else?"

"A lot of people were at the races, of course, but Lily came in to change her library books. She's invited me to tea tomorrow afternoon. I've said yes, that's all right, isn't it? I think she's lonely."

"She deserves to be," Rachel snapped, for Marigold still succumbed regularly to bouts of weeping.

"Mama, what's done is done. Everyone is being horrible to Lily, her sisters won't visit her and she's dying to show off her new house. Besides, Marigold will probably meet someone else eventually."

"I'm not so sure."

"I don't think Septimus is such a bargain anyway, with all that fat. I'd want my husband to be slim," said Emily, thinking of Adam, young, taut-muscled and handsome.

"There are more important things to consider when you marry. Septimus is overweight I'll grant you, but he's still got a healthy order book," Jed replied. "People as far away as Newcastle and London are buying his furniture. Lily's on to a good thing."

"I hope I never marry a man because he's got a healthy order book." Emily's young voice rang with disdain.

"But then you see, you've been blessed with your mother's beauty." Jed stroked his daughter's dark head affectionately. "You'll never be called upon to make that choice. But what about girls like Marigold and

Primrose, without much in the way of looks and stuck at home with their father? Ponder on that a bit and while you do, be a good lass and make your mother and me a cup of tea."

The following day, with the florin her father had given her, Emily went to the market and bought some yellow ribbon and a spray of artificial daisies. She sewed them on to her bonnet and just after two o'clock, set off for Lily's house. Shopkeepers' sons lounging in their doorways straightened in astonishment as she passed, wondering how it could have slipped their notice that she'd grown into a stunning young woman.

Emily didn't hurry and, in the High Street, she paused every now and then to study the goods displayed in the shop windows.

"Good afternoon."

"Mr Bennett, what are you doing here?" Emily swung round feigning surprise.

"Looking for you."

"But I'm on my way to visit a friend."

"I know, I heard you making your arrangements yesterday."

"You mean you eavesdropped, Mr Bennett?" The reprimand was diluted by a giggle.

"Well, unintentionally. But you can't turn me away, not after I've been waiting two hours," Adam pleaded, and moved closer, enchanted by the face under the bonnet. "You must let me walk with you."

"Oh . . . eh . . . well perhaps just a little way. But through the back streets." Never having practised deception before, Emily's early courage began to seep away. With a quick glance about her, she scurried across the road into Loseby Lane, leaving Adam to follow.

"Where does your friend live?" asked Adam catching up with her.

"In Orchard Street. But she mustn't see you." Emily was breathless now from nerves and guilt.

"Why not?"

"She might tell my parents."

"Would that be so terrible? I've no dishonourable intentions."

"Well . . ." How could she explain, without hurting Adam, that from stories half told, half listened to, she knew that old emnities lay between their families. "They're very strict," she lied.

"I see. So I mayn't write to you when I go up to Cambridge?"

Emily's brow creased with alarm. "Heavens, no." By now they'd now come out into London Road and Emily felt particularly vulnerable. "You'd better turn back here."

"Can't I wait for you?"

"Oh no, no." Race week drew people in from all over the County so the streets were crowded. Stalls had been set up along London Road and there was a steady sale of pies, lemonade and hot potatoes. She was bound to meet someone who knew her. "I'll probably be ages."

"I don't care. I'd wait a lifetime for you, Emily." Adam took her hand, and drew her to him. "Please say I can wait."

In the thrall of Adam's sapphire blue eyes, Emily was about to succumb to his pleas when behind her a voice trilled, "Ooh-hoo." Pushing him urgently away from her, she hissed, "Go, it's Lily."

"Too late, she's coming this way."

Emily groaned. Her small transgression would go straight back to her parents.

By now Lily was upon them, and already chatting

amiably. "I was watching out for you, in case you weren't sure which was our house." Although she addressed her remarks to Emily, Lily's eyes were fixed on Adam and they were bulging with curiosity. "Well, aren't you going to introduce me?" she simpered and patted her curls.

"Uhm . . . ah . . . yes," stuttered Emily, made the introductions then added, "but you're just going, aren't you Adam?"

"What a pity. You'd be very welcome to join us for tea, Mr Bennett."

"No, he can't." Emily gave Adam a small shove as if to push him down the street.

"Why not?"

"Because . . ." But Emily could think of no valid reason.

"Perhaps Mr Bennett should be allowed to decide." As well as being eager to show off her house to as many people as possible, Lily found it difficult to understand why Emily should wish to rid herself of such a fine specimen of English manhood.

"I'd be delighted to have tea with you, Mrs Rodway," answered Adam, not daring to look at Emily.

"Right, come along then." Lily beckoned the young couple up the path and through the door, where they were given a tour of every room in the house, including the wash house, broom cupboard and cellar. As was expected of them, they exclaimed over the furniture, admired the Turkish carpets, solid silver candlesticks and Royal Worcester dinner service, until their tongues finally ran out of superlatives.

"Your husband is a fine craftsman, Mrs Rodway," said Adam, when they returned with parched mouths to the sitting-room and Lily rang for tea.

"He is indeed, and he denies me nothing. Cake, Mr

Bennett? I made it myself." Lily offered Adam the cakestand and he took a slice of Madeira.

"Last night he came home with tickets for the Ball at the Assembly rooms on Friday. Remind me to show you my dress before you leave, Emily."

"Perhaps you'll honour me with a dance then, Mrs Rodway," said Adam gallantly, "for I shall be there as well." He turned to Emily. "You'll dance with me, won't you?"

Emily shook her head. "I'm not going."

"Why ever not? Are your parents against it?"

"Not particularly, but I can't go alone."

"Well that's easily sorted out," said Lily. "You must come with Septimus and me. There will be quite a party of us there, mostly business friends and their wives."

"But I haven't anything suitable to wear."

"You could borrow one of my dresses, we're about the same size, and stay for the night as well. It will be the first time the guest bedroom has been used. Oh isn't this exciting?" Lily clapped her hands with delight. "Now come upstairs, and see if you can find a gown that takes your fancy."

Pulling dresses of every material and colour from her wardrobe, Lily piled them on the bed and invited Emily to take her pick. A dress of moss green taffeta caught her eye and she held it in front of her.

"Try it on," Lily urged, helped Emily undo the buttons of her own dress, then slipped the evening gown over her head. "There you are." Head on one side, Lily studied Emily's reflection in the pier-glass then pulled in a handful of material at the waist. "Some stitches here and there and it'll be a perfect fit."

"The colour quite suits me, doesn't it?" Emily didn't

want to appear too vain, but she thought the dress lovely.

"The men will be lining up to dance with you."

"My parents haven't said I can go yet," Emily reminded her, although after all the money they'd spent sending her to dancing classes, she could hardly see them objecting.

"Don't worry your head about that. Septimus is a lamb and does whatever I ask. I'll send him round this evening to have a word with your father. He knows there's no one more trustworthy."

"Please, one thing Lily. Will you promise not to mention Adam to Septimus, or my parents? Or anyone in fact."

Lily laid her hand over her heart. "I won't tell a soul. On my honour." Remembering the tyranny of long, empty days she added recklessly, "You and Adam can always meet here, you know. When Septimus is at his business, of course." Forbidden love, intrigue, romance, just like a novel. Lily sighed and her own unfulfilled longings brought the colour to her cheeks.

"Could we really? You see he's going to university soon and I won't see him again for ages, and I daren't let him write to me."

"I'll act as your go-between. Tell him to send his letters here." Living vicariously now, Lily's eyes were bright with excitement.

Her sins forgotten, Emily leaned forward and kissed Lily. "You're an angel and I shall love you forever."

The footman in his powdered wig opened the coach door, let down the steps, took Emily's hand and helped her alight. More coaches rolled up and the Assembly Rooms' lights blazed down on town worthies, the titled of the County and military men, as well as onlookers come to enjoy the spectacle even if they couldn't participate. Many of the gowns must have been ordered in London and never had Emily been in such grand company. She remembered how, as a child, she too had stood outside with her mother, watching guests waft in on clouds of silk and perfume. How she'd loved the glitter and magic. How it had stayed with her for days afterwards. And now, incredibly, she was in a similarily enviable position, and being gaped at by a bunch of verminous looking urchins.

"Gee'us a penny, Mister," a small scarecrow of a girl called. Septimus generously obliged, threw a handful of coppers, and there was an undignified scramble for the coins.

Lily took Emily's hand and squeezed it. "Isn't this just the best day of your life?"

Tremulous with nerves and excitement, Emily could only nod.

"Grab hold, girls," Septimus ordered, extended his arms like wings, and the three of them sailed in through the porticoed entrance and up the stairs to the ballroom.

"Well, what do you think of it?" asked Septimus.

"Wonderful, my dear," answered his wife, while Emily stood silently absorbing the scene she'd so often imagined. The scent of hot-house flowers filled the room and above them, on a balcony, musicians were playing a waltz tune. At either end of the room were large gilt-framed mirrors. In them the dancing couples, and two chandeliers suspended from the ceiling like lakes of fire, were duplicated, triplicated . . . on, on into infinity.

"There's our party over there, let's move round a bit," said Septimus, guiding them to the other side of the room, where a group of men and their wives stood.

Here Lily, tonight very aware of her status as a married woman, introduced Emily.

Many of the people Emily knew through the bookshop so when the waltz ended and a *quadrille* was announced, she found herself partnered off with a pale young man with damp hands called Leighton. But she'd come here to enjoy herself and enjoy herself she would. She'd intended to keep a look out for Adam while she danced, but the complicated figures of the *quadrille* needed all her attention. By the time they reached the galop, Emily had quite forgotten Adam, and she bounded down the room laughing immoderately, both from high spirits and the sight of Septimus's cheeks wobbling like blancmange.

When the dance ended, the ladies collapsed into chairs and, all round the room, fans fluttered like giant butterflies. Then Septimus, after wiping the sweat from his forehead, declared that they must all have an ice. As he went off to order them, Lily tapped Emily's forearm with her fan. "See who's just arrived, at the far end of the room," she murmured.

Emily's heart began to beat erratically.

"Isn't he handsome?"

Emily nodded for, in her eyes, Adam, tall and self-possessed, outshone every other man in the room. From the coy glances behind fans, it was also obvious that many other young women shared this view. For the first time in her life, Emily tasted that demon jealousy; the insecurity of love, the terror of loss.

With Adam were Clare, an older man, larger even than Septimus, and a handsome woman wearing a sapphire necklace which exactly matched her blue silk gown.

"That must be his mother. He said he'd dance with us, but I wonder . . ." Emily's voice trailed away, for why should he even give her a second glance when he could take his pick from some of the most beautiful, and wealthiest, girls in Leicestershire.

While Emily was nursing her doubts, Harry arrived, gazed round the ballroom, searching every face until he saw Matilda. He stood studying her and thought, by God, she's a stunner, and every inch the lady. Fortunately, she'd lost the silliness that had been such an irritating part of her character when she was younger. In no way could she be described as matronly, though. On the contrary, she was like a good wine that matures with age. A woman in her prime, self-assured, beautiful, rich and dying for sex.

Matilda was talking to Adam, but she must have sensed she was being observed because she turned. Her lips were parted in a half smile of greeting, but then seeing who it was, they tightened, then she turned back to her son.

The rebuff stirred the old sexual urge in Harry. I'll dance with you tonight, see if I don't. And rekindle that passion so that you're crying out for it my haughty lady, Harry vowed, then thought how fortunate it was that Charlotte had developed a chill which had prevented her from coming tonight. Initially, he'd suspected it was another of his wife's excuses to avoid a social event, but an unbecoming red nose and a croaking voice convinced him.

"I'll stay with her if you like, Papa," Judith offered, who found the idea of dressing up in frills and flounces and parading herself at a ball rather bothersome.

But Harry was having none of it, he had too much invested in this evening. "No, my dear, that isn't necessary. We pay servants to do that. And Max and Gregory will be arriving soon so go and get yourselves ready."

With two girls to find husbands for, Harry engineered

social contact between them and Sylvia's boys as often as possible, ignoring the fact that Olivia obviously found Max's devotion tiresome. There wasn't a glimmer of interest between Judith and Gregory either, but he had to plod on. Marriage was a business contract, an alliance which would be beneficial to both parties, one hoped, but it had nothing to do with love. This sad fact was something his girls would have to wake up to unless they intended remaining spinsters for the rest of their days.

In fact, Harry often wondered if Judith might. She was almost deliberately awkward in her manner and made little effort to make herself attractive. She even managed to look like a sack of potatoes in the dress which he'd gone to such expense over. He just prayed she wouldn't deliberately snub Max and Gregory, who'd been invited to stay overnight, the idea being that the more familiar they became, the fonder they would grow of each other. But there, children didn't always appreciate parents' efforts on their behalf.

The right impression was important though, and he'd made sure the family coach and upholstery were thoroughly cleaned, that the buttons of the coachman's blue jacket shone like gold pieces, and that they arrived at the Assembly Rooms in style. Gazing round the ballroom Harry thought, well we might have not have vast tracts of land, nor coal deposits, nor a title, but the family was gentry and equal to anyone in this room.

Max, Gregory and the girls had joined the other dancers on the floor and watching them, Harry indulged in a little fantasy. It could happen; two brothers could marry two sisters and all four of them walk up the aisle together. Harry glanced over at Matilda. She still wasn't dancing. He edged round the floor towards her. I've nothing to lose, he told himself, she can only refuse me, but still felt as self conscious as a schoolboy.

"Will you honour me with a dance, Matilda?" Harry gave a formal bow and he noticed she was slightly thrown by the offer, uncertain whether to refuse or accept. But the musicians struck up a waltz and Harry held out his arms. She went to him and as he clasped her round her waist and their fingers touched, he was aware of a faint sexual charge. Emboldened he murmured huskily, "It's a long time since I held you in my arms like this, Tilda. Too long."

Matilda leaned back and studied him with a cool eye.

"Still the same old silver-tongued Harry." She laughed but there was a bitter ring to it.

"But I mean every word." Remembering what an eager participant she'd been in all their sexual adventures, the risks she'd been prepared to take, Harry pressed his mouth close to her ear and whispered, "Rooks Spinney, remember? And the church and all those other places and how good it was."

Matilda gave a half-embarrassed giggle. "But we were young then, Harry."

"You're still young. In fact you're even more beautiful than when we first met. Let me show you." He swung her over to one of the large mirrors. "See what a handsome pair we make." Harry, now in his stride, saw small telling signs of arousal; a slight agitation in her breathing that caused her breasts to rise and fall, dilated pupils. "And we could have it all again, what's to stop us?" He pulled her closer and, already anticipating their reunion, he whirled her round the room and felt her relax in his arms. If he could bribe one of the attendants to find him an empty room, it would be sooner rather than later, Harry was musing, when he felt Matilda stiffen and move away from him.

"Who's that girl Adam is dancing with?"

Harry glanced indifferently in Adam's direction.

"There are so many girls here, I don't know half of them."

"There's something familiar about her face."

"Don't let it trouble you, Matilda."

"I don't want him mixing with anyone unsuitable."

"It's someone to dance with, that's all." Sensing she was slipping away from him, Harry cursed under his breath. And just when he'd been making such headway.

"He's had several dances with her already, I shall have to put a stop to it, otherwise people will talk." The music stopped and without a word, Matilda moved away, leaving him standing in the middle of the floor feeling slightly ridiculous.

Olivia, who had also been paying close attention to Emily and Adam, and noticing how totally absorbed they were in each other, waylaid him on his way back to his seat. "You haven't asked me to dance yet," she pouted.

"The next quadrille I will, I promise, Olivia," Adam answered, continued on his way, only to be met with a sharp look and question from his mother.

"Who was that girl you were dancing with?"

"Just an acquaintance," he parried.

"What's her name?

Adam frowned. "Mother, why the inquisition? I only danced with her."

"Do her parents keep a bookshop?"

"Since you ask, yes."

"She's Jed Fairfax's daughter isn't she?"

George jumped up in alarm. "Good Lord, don't have

anything to do with her, Adam. Our families are sworn enemies."

Adam gazed with steely eyes at his uncle. "Now why should that be?"

George hurrumphed loudly and sat down "Well . . . it's a long story . . ."

"Indeed it is – very long." Matilda gave her brother a glance that told him to shut up. She had no desire to conceal his crimes but this was hardly the occasion to be rattling family skeletons, not with half of Leicestershire present. "My objection is that her father's a dangerous radical, and her mother's a nobody. A bastard child who came to us from the workhouse as a maidservant."

"I would consider it a misfortune rather than a crime to be left an orphan, Mother."

Oh God, he wasn't getting cranky ideas as well, thought Matilda in some alarm.

"Who are you all talking about?" asked Clare, who had been standing a few feet away, chatting to a couple of young women.

"Emily," answered Adam, bold in the face of his mother's disapproval.

"Why, she's a kinswoman of mine."

As if I could ever forget, thought Matilda, then smiled weakly at her niece. "Yes, but so distant, dear, it hardly counts."

"But anyway, here are Olivia and Judith, come to dance."

Matilda saw the coquettish smile Olivia gave Adam and felt the hairs rise on the back of her neck. My God, what was happening? The room grew warm, the dancing more hectic, the laughter louder. The large windows were opened to the night, moths flew in and were incinerated in the flames of the candles and Matilda felt the past galloping towards her in fury.

"You've gone pale, Tilda, are you all right?"

Matilda actually heard a note of concern in Harry's voice, and she gave her head a small shake. "Yes, I'm fine, thank you." The resemblance was so strong, Matilda knew Harry must have a pretty shrewd idea that Adam was his. He'd asked her once, years ago, and she'd denied it and she would go on denying it. He'd inflicted such deep emotional wounds she'd vowed that a confession would never come from her lips. It was her only weapon. The element of doubt would be his punishment. But Adam and Olivia . . . it didn't bear thinking about. For a second she was tempted to confess all, then she remembered; soon Adam would be going up to Cambridge and out of the clutches these young hussies. The knowledge helped her to breathe freely again.

"Well, come and dance, then." Harry went to pull her on to the floor but she resisted.

"I'd rather not."

"But you must, Auntie, we need four couples," Clare exclaimed.

"Oh, all right. But I'm tired so if you don't mind, after this dance, I think we should go home."

Adam, who put his mother's strange mood down to his dancing too often with Emily, couldn't hide his dismay. "But the evening's hardly half over. At least wait until after supper, Mother."

"We'll see," said Matilda and gave Adam a look that said, as long as you toe the line.

Chapter Twelve

As Adam hoped, by the time she'd had supper and a glass or two of wine his mother had relaxed, forgotten her threat to leave early, and went on to dance almost every dance right up until the Sir Roger de Coverly brought the Ball to its conclusion. In fact, the musicians had packed away their instruments and yawning attendants were snuffing the candles on the chandeliers when they finally came out into the dark streets to await their carriage to take them back to Halby.

After the interval, so as not to appear to be favouring one girl above the other, Adam danced in strict rotation with Clare, Judith and Olivia. But while he swung them around the room he tried to gain Emily's attention. But she refused to look at him and, from the dejected droop of her shoulders, Adam could guess her thoughts; with three other attractive young women to entertain, he'd lost interest in her and she'd been ruthlessly abandoned.

As the evening advanced, so did Adam's conviction that he'd been reduced, in Emily's eyes, to a slimy, loathsome toad. That he couldn't bear and he was growing desperate when a *mazurka* was announced. At last, an opportunity he'd been waiting for. A chance to speak to her, to explain what had happened and let her know that he wasn't empty, fickle and vain. Emily remained determinedly seated, though, refusing all requests to dance.

His one piece of good fortune was to partner Lily in one of the figures. "Please, Lily, tell Emily it's not what it seems, I haven't forsaken her."

"Oh no?" Lily, who'd had to deal with her friend's bewildered misery, gave Adam a less than friendly glance. "Look, she's breaking her heart over there," she went on, and drew some comfort from Adam's stricken countenance.

"Say it's family, she'll understand then. Can I come round tomorrow to see her?"

"Well . . . there is Septimus to think about. You see, we'll be rising late."

"I beg of you, Lily, this is a matter of life and death," Adam declared, in an excess of youthful emotion.

"All right, but not before midday. He'll probably have gone to his business by then."

Adam squeezed her hand. "You're a brick, Lily."

"I know," Lily answered, and moved to her next partner, wondering wistfully if she would ever awaken such passion in a man's heart. Even in her husband's would do for a start.

In spite of all the dancing and going to bed almost at dawn, Adam slept badly and had confused, unsettling dreams in which Emily was running away from him and, although he almost burst his lungs trying to catch up, the distance between them never lessened. Seeing this as a bad omen, he rose early and in a state of anxiety, made his way back to Leicester. Even after he'd breakfasted at the Bell Hotel, he still had time on his hands, so he walked as slowly as possible along Granby Street and up London Road. He stopped a few yards short of the Rodway residence and waited. My little love is in that house, perhaps still asleep, he thought tenderly, and imagined a slim arm flung across the bed, her hair a tangle on the pillow.

Adam stood waiting for over an hour. Finally at ten to twelve, his patience was rewarded, the door opened and out stepped Septimus. He turned, kissed his wife on the cheek then picked his way down the street with the precise balletic steps of a dancer, which struck Adam as faintly ludicrous in a man with his porcine girth. Lily waved like a dutiful wife, but as soon as her better half had vanished round the corner, she extended her hand and beckoned to Adam.

Adam bounded across the street in long eager strides. "Is she angry with me? Did you pass on my message?" he demanded, gripping Lily's hands.

"Yes I did and no, she isn't angry with you. Once she knew it was family she understood and forgave you absolutely."

"Thank heaven."

"I've given Bertha, my maid, a few hours off. You'll find Emily in the morning room. Go and make your peace with her while I prepare us all some sandwiches. I shall be about a quarter of an hour." Lily gave him a quick, knowing smile and enjoying her role as intermediary, she trotted off to the kitchen.

Adam opened the door with caution, still uncertain how he would be received. Emily was sitting by the fire nursing a tortoiseshell kitten and reading a book. When she heard his step, she looked up with a smile that spoke of total forgiveness.

In one eager step, Adam reached her. Emily laid her novel aside and Adam knelt and pretended to tickle the kitten's ear. Instead he grasped her hand, only to pull it away with an "Ouch!" when sharp feline teeth punctured his skin.

Emily laughed. "She doesn't like you."

Adam leaned close and stared deep into her eyes. "But do you?"

"Oh . . . yes!" Emily answered fervently.

"Truly?"

"Truly."

"I have to know you see, because my mother, like your parents, is making objections, which means we aren't going to be allowed to be open about our feelings. Will you be able to stand that, Emily? Having to meet in secret, tell lies."

"I'll do anything for you, Adam," Emily answered simply. "And we have Lily, she is a good friend to us. So we'll always find a way."

"Dearest Emily." Adam was leaning forward to seal their covenant with a kiss when there was the clatter of teacups.

"Can someone help me please," Lily called diplomatically.

Adam leapt up, cleared his throat and tried to compose himself before opening the door and taking the tray from her. Lily entered with a bright enquiring look. "Everything all right?"

A secret glance passed between Emily and Adam, then they both smiled and answered in unison, "Yes thank you, Lily."

"Good." Lily poured the tea, served it then settled down for a gossip. "Now let's talk about last night. Wasn't it a grand Ball? And what did you think of Lady Paget's diamonds? And that son of hers, isn't he handsome? Although I've heard he's a confirmed bachelor." And so it went on, hairstyles and gowns were discussed, people's characters, manners and behaviour dissected and put under the microscope, while the pile of sandwiches gradually disappeared.

Adam grew desperate. Here they were, sitting talking

about matters of no consequence, when all he wanted to do was take Emily in his arms and cover her face with kisses. By three, Lily was glancing at the clock and he knew he was in danger of outstaying his welcome. He stood up. "I must go."

"I'll see you out," said Emily and walked with him to the door.

"When can I see you again?"

"The books you ordered have arrived."

"I shall come and collect them on Monday." Kissing her dear, sweet little hand, Adam departed. But he rode back to Halby punching the air every now and then with his fist and singing lustily.

Adam spent a good ten minutes striding up and down outside the bookshop, stopping occasionally to peer through the window and check if Emily was alone. When he was certain the coast was clear, he pushed open the door. The bell seemed to clang as loudly as the bell in St Nicholas's church tower and he squinted into the dark corners of the shop, half expecting an irate father to leap out at him. "Where are your parents?" He heard his own voice, gruff and nervous.

"Papa's gone to a book sale. My mother is cooking dinner."

Adam's shoulders relaxed and in one stride he reached the counter and took Emily's hand. "Can you see me for a little while, dearest? In the Newarke, where it's quiet. It will be our last chance, I'm afraid. My mother has decided to take Clare and me to Bath for the week. She seems to think I need a holiday before I go off to Cambridge."

Emily flicked over the pages of a book with anxious fingers. "Oh, I don't know. You see, with Papa away, my mother needs me in the shop. Anyway, what reason would I have? I can't say I'm visiting Lily again, she might grow suspicious."

Adam, who wasn't without his father's persuasive charm, leant across the counter, in his eyes an expression so intense it burnt into Emily's soul. "It will break my heart if we have to part without saying goodbye."

A passer-by paused, peered through the window and looked about to come in. Emily busied herself tying up the books that Adam would take away with him to college. A place far away where he would make new friends and meet well-bred girls who would find him as irresistible as she did. How long would it be before he forgot her, she wondered sadly. One month or two?

The potential customer walked on, Emily handed Adam his parcel and made up her mind. "I'll tell Mama I want to buy flowers from the market for Lily as a thank you present," she said, bothered that she was becoming such an adept fibber.

"Say four?"

"Emily, come along, it's dinnertime," Rachel called down the stairs,

Emily jumped. "Coming, Mama." Then, to Adam, "I'll try, but I can't promise anything." And with that he had to be satisfied.

The Newarke was where the really prosperous families of the town resided: lawyers, doctors, rich hosiers and the like. Many of the houses were surrounded by high walls and had solid iron gates designed to keep at bay the half-starved hordes and dangerous radicals that littered the town. Here everything was muted, damped down by respectability and apart from a dog sniffing its way along the gutter, and a chimney-sweep doing the rounds with his cart and his small climbing boy, the street was deserted.

So, as he often had to, Adam leaned against a wall and waited. After a few minutes the sepulchral silence was broken by the creak of rusty hinges and a man stepped out into the roadway. Although Adam wore the dress of a gentleman, he felt himself being regarded with deep suspicion. To his relief, Emily's small figure came hurrying along the road and he moved towards her with arms outstretched. Satisfied that Adam probably wasn't bent on stealing the family silver, the man walked on, even managing a tolerant smile when Adam swung Emily off her feet, and her carefree laughter cracked the gloomy gentility of the place.

"Little one, I was so worried you wouldn't come!"

Emily, growing anxious again, glanced over her shoulder. "I mustn't stay long, or my parents will begin to suspect."

"Give me a little while at least," Adam pleaded. "After today we'll be parted until Christmas, which seems like a lifetime."

"I know, and I don't know if I can bear it." Tears weren't far away and Emily's head fell on his shoulder. Adam held her away from him and lifted her chin. She trembled in his arms and her eyes, large, luminous and uncertain, stared up at him. Unable to control himself a moment longer, Adam bent and kissed her, covering her until now unkissed mouth with a hungry urgency. A charge of hot desire shot down his body and into his loins. With a moan, he began pulling roughly at the buttons on Emily's dress then at the hem, wanting to engulf her with his passion.

"No." Visibly shaken, Emily pushed him away. "I must go."

"Not yet," Adam entreated, for his body was still hot and hard.

"Yes." Emily began to walk away. "You shouldn't have done that, you know."

"Done what?"

"You were rough and you tried to touch me." The anger Emily directed at Adam, was all tangled up in the shame of her own response; at the almost uncontrollable urge that left her wanting him to go on, to take them to the mysterious limits of their desire for each other. So agitated was she that Emily wove an erratic path down the street, as if trying to shake off the smirking, know-all devil that was frolicking at her heels.

Finally Adam reached out and caught her by the shoulder. "I beg you, Emily wait." He turned her round to face him. "I promise I'll never do anything like that again. Not unless you want it."

Moved and humbled, Emily reached up and traced her fingers around the outline of his mouth. "We've got plenty of time you know."

Adam kissed her again with a deep tenderness. "You're right, my love, all our lives."

Chapter Thirteen

For as long as Clare could remember, Adam had been her constant companion, then suddenly he had gone, leaving a great yawning gap in her life. It hit her badly to know that there would be no morning rides together, no more opportunities for childish games with Olivia and Jude away from adult eyes. Life was dull beyond reason, so to alleviate her boredom she teased Christopher Harcourt unmercifully, her remarks growing more provocative by the day. At first it was gratifying to watch him blush a peony red, but soon even this palled and, instead, she took to wandering round the house sighing lustily.

By now her grandmother, the most tolerant of women, had lost patience with her. "What is the matter with you, dear?" she asked one afternoon as Clare sat in the kitchen tantalizing an elderly cat.

"I'm bored."

"Well that can soon be rectified. You can give me a hand. Here, cut up these crab apples, then when you've finished, write out some labels for the pots."

"But the apples will stain my fingers!"

"Poppycock!" Having none of it, Esther Pedley pushed a basket of small apples and a preserving pan across the table to her granddaughter and Clare had no choice but to start chopping.

Right through childhood, Clare had watched her grandmother make crab-apple jelly and it was a tedious job. After the fruit was cut up it had to be cooked to a pulp then strained – never squeezed – through a jelly bag with a slow drip, drip which took all night. The following day the juice would be measured, then after the appropriate amount of sugar had been added, it would be boiled. It was then that a wonderful alchemy took place and the small sour apples were transformed into a clear, sharp tasting, amber jelly which was delicious eaten with goose and cold meats at Christmas or spread on bread and butter.

"I start on the Christmas puddings next week," said Esther, measuring water into the pan. "You can help Prudence and me with those as well. After that it's the Christmas cake and the mincemeat. With all the fruit, peel and suet to cut up and clean, you won't have time to be bored."

"Who's bored, then?" asked George, strolling into the kitchen and peering into the preserving pan. Finding nothing edible there, he helped himself to a tankard of ale from the pantry and sat down at the scrubbed table.

For all her sweet ways, Clare sometimes betrayed characteristics that reminded Esther uncomfortably of whose child she was. "Your daughter."

"I'm inclined to sympathise, Halby is a damned dull place and Leicester is hardly better."

"Language, George," his mother reprimanded.

"Sorry, Mother but that's the truth of it. Always was, always will be. In fact I'm thinking of taking myself off back to London for a while."

Clare, looking suddenly animated, leapt up, linked her arm through her father's and gave him a winsome smile. "Oh take me with you Papa . . . please."

George, who'd had a run of luck at the card tables and a cockfight and was feeling unusually prosperous, looked at his mother for affirmation. She was very comely, this daughter of his and he knew several elderly widowers looking for a young bride. Much as he loved his little girl, for a cash inducement, he could probably be persuaded to part with her. The time to strike the bargain was now, with Adam away, although it wouldn't do for his mother to get wind of his plans or the game would be up. "Well . . . I don't know," George mused, stroking his moustache and pretending to sound doubtful.

"Please, Papa." Clare jumped up and down in frustration.

"If she's going to moon around here, probably a couple of weeks away would do her no harm," observed Mrs Pedley.

"Oh Grandmama, thank you." Clare ran to her grandmother and kissed her. "When do we go, Papa?"

George patted Clare's cheek in a fatherly manner. "Let's say Friday, that will give you plenty of time to get packed."

With Adam no longer under his tutelage, Christopher Harcourt's routine had changed and he now gave Clare her daily lessons at Thatcher's Mount. It was history that day, not her favourite subject, and she was doodling on a piece of paper, her mind obviously not on their chosen period, the Roman occupation of Leicester. When she yawned, he was finally moved to rebuke her. "Miss Clare, pay attention, please."

"I'm sorry Mr Harcourt, but I'm finding it hard to concentrate today."

"I had noticed."

"You see, Papa is taking me to London on Friday, and I'm so looking forward to it, I can hardly think of anything else."

This news came as an unpleasant surprise to Christopher. Being a sensitive young man, given more often than was good for him to gloomy introspection, he feared that his days in Halby were numbered. He would be desolated if he were parted from Clare, but it was inevitable unless he found another post in the area. Unfortunately, tutors were two a penny, so his chances were slim. Sometimes he even considered throwing himself upon Clare's mercy, declaring his love and seeing what happened. But in his more lucid moments, Christopher realised it would be a pointless gesture. After all, what had he to offer any young woman? His future prospects looked bleak and he was as poor as a church mouse. His Aunt Tabitha, who raised him after his parents died, had been a pious spinster who resented being palmed off with her brother's child, and he found what affection there was in the servants' quarters. The small inheritance his father had left saw him through Oxford, but when his aunt died he discovered she'd left her considerable wealth to the Missionary Society, with strict instructions that they were to take the gospel to a remote tribe of pygmies in equatorial Africa. Anyway, even with money he doubted if he was the sort of man to set Clare's pulses racing. Oh she teased and flirted with him, but what she was really doing was testing her feminine powers.

Christopher always made a point in going in through the back way at Trent Hall. This gave him an excuse to pause in the kitchen and have a chat with Mrs White, the cook, a kind woman who was inclined to mother him.

"A scone, Mr Harcourt?" she asked, as Christopher hoped she would. She stopped rolling pastry and pointed to a batch nestling, warm and floury, on a clean white cloth.

"Yes please, Mrs White." Christopher sorely needed cheering up, and he watched with a sense of gratitude as she split the scones in two, buttered them and then poured him a glass of cold milk. He spent more time than anyone might have guessed in the warm kitchen, for it reminded him of his childhood and he was at home here. The servants' banter and gossip, their comings and goings, all helped ease his loneliness.

"You look worried, me duck, everything all right?" Mrs White gazed at him with concern.

Christopher took a drink of milk and resisted the urge to confide. If it got back to Mrs Bennett, more than likely he'd be shown the door. "I'm fine, thank you Mrs White, and these scones are delicious."

"Think nothing of it, Mr Harcourt." She leaned confidentially over the table. "And if you happen to be around at four o'clock I've made a very nice fruit cake."

"I'll remember that." More cheerful after the small spoiling, Christopher was whistling quietly to himself as he passed Matilda's office. The door was open and she was busy writing but she looked up when she heard his footsteps. "Mr Harcourt, may I have a word?"

This is it, thought Christopher, his mouth turning dry with apprehension. By the end of the month he'd be out on his ear and destitute. "Yes, certainly, Mrs Bennett."

"Take a chair, Mr Harcourt," Matilda invited. Christopher did as he was bid, but sat poised on the edge and tapping his foot in an agitated manner.

Matilda swung round and studied him. "How long have you been with us?"

"Three years."

"It's amazing how times flies and now Adam's up at Cambridge and Clare is eighteen," she mused.

Christopher braced himself. Here it comes, he thought. Now, take it on the chin like a man.

"You have little in the way of family, I believe."

"My Aunt Tabitha, who raised me, died some years ago. There might be distant cousins, but none that I have any contact with," Christopher answered, puzzled by the line of questioning.

"Obviously I'm not going to need you here much longer."

"I had rather presumed that, Mrs Bennett."

"Don't look so glum, I have a proposal to put to you, Mr Harcourt. As you must be aware, most of the people in this village are born ignorant and die ignorant, a state of affairs I want to rectify. It is a matter I have given considerable thought to and I've decided to open a small school. It will be modest, no Latin or Greek, just the three R's, but a move in the right direction. A cottage on the Green belonging to the Estate has become vacant, and I was wondering if you would consider taking on the task of setting up the school, buying the primers and slates and whatever else you need to teach the children? I'm sure you could make a success of it. Your salary will remain the same and you'd keep your room here. Of course you may have already made other plans . . ." Matilda's voice trailed away but she watched him closely, for she was most anxious to keep this young man in Halby. He was in love with Clare, and although there was no money, neither were there any relatives to ask awkward questions about Clare's parentage. Although she was extremely pretty, her niece had never been courted, and she guessed it was because round here people remembered her mother, the simple Polly. If she could encourage Clare to get involved in the school they'd be thrown together and nature, she hoped, might take its course.

It took Christopher a few seconds to absorb what Matilda was offering him, then slowly his intense young features relaxed and he felt the urge to do something impulsive, like jump up and dance round the room. Imagine, he wouldn't have to face the humiliation of applying for positions and being turned down and, joy of joys, he could stay here beside his beloved. "I've no other plans Mrs Bennett, and I should be delighted to accept your offer. When do we start?"

"Make me a list of what you think you might need, but don't be too extravagant, there aren't unlimited funds." (Matilda had actually sold a pair of fine diamond earrings to pay for this project). "Bring it here and we'll discuss it, then you can go into Leicester and order what is required. How long do you think it would take to get the school up and running?"

"About a month." A cold, uncaring world no longer beckoned. If he made a success of the school he could have a job for life. Brimming with enthusiasm, Christopher slapped his knees and stood up. "If you don't mind, Mrs Bennett, I'll go to my room right now and start drawing up a list, and I promise you I shall be most prudent and not overspend."

Matilda had reacted unnecessarily strongly, in Esther Pedley's opinion, to the news that Clare was off to London with George.

"I don't know what all the fuss is all about, Tilda, after all, he is her father and she has been down there with him before."

"Not on her own. You went too, and Adam," Matilda reminded her.

"You seem to be implying that George is incapable of looking after his own daughter."

"He mixes with very low characters, you know that."

Mrs Pedley bristled. "You're not suggesting he's going to take Clare amongst these so called, *low characters*."

"I hope not, but I really think you should have

discussed it with me first. Besides I was hoping to get Clare interested in this school I'm opening for the village children. Mr Harcourt has agreed to run it, but he'll probably need assistance. There's been enough money spent on her education so it might as well be put to some use."

"Matilda, my dear, I've agreed to Clare going to London for two weeks, that's all. When she comes back I'm sure she'll give Mr Harcourt whatever help is needed. At least it will keep her occupied because she's forever complaining she's bored now that Adam's not here to keep her company."

The day before she was due to leave for London, Clare received a very homesick letter from her cousin. It was a sustained, heart-rending lament and in it he declared that he loathed Cambridge and hated every minute of his studies. His tutors didn't get off lightly either and he appeared to despise them almost as much as he did his fellow undergraduates, pompous fellows, each and every one of them, was how he described them.

He harked back to carefree summer days spent with Judith and Olivia, then the Ball. He begged her to write and finished by saying: "I'm just longing for the Christmas vacation when I'll be back with you all. By the way, if you do bump into Jude or Olivia, tell them how much I'm missing them."

What a pity that she wouldn't get the chance to pass on his message, thought Clare, as she locked the letter away in her escritoire. Unfortunately she didn't enjoy the same freedoms as the sisters, who seemed to be allowed to gallop about the country-side like gipsies. Christopher would want to know how Adam had taken to the academic life, though. She knew where she was likely to find him, as well.

Working his fingers to the bone to get the school ready in time.

Even before it opened the school was already the subject of much debate. Did they want their children "edgimicated," the villagers were asking. Would they get above themselves once their minds were crammed with new-fangled ideas?

Her packing was done, for she and her father were catching the midday coach, and if her grandmother found her idle, she would no doubt find her something useful to do. Wrapping a shawl round her shoulders but hatless, Clare set off down Blackthorn Lane. It was a blustery day with scudding cloud, but on the Green children were busy hurling sticks into the huge horse chestnut tree, then scrambling to pick up the shiny brown conkers as they fell. Make the most of it, Clare thought as she passed, for some of you at least, your days of freedom are numbered. Soon you'll be sitting at a desk learning your letters and numbers and yawning over sums.

The cottage in which Christopher would try to drum some knowledge into their unschooled minds stood three doors down from Woodbine Cottage, where she'd been born. Pushing open the door, Clare found him up a ladder lime-washing the walls, a fair amount of which he'd managed to splatter over his clothes and hair.

"Hello, Mr Harcourt." She smiled, waiting for his fair skin to stain red.

But Christopher had so many things on his mind he forgot to blush. "Hello, Miss Clare, come to help?"

"Well . . ." she stumbled.

"Good, there's a cloth over there, get some water from the pump and clean the windows if you wouldn't mind. There's still heaps to do before we open."

Lost for words, Clare did as he ordered, thinking

wryly as she pumped water that she'd escaped one set of chores only to be landed with others. "I had a letter from Adam today," Clare said, bending to wring out a piece of rag.

"How is he?"

"Unhappy."

"He'll get over it, everyone does. Next term he'll be taking girls punting on the river, going to parties and Balls, in fact having a grand time."

Clare straightened. "Did you ever take a girl punting on the river at Oxford, Mr Harcourt?"

"Sadly no, I had to study. You see I couldn't afford to fail my exams. But I was the exception, most undergraduates count their years at university as some of the happiest of their lives."

There was no self-pity in Christopher's voice, it was just a statement of fact. Had he ever had any fun, Clare wondered, or had it always been work? Suddenly she felt intensely sorry for her tutor, and guilty at her past behaviour, and swore never to tease him again. To make amends for past sins, when every diamond pane shone, Clare went into the garden and applied herself with even greater diligence to the outside windows. She was buffing away when she noticed a horse come out of the smithy's and amble down Main Street. Recognising the oddly dressed figure, she threw down the cloth, called to Christopher, "I won't be a minute," then ran across the Green, waving frantically and shouting into the wind, "Jude, Jude, wait!"

Judith turned and, seeing Clare running towards her, she dismounted and stood waiting, her plain features transformed by an undisguised joy. "My dear, how lovely to see you, it's been such ages."

Clare paused to draw breath. "I've got some news for

you, so I'll walk with you some of the way if you're not in a hurry."

"I brought Star in to be shod, but that's done so I've all the time in the world."

"I've had a letter from Adam. He's very miserable, poor dear, and he says to be sure and tell you he really misses us all."

"Livvy will be pleased. But I can't understand why he went away, if he hates it so."

"My aunt wanted it."

"So it's her I have to blame for spoiling all the good times we had together?"

"Apparently he had to be educated."

"Things never stay the same, do they? Not even the good times," said Judith in a wistful tone. "Look how you've dropped out of our lives."

"I'm not permitted to go out riding on my own."

"Couldn't you sneak out early, before anyone's up?" asked Judith, for whom breaking rules was a matter of honour.

Clare looked doubtful. "Oh, I don't know."

"Please, meet me tomorrow, just once."

"My father's taking me to London, I can't." They had now turned into Halby Lane and Clare stopped. "In fact, I'd better be getting back. Mr Harcourt is opening a school for the village children and I'm supposed to be helping him."

"No, you mustn't go yet." Judith reached out and took Clare's hand, imprisoning it in a firm grip. "Walk a little further with me."

"Well, for a short way perhaps," said Clare and allowed Judith to lead her through a gate and onto the bridle path that would take her back to Fern Hill.

"I popped in to see Miss Dobbs while I was waiting for Star. I really envy her, working with horses, running her own affairs. I'd do anything live like that."

"Does that include dealing with Reuben?" Clare said, laughing.

"I think people are very snobbish about that man. But Miss Dobbs really values him." Judith turned to Clare, her expression tense. "I hate the idea of marrying, don't you?"

Clare, who'd always imagined marriage to be every girl's dream, was slightly nonplussed by her friend's outburst. After all, what was the alternative? "Not really. I just take it for granted. And it's what happens to most people, isn't it?"

"But why should it?" Judith pursued. "Why do we girls have no say in the matter? Why do we have to marry a man our parents consider suitable?"

"I don't know, Jude, I really don't." Clare found Judith's questions unsettling and, anxious to change the conversation, she paused and held her palms heavenwards. "It's beginning to rain, I'll get drenched if I don't turn back."

On cue, the skies opened. "Quick, over there under that tree," said Judith and they sprinted for shelter, the horse shaking her mane and giving a small whinny of complaint at being caught in the rain. Normally the foliage would have protected them but it was now autumn and the leaves were beginning to fall and Clare, without a shawl, was soon shivering. "I'm cold," she complained, massaging her arms.

"Here, put this round you." Judith shrugged off her father's voluminous coat and draped it protectively round Clare's shoulders. "Is that better?"

"You'll get wet now, you silly goose, come under as well," Clare invited, holding open the coat.

Judith wriggled under the tent-like garment and,

gripping the collar with one hand, slid her other arm round Clare's waist.

"There, snug as two bugs in a rug," giggled Clare.

But Judith's emotions were in such turmoil, she was in no state to join in the laughter. Never had she and Clare been so physically close and pressed together under the coat, the faint smell of damp clothes was more erotic than any perfume. Clare's face was half in shadow, but her lips, pink and soft, were invitingly near. Her heart beating frantically and moved by an inner compulsion she hardly understood, Judith leaned forward and kissed Clare full on the lips. As she drew away, she saw that Clare's brown eyes were wide and startled. But she was reckless in her need and without heeding the warning, Judith pulled Clare close again, murmuring against her cheek, "Oh my dearest, dearest, dear."

"No!" Clare protested, pushed Judith hard against her thin chest, threw aside the coat and, sobbing wildly, tore off into the rainswept countryside.

"Clare, Clare come back, please."

But Clare ignored her. Grief-stricken, the rain beating into her face and mingling with her tears, Judith watched her stumble down the bridle path as if pursued by demons. Judith longed to run after her but knew there was no point. By her stupidity she had ruined everything. Instead she called broken-heartedly, "I love you, Clare, truly and deeply, and I always will." But the rising wind picked up the words and tossed them over Judith's shoulder and they were carried away up, up into infinity.

Chapter Fourteen

Women kissed, but only on the cheek, not on the mouth and certainly not in the lingering way that Judith had. That was a privilege granted to a man only when you were betrothed, at least that was how Clare understood it. After her flight she'd been in such a distressed state, she hadn't dared return to the cottage and Christopher's inevitable questions and she'd left Halby without even saying goodbye to him.

But Clare had been glad to get away. Pushing aside unanswerable questions, she threw herself into London life with such verve she never paused to question George about the dubious places he was taking her to.

"Stand behind me, my dear," her father would order, when he was seated at a gaming table, "you might bring me luck." Or "Take my arm, Clare," he would demand as he swaggered with her along Oxford Street, doffing his hat to all and sundry and enjoying the lascivious glances directed at Clare by young bucks of his acquaintance. But it wasn't a young man George had in mind for his daughter, for they had a habit of dissipating their fortunes on whores, horses and in gaming dens. Besides, no marriage portion would go with her, so what he needed was a besotted old codger he could touch for a hundred every now and then, or, even better, someone likely to kick the bucket pretty soon after the marriage and leave his daughter a wealthy heiress. He also happened to know of such personages and where he was likely to bump into them.

So to Astley's they went. With its amphitheatre, three tiers of gilded boxes, musicians, rowdy audience and the smell of sawdust and horses, for Clare, who'd never set foot in such an establishment in her life before, it was a heady, exotic mix. When the orchestra started up, she leaned forward, totally engrossed in the spectacle of bareback riders in spangled tights performing their daring tricks. She'd never seen her father enjoy himself so much either, and he slapped his thighs and roared with laughter at the antics of the clowns. There were dancing dogs, and acrobats whose stunts had the audience gasping in admiration. But they were equally quick to judge and when the curtain went back on the stage to reveal a large lady who had trouble singing in tune, they began to chant, "Gerrorf! Gerrorf!" and the unfortunate woman exited under a hail of bottle corks. In contrast, a ballet performed by a group of skimpily dressed girls, was greeted with appreciative whistles and yells of approval from the gallery.

As much as she was enjoying it, by the time the interval came, the noise, heat and smell were making Clare feel slightly sick. As they went for refreshment she put her hand on her father's arm. "Papa, I don't feel well. Can we go back to our rooms?"

"At this time of night? Why the evening's hardly begun," George huffed, sounding quite bad-tempered. "Let me have some refreshment at least before we go."

Without waiting for his daughter's reply, George wandered off, leaving Clare alone and vulnerable. Men stood around in groups, smoking and drinking, and it was impossible to ignore the behaviour of many of the women, brazen, gaudy types, who accosted these men at will. Encouraged by the women, and amid much coarse laughter and lewd jokes, the men began fondling their breasts, some even going as far as to plunge their hands down the front of the women's dresses. With a gasp of distress, Clare averted her eyes and, greatly agitated, searched the foyer for her father. She must get out of here, immediately. But even standing on tiptoe she found it impossible to pick out anyone amongst the thirsty crowd pushing its way to the bar, and a fear lodged itself in Clare's mind that her father had abandoned her and gone on somewhere else. Feeling tainted by the company she was in, but not sure what she should do, Clare was hovering uncertainly when a middle-aged gentleman with elaborately pomaded hair, sauntered up to her. He leaned back, studied her through his eye-glass as if she were livestock at the market, then declared, "Dammee, you're a lovely little filly."

Hot with anger, Clare shot back, "Go away you horrible man, my papa's over there and he'll deal with you."

The man laughed and walked on but it was now quite clear to Clare that for her own safety she should move. What sort of person did he think she was? In great indignation she elbowed her way towards the bar where, by some miracle, she found her father. He'd just been served and he handed his daughter a glass of claret while gulping down his own.

But Clare was so agitated the red wine spilled down her white dress and she thrust the glass back at him. "I don't want it, take me home, this minute. I've just been accosted by a most vile man."

George pulled a linen handkerchief from the sleeve of his coat and dabbed his straggly whiskers. "My dear have a drink and calm down. He would be admiring your beauty, that's all. You forget, this isn't Halby.

In London, men are quite open in their admiration of women and it's something they come to expect and don't take offence at."

Her father seemed to be implying that she was some sort of country bumpkin, which Clare didn't care for at all. She wanted to been seen as a young lady at ease in any company, which was why she was persuaded to drink the glass of wine her father pressed back on her and why she allowed him to lead her back to their seats after the interval.

It was late when they finally left the theatre. By now, as well as feeling sick, Clare also had a headache and couldn't wait to get to bed. Thankful to breathe fresh air, they'd reached the street where George was trying to hail a cab, when behind them a voice exclaimed, "Why blow me if it isn't Pedley."

George turned, and his face took on an unusually jovial expression. "Hello, Bryanston, old chap," he replied in greeting and thumped his acquaintance heartily on the back.

Clare, on the other hand, recognising him as the man who had publicly insulted her earlier in the evening, froze as he drew near. But if he remembered her, not by a flicker of a muscle did he show it, and when George introduced Clare as his daughter, Henry Bryanston bowed and said suavely, "Charmed, Miss Pedley."

Clare, who felt defiled by his mere presence, refused point blank to acknowledge him. Instead, hoping to shame the gentleman, she stared at him with a pale, fixed face. However, it seemed to amuse, rather than rattle him, for a faint smile played around his mouth, which Clare felt a compelling urge to wipe off with a hard slap.

"Where you off to then, George?" Bryanston enquired.

"Back to our rooms."

"At this early hour?" Bryanston pulled a gold watch from his waistcoat pocket. "Why, it's not even midnight yet." He draped an arm round George's shoulder in a friendly manner. "I'm in need of company, so why not let me take you for a bite of supper and some fun, eh m'boy."

George glanced at Clare. He rarely turned down an invitation, particularly if it meant he wouldn't need to dip his hands in his own pockets and Henry's family had grown rich on slavery and sugar. He also knew how to spend, and have a good time, by thunder he did. "Well . . ." He paused, pretending to consider.

"Go, Papa. Just get me a cab and I will find my own way home."

"If you insist." George hailed a cab in double-quick time, gave the driver their address and handed Clare some money. "See you in the morning, my dear," he said, opened the door, bustled her inside, saluted and was gone, off with the older man to various long rooms, finishes and taverns, and a night of drink and debauchery.

The following day George didn't rise until well into the afternoon, leaving Clare twiddling her thumbs and growing more and more frustrated and angry. Finally, unable to stand being cooped up any longer, she put on a cloak and went shopping, spending money on fripperies and trinkets she neither wanted nor needed.

When Clare returned at three, her father was up, but still in his dressing gown, unshaven and nursing a sore head. She took one look at his ashen face and ordered tea and bread and butter to be brought. George drank his tea in silence and she watched him with a growing contempt. These past days alone with him, she'd really begun to see her father for what he was: a drunken scrounger. "You had a good time last night by the look of it," she commented dryly.

George grunted a reply, and Clare thought, he's my father and yet I don't feel an ounce affection for him. In fact she was beginning to thoroughly dislike him. She was lonely too, and missed her grandmother and Aunt Tilda more by the day. After her experiences of the previous night, London now seemed a tawdry, threatening place and she pined to return to the familiarity and safety of Halby.

"I want to go home, Papa."

George looked up sharply. "You can't do that."

"Why not?"

"Well . . . our return seats are booked for next week, that's why," he blustered. Grasping the table, George eased himself up gingerly. "Now, I want no more such talk, tonight we are going out to be royally dined. I must go and get bathed and dressed and so must you. Wear that white satin dress, you look very pretty in it," said George, who was aiming to flatter his daughter and stop her asking awkward questions.

"Who's the invitation from?" Clare enquired.

George flapped his hand vaguely. "Friends, just friends."

The carriage was rolling down Whitehall, a bustling thoroughfare of Government offices where Ministers and civil servants laboured over affairs of state. Down its whole length the road was illuminated by gaslights and in front of them was the Houses of Parliament.

"Is it far, where are we going, Papa?" Clare asked.

"No, College Street is just by Westminster Abbey. We'll be there very soon." George patted his daughter's hand in a show of affection. Although she'd been rather tiresome of late, tonight he was feeling kindly disposed towards her. Marriage wasn't on the cards but if all went to plan, by the end of the evening she would make him the richer by one hundred pounds.

In a short while they pulled up outside a tall house and the door was opened by a liveried footman who invited them to step inside. He then led Clare and George up a wide staircase with walls covered in oil paintings. On the first floor the footman threw open two doors and displayed a drawing room of some opulence but to Clare's eyes, little taste. She had an impression of a mish-mash of periods and styles; English and French furniture, golden cherubs and ormolu clocks, porcelain ornaments, Persian carpets and even more paintings. The room appeared empty, but then a man rose from a wing-backed chair and turned to face them. "Good evening," he said with a smile.

Clare gave an audible gasp and took a step backwards, but George was having no nonsense with his daughter and, gripping her elbow, he steered her forward into the room.

"Come to the fire, Miss Pedley," said Henry Bryanston, with a air of great solicitude. "Sit down, have a glass of Madeira."

"No thank you." Clare tried with frantic eye signals to catch her father's glance but he refused to look in her direction. Instead, he went and stood with his back to the fire, pushing up his coat tails and warming his large behind.

"Had a devil of a head this morning, don't y'know," Clare heard him say to his host, which was about the general level of her father's conversation.

"So did I, but by gad it was worth it," his friend mused, lifting his glass and downing the contents in one go. "Now, shall we go into dinner?" Henry Bryanston stood up. "Take my arm Miss Pedley."

Clare stared at him with haughty disdain. "No thank you."

"Clare!" her father reprimanded. "Take Mr Bryanston's arm."

Clare laid her hand upon Henry Bryanston's sleeve as if she expected to be infected with some particularly nasty disease, then, her features a mask, she walked with him into the dining-room. He held the chair for her and she sat down. In front of her was an oval expanse of highly polished wood set out with candelabra, silver, cut glass and bone china, all for three people.

By her father's conduct, bringing her to this man's house, two things became apparent to Clare; one was that that he was indifferent to her sensibilities, the second was that she could no longer count on his protection. She scowled at him across the table and thought; but he'll be singing to a different tune tomorrow when he wakes up and finds I've gone. Clare regretted the money she'd wasted on trinkets, but she did some quick sums in her head and reckoned that, if she rode outside, she had enough for a coach to Leicester. And by hook or by crook she intended to get back home, even if meant walking every step of the way. Anything to put distance between her and a father she had grown to detest.

The servants were now bringing in the food and setting it down in front of her. But no one could force her to eat and, as course followed course, Clare stared straight ahead, obstinately refusing to taste even a morsel. It was the same with the wine, not a drop touched her lips.

George's florid jaws wobbled with fury, which gave her a small measure of satisfaction. Henry Bryanston appeared completely indifferent, although occasionally a viper's smile would play round his lips. Clare's abstinence didn't affect the appetites of either man, who gorged themselves on the rich food. Time ticked by, and as the wine in their glasses was constantly topped up, so the conversation became more dubious, the laughter heartier, the jokes, to Clare's distress, coarser.

Finally, the port and cigars were brought in. George went through the ritual of piercing and lighting his, then looking across at his daughter, he said smoothly, "Off you go into the drawing-room, my dear, we'll join you in a little while."

Clare made her escape with relief, sat down on a hard armchair, stood up again, thought: I'm not staying here a moment longer, moved swiftly to the door and turned the handle. It appeared jammed, so she began to tug, rattling it frantically when it refused to budge.

"It's locked," said a voice behind her.

Clare swung round and masking her fear, asked in a calm voice, "Where's Papa?"

"Don't worry m'dear, he's not far away." Henry Bryanston strolled into the room, a cigar in one hand, a glass of brandy in the other, and went and sat down by the fire. Patting the seat beside him, he said, "Come and sit by me."

"No."

"Don't be a silly girl, I shan't do you any harm."

But Clare cowered against the door with the terror-struck look of an animal about to be pole-axed and refused to move. Losing patience, Henry Bryanston stood up and moved in on her. His eyes were glassy with drink, and the sickly smell of patchouli made her shudder with disgust.

"However, I don't care to be disobeyed, either," he went on, and gripped her wrist spitefully.

"Let go, you're hurting," she cried.

"Don't you like that? To be hurt? Some women love it." While he spoke he dragged her towards the fire.

"Papa!' Clare screamed. "Help m—" A hand was clamped over her mouth. "Be sensible. Don't waste your breath. I'm paying your father a hundred pounds for the privilege of your company tonight, so it's naive to imagine he will come to your aid. Surely you know him better than that? And the servants have been dismissed for the evening."

Her own father had sold her, as if she were some common harlot! At the stark reality of his betrayal, steel entered Clare's heart. Her father would not get his thirty pieces of silver, and if she had to fight to her last breath, she would not surrender to this odious creature.

Clare gave a small sigh and allowed her body to go limp, as if in compliance, offering no resistance as he pulled her down on his lap.

"That's a good girl, do as your daddy says and there'll be no trouble." Breathing heavily he began to fondle her breasts. Clare endured it for a half second then with venom in her heart, she lifted her hand and raked her nails down his cheeks, drawing blood.

"You bitch!" Bryanston slapped her so hard round the head her ears rang but she retaliated by throwing the glass of brandy in his face. Spluttering with rage, he loosened his grip and she fled to the far corner of the room where she picked up a large vase and swung it high above her head.

"No!" Bryanston exclaimed, "don't throw that, it's Ming and priceless."

"Good," Clare answered and hurled the vase straight at him.

"Now look what you've done!" he cried as it shattered at his feet, so genuinely distressed he didn't see an identical piece follow. It caught him hard on the chest and sent him staggering back before it too splintered into a hundred pieces.

Enraged, he advanced on Clare. Her brain was almost addled with fear and she was shaking violently, but her hand went round a lighted oil lamp. "D-don't take a . . . a . . . step nearer." She held it defensively in front of her and, wisely, Bryanston paused.

At first, Clare thought it was her own heart pounding in her ears, but then, through her dazed senses, she realised someone was hammering on the door. Her father. "Bryanston. We've got to get out of here. Parliament's on fire and we're in danger of being burnt to a cinder!" As he spoke, George Pedley's voice rose several octaves and ended in a squeak of terror.

"Don't talk such damned nonsense." Thinking it some trick, Bryanston strode to the window and drew open the heavy velvet curtains. "My God!" he exclaimed and took a step back. Clare, who was standing behind him, stared in disbelief. This was no joke. It was impossible to know, from where they stood, the exact source of the fire, but flames and smoke were spiralling up to the night sky and the house reverberated with the sound of running feet, shouted orders, fear and panic.

Concerned now only for his own safety, Bryanston raced to the door and unlocked it. George was standing there with his hand held out like some mendicant. "My money please, old chap, if you don't mind."

"Go to hell, George. You owe *me*. That stupid wench of yours ruined two priceless vases."

George moved closer and gripped his friend's collar. "You promised."

This altercation gave Clare her chance. Slipping past them, she hoisted the skirt of her satin gown high and flew down the stairs and out into the street. Realising, too late, that his prize had escaped, behind her George roared, "Clare come back here, this instant."

The devil she would! Clare heard George's heavy body come pounding after her, but he wasn't in good shape, whereas she was young and fleet of foot. Pushing her way through the crowds, she quickly outstripped her father. A stitch in her side eventually forced her to slow down, but people were closing in on her until she was just one more person in an anonymous crowd. Clare knew it would be foolish to be lulled into imagining she was safe, so with no idea where she was headed, she turned a corner and was brought up short by the fire. She'd expected nothing of this magnitude and she gaped in awe at the great blazing pile that had once been the Palace of Westminster. It was like some huge firework display. Orange tongues of fire burst through windows, fiery particles shot into the sky, and everywhere was chaos and panic. But where are the fire engines? Why aren't they here? Clare wondered. Various official-looking men rushed around shouting orders, and at the same time tried to stem the flow of sightseers. However, these were the elements at their most remorseless and a rising wind was whipping up the fire into an angry, roaring inferno. Dumbstruck and helpless, the citizens of London watched as the fire made a funeral pyre of their nation's pride and history.

The building was now a fire-ball, but Clare hobbled gamely on until she was finally brought to a halt by a line of policemen, arms linked, and forming a barrier across the street.

"Move back please," they were ordering the crowd, in self-important tones.

"But I must get through, it's a matter of life and death," Clare pleaded.

"It'll be your death if you goes in there. In that heat you'd pop like a roast chestnut. Take a look fer yerself. There's debris falling all over the place. Anyway once they're 'ere, we'll need ter get the engines through before the fire reaches the Abbey."

"Clare! Wait!" In spite of the intense heat, the command chilled her blood. Fearing her father more than falling masonry, Clare ducked under the policeman's arm and ran for dear life.

"Hey, come back!" the Peeler bellowed, then shrugged and thought to himself; well if she wants to risk 'er neck let 'er, but he was damned if he was goin' chasing after the silly young miss, not wiv 'is bunions.

After the man's warnings Clare expected to find herself pursued by half the police force and hauled back. But she found herself completely alone. Realising it was unlikely anyone would follow, she paused and took stock. Her dress was pitted with scorch-holes, her soft kid slippers were in tatters, and the white-hot heat seared her skin. But she had no choice but to keep moving. Suddenly she was struck by how eerie the street seemed, its emptiness filled by the crackle and roar of a great building being inexorably reduced to smoking rubble. Clare could see dark masses of people outlined on house-tops, the leaping flames had sucked the colour from everything and trees and grass had turned a ghoulish white. To Clare it was unreal, nightmarish, like moving through Hades.

Then just when she thought she was safe, across the empty wasteland she heard the hated voice. "It's my daughter, she'll be killed, I must get to her."

"No you won't. I'd rather die first," Clare shouted and ran for it, zig-zagging between lumps of charred wood and falling debris. Coughing, her eyes smarting from the acrid smoke, she didn't see the lump of brick until she went flying. With a cry of pain Clare picked herself up and hobbled on, now so dazed she wasn't even sure in which direction she should be going. Despair seeped into her soul and she began to stagger from fatigue. It was all up for her. She couldn't go on and her father was gaining ground.

Clare had never heard a tumult like it. It was as if the heavens were being torn asunder. The earth trembled under her feet and she gazed stupefied as the great roof finally collapsed and was transformed into an immense pillar of fire and smoke. Too late she heard the jangle of fire engine bells.

The building was now illuminated from base to summit and masonry and flaming beams exploded into the atmosphere. Common sense told her to run for cover but she was transfixed by the terrible beauty of the scene. Clare had all but forgotten about her father until a scream to chill the soul rent the air. Slowly she turned and her heart seemed to stop. Several yards from her lay a body, crushed under the weight of several tons of wall. She knew it was her father, although there was little to identify him, for his skull had been smashed to pulp and his brains, spilling out white like cods' roe, floated in a pool of blood. An extended hand gave one final convulsive twitch and then George was gone, to a place where he could harm his daughter no more.

Chapter Fifteen

When her benefactor wasn't in town, Harry had slipped into the habit of spending his evenings in London with Adele. Unfortunately, of late, she'd grown so possessive and demanding, he knew the time had arrived when he'd have to think seriously about ending their relationship. This would be a shame because he enjoyed her receptive young body. Tonight, though, her tantrums and sulks had been more than he could take. Guessing a scene of volcanic proportions was brewing, Harry made his escape early and let himself out into the street with a sense of relief, a move quite out of character, for Harry usually left a woman's bed with the utmost reluctance.

People were making their way to theatres and taverns, so the streets were busy. Harry paused on the step to light a cigar. He was buttoning his coat when he noticed that the flow of the crowd appeared to be in one direction. They also moved with an unusual sense of purpose. Curious to find out what it was that so caught their interest, he began walking at a brisk pace along Piccadilly. The Haymarket was so clogged with people it was hard to move, but Harry pushed on and finally caught up with a policeman. "Where's everyone off to in such a hurry then, constable?" he asked, falling into step beside him.

"Haven't your 'eard, sir? The 'Ouses of Parliament is on fire."

"What on earth are you talking about?" Harry demanded, thinking that the man was having a joke at his expense.

But the policeman's expression was deadly serious. Sniffing the air like a bloodhound, he said, "Can't yer smell it? And see that glow in the sky? What do you think that is? Anyway, if you don't believe me, sir, go and see for yerself."

"I'll do that," Harry answered and tried to tell himself it must be a scurrilous rumour put about by radicals wanting to see the downfall of parliament. But what he couldn't ignore was the smell of burning, nor the unaccountable brightness of the sky. With much frantic elbowing, Harry finally reached Whitehall. Confronted by the unthinkable, he stopped. "Oh my God," he exclaimed and stared in horror.

"By all accounts it's too late for Him to be of any help," a passer-by commented. The news had spread as quickly as the fire, and the entire population of London appeared to be flocking towards Westminster, carrying Harry with it and finally depositing him in Parliament Street. The bridge was choked, side streets were impassable, and it was obvious the building was beyond saving. Harry began to grieve for what was lost. It was a place whose customs, he was ashamed to remember, he sometimes mocked. A place where he'd listened to riveting debates, or snoozed through boring speeches. But it was also an institution that he loved and believed in and to have to stand helpless while greedy flames reduced it to ash, was so unbearably poignant, hot tears of emotion blurred his eyes.

Pull yourself together man! Harry berated himself. Women cried, not ex-soldiers. Imagine the shame if he bumped into a fellow MP. As he surreptitiously rubbed away a tear, Harry's attention was drawn to

Westminster Abbey. Illuminated to its topmost pinnacles by the fire, it stood alone and vulnerable. A spark blowing in the wrong direction and *whoosh*, it would be ash too. Harry shuddered. But he wouldn't stand there passively and watch another noble building and its treasures destroyed, he decided, and pushed his way forward.

"Let me through please, I'm a Member of Parliament." Harry's authoritative tone did the trick and people made way for him. In Palace-yard the lurid glow picked out firemen unwinding their hoses, hoisting ladders and making a gallant attempt to douse the blazing pile. But the water seemed little more than a pathetic trickle and they were constantly beaten back by the scorching heat.

Harry could see they were wasting their time. There was still the Abbey though, if he could get through. Harry was about to move on when his attention was caught by a commotion, and a young woman apparently in some distress. A small group was gathered around her and some instinct drew him towards them. By their clothes Harry could see they were working men and there was something awkward in their stance, as if they were in a situation they were unsure how to handle. Harry understood why when he drew nearer. A body, covered by a shabby coat and obviously dead, lay stretched on the ground in a pool of blood. But it was the girl who caught Harry's attention. Violent spasms shook her slight body, the flames cast their unforgiving light on eyes that were bright and wild and had a touch of madness in them.

If the girl's white satin gown hadn't told him otherwise, with her soot-streaked face and rebellious hair, Harry might have mistaken her for a whore caught up in some violent altercation which had ended in tragedy.

Studying her more closely, Harry had a notion he'd met her before, although it took several seconds to place the girl. Then it all came back to him. Of course the race-week Ball. Matilda's niece. Her name escaped him though. Concentrate, he thought, tapping his forehead as a memory aid, it could help. Suddenly it came to him. Clare, that was it!

Cautiously he approached her. "Clare?"

She stepped back and gazed at him with a look of blank terror.

At a loss, Harry turned to the men. "Can someone tell me what has happened here, please?"

"We dunno for sure, but the young lady, she ses it's her pa." The man who'd answered pointed to the corpse. "Flattened by a piece of wall, 'e was. We couldn't do nuffink, guv, the poor so-and-so was a gonner by the time we arrived."

"Good God!" But how on earth did they come to be here? "Is it your father?" Harry asked Clare gently.

She nodded dumbly, but when Harry reached out in a spontaneous gesture of comfort, she flinched back from him. "Clare, do you remember me? I'm Judith and Olivia's father. We met at the Ball in Leicester, you were with your Aunt Matilda and Adam."

The familiar names obviously made some connection in Clare's confused mind because she stopped tugging compulsively at her hair and allowed Harry to take her arm.

"Look, we'd better move away from here. More of the building could collapse." Harry handed each man a sovereign. "Can you bring the body please? And do you know of an undertaker nearby?"

"Bert Figgins at the Lion and Lamb in York Street, 'e does burials, and 'is missus lays 'em out. Very particular they is too, with lead-lined coffins to stop the resurrection men," their spokesman replied.

So the cortege set off in the direction of the ale house, where George's body was deposited in an upstairs room to await interment. Harry reimbursed Bert Figgins and assured him he would return soon with instructions and money for the burial from the family.

He thanked the men and slipped them a few more coins for their trouble, then began to concentrate on his next problem; Clare and what he was he going to do with her. "Where are your lodgings, Clare?"

"Somewhere . . . I . . . can't remember."

Harry was staying at his club and he couldn't take her there, but neither could they walk the streets all night. Then he remembered Sylvia. She would help him out. In a street where the crowds were less dense, Harry hired a cab and instructed the driver to take them to Sylvia and Basil's residence, praying all the way that they would be at home. Clare, who hadn't spoken a word, sat curled up on her side of the carriage, and Harry decided to leave her like that. There were questions he needed to ask, but now was hardly the appropriate time.

Harry's first words, when an astonished footman opened the door to them were, "Is Lady Sylvia at home? If she is tell her it's extremely urgent that I see her."

Clare was staggering with fatigue now and Harry half carried her up the steps and into the hall. He was still holding her when Sylvia came running down the stairs, her face puckered with anxiety and appearing not to notice the girl. "Is it about the fire? Has something happened to Basil?"

"I didn't know Basil was down there, but as far as I know he's all right."

Sylvia's expression cleared. "Thank heaven, I was expecting the worst. But Parliament, what about that?"

"A gonner, I'm afraid."

"Oh no!"

"It will be re-built, and bigger and better," Harry, assured her, "but I have a rather more immediate problem. Sylvia, this is George Pedley's daughter, Clare."

Sylvia moved forward and peered at the girl. "So it is. But why is she in such an appalling state?"

"I'll explain later, but she's been through the most horrendous ordeal and needs looking after for the night. Can you help?"

"Of course. I'll get my maid to see to her. Come, my dear." Immediately sympathetic, Sylvia took Clare's hand. Mute and compliant, Clare allowed herself to be led away.

Harry sank down in a chair in the drawing-room and tried to sort out in his mind what he should do about the tragedy in which he'd become unwittingly entangled. But his brain was addled with fatigue and he was just drifting off when he heard Sylvia return. She poured him a whisky and handed it to him. "My maid is having a bath filled for Clare, then she's putting her straight to bed. But what on earth happened to the poor lamb? She appears to have lost the power of speech and not a word could I get out of her."

"Something pretty gruesome. For a start she saw her father killed. His head was crushed in."

"George? Dead? How many more shocks do you have for me tonight, Harry?"

"Not many more, I hope."

"But how did all this happen?"

"Until she feels able to tell us, I'm about as much in the dark as you. I came across the poor child, by chance, amidst all the mayhem of the fire. How either of them came to be there is a mystery. I'm banking on her youth and a good night's sleep to repair some of the damage, so we'll just have to be patient and hope she'll start to talk in the morning. In the meantime I'm going to ask another big favour of you, Sylvia. Can I leave her with you for a day or two? A letter could take days to reach her family, and I'd find explaining what's happened on paper difficult. On the other hand, if I catch the midnight coach, I'll be in Halby by tomorrow and probably back here with her aunt by the following evening."

"I'll be happy to look after her. But you look done-in yourself Harry. Go in the morning after you've had a night's sleep."

"I can't, Sylvia. I dread it, but the news has to be broken to George's mother and father, then the funeral arrangements made." Harry stood up. "I'd better be on my way. I know I can depend on you to be tactful, but see what you can get out of Clare after she's rested. Her family will want to know the full facts."

"I won't push the child, though. I'll let her tell me in her own good time."

On the coach back to Leicester, Harry had slept, after a fashion, but there'd been no time to refresh himself and his eyes were gritty, his mouth dry and he desperately needed a bath and shave. As the chaise he'd hired jogged up the drive to Trent Hall, he was aware that he nowhere looked his best and he was troubled by the task ahead. He'd had to write sad letters when he was in the army and, although it was never a task he relished, he maintained a certain detachment. But this was a different situation, these were people he knew, he was the messenger of doom and he had a superstitious feeling it would do little to further his cause with Matilda. Then, amidst all the grief, he had somehow to get the family back to London.

Having more or less prepared himself mentally, Harry

was disconcerted to be told that Matilda was not at home but down in the village, helping organise the school she would shortly be opening. He'd had the driver wait so he now ordered him to drive back down to the village. Passing the church Harry remembered that first time he'd set eyes on Matilda, young and pretty and oh so malleable. How times changed.

The cottage door stood half-open and Harry could hear Matilda talking to someone. "I think we'll hang the map of the world on this wall Mr Harcourt, what do you think?" Her voice sounded cheerful, and he dreaded the knock that would change all that. But it had to be done. Harry raised his fist and was about to bring it down on the wood, when she unexpectedly appeared at the door and stared at him with a perplexed expression.

"What are you doing here?"

"Matilda, can I speak to you somewhere quietly. I've driven all night from London to get here and it is rather personal."

A young man Harry didn't recognize came and stood behind Matilda, his unworldly face scarred with anxiety. "It's Clare isn't it? Something's happened to her."

"Clare is reasonably well and in safe hands."

"She's with her father, so what do you mean by safe hands?" Matilda eyed him with suspicion and seemed reluctant to let him in.

"This matter is really too serious to discuss on the step, Matilda."

"Sorry. Come in. Let's go upstairs, we can talk there."

In the small low-ceilinged bedroom, Matilda turned and faced Harry, obviously preparing herself for bad news. "Well, go on, tell me; what hole has my brother dug himself into this time?"

"There's no way of saying this easily, Matilda, but I'm sorry to say George is dead."

"Oh no!" Her eyelids fluttered in agitation and she took a step backwards and gripped the windowsill. "But Clare?"

"She's in quite a bad way, but staying with friends of mine."

"Was it a duel?"

"No. An accident. It is a very long story." Harry told her as much as he knew. "I still don't know the half of it, but can I leave it to you to tell your parents and express my condolences?"

"Yes, of course. But Mama will take it especially hard and it seems so cruel of fate to give her son back after all those years, only to steal him from her again. In spite of all the heartache, she had a true mother's love for George." Matilda's voice broke and Harry gripped her hand.

"The next few weeks are going to be difficult for everyone and I'll do all I can to help, but right now Clare needs someone from her family beside her. There's also the funeral to arrange, so I'll have to ask you to return to London with me. Can you manage that?"

Matilda nodded.

"Good. Now if you'll excuse me, Matilda, I'm off home to catch up on some sleep. I suggest you put up at the Bell this evening then you'll be ready to catch the four o'clock coach. I'll meet you there and on the the way to London I'll tell you as much as I know about George's death."

"Thank you, Harry, for what you've done."

Before he turned to leave, Harry risked leaning forward and kissing her cheek. "Let us say it was all for old times sake."

Harry found the young man hovering at the bottom

of the stairs where, he suspected, he'd been listening in on the conversation.

"Will you give Clare my regards, please, when you see her?"

"What name shall I say?"

"Harcourt. Christopher Harcourt. I was tutor to Adam and Clare. Mrs Bennett is opening this school for the benefit of the village children, and I'm to run it. Education will make an enormous difference to their lives."

"It will," Harry agreed, and thought how earnest Christopher Harcourt sounded for one so young. But a good egg and reliable and it was obvious he cared deeply for Clare. And Harry was glad about that for he had the greatest faith in the healing power of love.

Chapter Sixteen

It was an ordeal Matilda hoped she would never be called upon to repeat; walking up to Thatcher's Mount, stumbling for the appropriate words, but finding no easy way of telling her parents that George was dead. Afterwards there was their grief to deal with, while at the same time trying to remain clear-headed enough to make the funeral arrangements and explain to them about Clare.

Matilda felt guilty about it, but in the end it had been a tremendous relief to board the coach for London and escape from the desolation of Thatcher's Mount. The talk in the coach, like everywhere else in the British Isles that day, was of the calamitous fire, and it remained an excited topic for the entire journey. But to Matilda parliament was only a building; bricks and mortar which could be re-built. Her preoccupations were with matters personal, the circumstances of her brother's sudden death and its effect on Clare.

She waited until the horses were rattling along at a good pace, then she turned to Harry and keeping her voice low, said "Tell me exactly what happened, but try not to let this gossipy bunch hear."

"I can only tell you what I know," said Harry, moving a little closer. "It was sheer chance, me stumbling across Clare that night, but it's fortunate I did, although it's still a mystery how she and her father got themselves into such a dangerous situation in the first place."

"Knowing George and his cronies, he probably did it for a bet."

Harry rubbed his chin reflectively. "Do you know, that's a possibility. Although if George did take her into that inferno it was an act of sheer criminal folly."

"One shouldn't speak ill of the dead, but my brother would do anything for money. Even put his daughter's life at risk."

"The poor child was stumbling around half out of her mind. But she's staying with friends now and is quite safe."

Matilda patted his hand. "I appreciate all you've done, Harry and no doubt we'll get the full story from Clare before long." Disinclined to talk further, Matilda turned and gazed out of the window. Through the dust thrown up by the horses and the carriage wheels she could detect a hint of daylight. The Boots at the Bell Hotel had roused her at half-past three and there was still hours of uncomfortable travelling to be endured. The mere contemplation of it induced in Matilda such a weariness of spirit, she closed her eyes.

As befitting a sister in mourning for her brother, Matilda wore dark clothes. Although in an overloaded coach it could hardly be said they were alone together, it was years since Harry had been this close; swaying against her when the wheels juddered through ruts, thigh pressed against thigh. Through the smell of infrequently washed bodies, he caught a faint hint of attar of roses which stirred in him memories of secret assignations; of outwitting parents but not, in the end, mother nature. It was Harry's instinct to take advantage of their enforced intimacy, except with George hardly cold even he could see it would be rather bad form. Hold your horses, old son, he told himself, you're in favour with her now. Gratitude could manifest itself in many ways, a warm bed for example, so let events take their course. Harry closed his eyes and contemplated the gratifying prospect Matilda falling as eagerly into his arms as she had done as a young girl. And the many variations on this theme occupied him quite happily until the next change of horses.

Harry had wondered if Matilda might be rather overawed by Sir Basil and Sylvia, but there was a dignity about her he found impressive. But then, why not? he thought. After all, he had to remember that she was no longer a hosier's daughter, but a woman of means who moved among the County set with ease.

Matilda's first anxious words after she was introduced were, "My niece, Lady Sylvia, how is she?"

"She slept for the best part of the day, and she's eaten a light supper, but I've got little out of her. You being here is probably the best medicine."

"May I go up and see her?"

"Yes of course, Mrs Bennett." Sylvia led her up a flight of stairs and opened a door quietly. The lamps were lit and Clare sat, her hands idle in her lap, staring into the fire. In the half light and with hair falling around her shoulders, she looked shadowy and insubstantial, as if she might dissolve into nothing and Matilda was alarmed.

"Clare, my dear, a nice surprise, your aunt has come to visit you," said Sylvia in a bright, encouraging tone.

Clare lifted brooding eyes. "Hello, Aunt Tilda." Her voice sounded hoarse, the effect, Matilda imagined, of inhaling smoke.

This wasn't the lively, sparkling girl Matilda knew

and she drew up a chair and took her niece's hand, while Sylvia quietly withdrew. "I came as soon as I heard. I'm so terribly sorry about your father, my dear." Matilda stroked her cheek in a gesture of comfort and tenderness.

Clare's body went rigid and snatching her hand away from Matilda, she half rose in her chair. "Don't be, I'm glad he's dead!" She spat out the words with such uncharacteristic venom Matilda was shaken rigid.

"Clare, how could you say such a thing, and with your father not in his grave yet!"

"I can say it because I mean it and because my own father tried to sell me to some vile friend of his for . . . for a hundred pounds!

Matilda's head reeled. "He couldn't have, no . . . not even George could stoop to such depravity . . ." she protested.

"Well, he did." In her agitation, the words erupted from Clare in an unstoppable flow. In sickening detail she told of her ordeal and as the horrifying story unfolded, and Clare's likely fate in that house became clear, Matilda longed to block her ears against it in denial.

But she knew her brother too well. That blackguard had behaved in character. He cared for nobody and was driven by one emotion only, greed and the acquisition of money. For gain, he had been willing to sacrifice his own daughter's honour. Matilda thought she would vomit with disgust. And she was glad, glad like Clare, that he was dead. But even ten feet under, his malevolent spirit could still reach out and taint their lives and bring shame and dishonour to the family.

Matilda studied her niece closely. She was slumped in the chair and Matilda sensed her desolation of spirit, saw that her childish innocence and trust were gone forever. And now she thought, she was going to demand even more of her.

"Clare, after what you've been through I shouldn't be asking you this . . . but it's your grandmama you see. I'd cut off my right arm to spare her what you've just told me. She loved George, but he dumped a barrow-load of sorrows on her right through his life. If this story became public the disgrace would kill her. So please, for her sake, could this be our secret?"

Matilda held her breath and waited. She shouldn't expect so much of the child, it was cruel. But she was driven by the need to protect her mother, who'd never harmed a living soul.

Finally in an apathetic tone Clare answered. "I'll do what you ask, but only for Grandmama's sake. Not that I would want people to know I share that man's tainted blood anyway."

Matilda gave her a warm hug. "Oh bless you, sweetheart, bless you. You don't know how much this means to me, and we'll pull through this ordeal together, and win, I promise."

"Now I think I'd like to go to bed, if you don't mind, Aunt Tilda." Knowing she was being politely dismissed, Matilda tucked her niece in then kissed her goodnight. By the way she snuggled down and closed her eyes, Matilda could see that Clare gained comfort from these small childhood rituals and walking down the stairs, she reflected on her niece's future. It would be a long time before she was able to commit herself to any man. Even then she'd need someone who was kind, gentle and deeply understanding. Almost immediately Christopher Harcourt sprang to mind.

As she reached the bottom step, Matilda was aware of

three expectant faces. "Well? How did you find Clare?" Harry asked.

"Not too good, but she's sleeping now. She needs to be back home in familiar surroundings, she'll start to improve then."

"And did you get anything out of her?"

Matilda stared at the ground and thought while she talked. Hurriedly, almost dismissively as if the whole incident were of little importance, she said, "It seems they were caught up accidently in the fire. George had taken Clare to dinner at the house of a man called Henry Bryanston."

A knowing glance went between Sir Basil and his wife and Harry exclaimed, "Bryanston? Why the man's an utter cad."

"I must admit, George had some odd friends but there was nothing sinister about it. Unfortunately, they left his house at the wrong time and went slap, bang into the fire."

"Very unfortunate I would have said, considering George lost his life." There was more than a touch of sarcasm in Harry's voice and Matilda reciprocated with one of her chilly looks. But Harry wasn't fooled. Too much was unexplained and it was his bet that Matilda was covering up for George. But he would get to the bottom of it, the devil he would, by shortly paying a call on that bounder Bryanston.

Apart from the family, barely a half dozen people could be scraped together to attend George's funeral. As soon as it was over, Matilda thanked Sir Basil and Sylvia for their kindness and hospitality and whisked Clare back to Halby. She had the apothecary in to take a look at her and after a thorough examination this gentleman declared that there was nothing wrong that time and nourishing broths wouldn't heal. But in spite of his diagnosis, Clare continued to languish, so Matilda decided it would be best to let her remain at Trent Hall, where she could keep an eye on her.

During this period, and knowing Matilda could hardly object, Harry was a frequent visitor. It was now early November, the trees were stripped almost bare, but after an early morning frost the country was being treated to a rare and perfect late autumn day of blue skies. In the lee of the house it was warm enough for Clare to sit out and she was alone reading one afternoon when Harry arrived with Judith.

Clare could no longer see Judith as a friend and her very presence was an embarrassment, so to look up and find her rushing across the lawn with an expression of deep solicitude on her plain face, made Clare cringe.

But Judith seemed not to notice that anything was wrong. Clasping Clare's unresponsive hand, she scanned her face with a tender expression. "You poor, poor dear, I was so sorry to hear of your sad loss. How you must have suffered."

Clare who saw no point in playing the grieving daughter, removed her hand from Judith's and replied matter of factly, "It was a while ago, I'm quite over it now."

"Are you sure?" asked Judith, who knew she would never recover if her own father died. She didn't want Clare sick, but oh, to have the chance to smooth her pillows, cool her fevered brow with compresses, to nurse her through a long night!

"Absolutely."

"If you two girls don't mind I'll leave you to chat. I want to have a word with Matilda." The chance of finding Matilda alone was so rare, Harry seized any opportunity he could and he was levering himself up when she appeared on the step with Jane. He cursed under his breath, sat down again, then observed *sotto voce*, "Lord, Jane's put on weight."

Matilda and Jane joined them, tea was brought out by a maid on a heavy silver tray and Clare handed round sandwiches while her aunt poured. When everyone was served Matilda sat down, and stirring her tea said, "Jane tells me she has some very exciting news for us."

"Don't tell me you've got another winner, Jane," Harry smiled.

"No, far better than that. I'm getting married." Jane's ruddy face split into a triumphant smile.

There was a silence, while the small party digested this astounding piece of news and tried to imagine who the prospective groom might be. She'd once nursed a soft spot for George, but her only real suitor had gone out to India and been killed on a tiger hunt.

Jane helped herself to a finger of anchovy toast, bit into it then said brightly, "Well, aren't you going to ask me who my husband-to-be is?"

"Of course, we're dying to know, dear," Matilda replied.

"It's Reuben."

"Reuben?" Matilda spluttered, staring at her friend as if she had gone out her mind.

But Harry, who was more tolerant of people's foibles, went over and gave her an affectionate kiss. "Congratulations, Jane."

"Have you thought about this carefully, Jane?" Matilda asked with a candour permitted by a friendship reaching back into childhood.

"Yes, I have," Jane answered a trifle defiantly. "I know exactly what you are all thinking: Reuben's a rough character, hardly suitable for a vicar's daughter. But he loves me and I love him. The banns will be read for the first time this Sunday and you are all invited to the wedding."

Harry gave her an encouraging smile. "Thank you, Jane, I would love to come."

"Me too," said Judith.

"And me," finished Clare.

The congregation of St Philip's was agog. They'd contained themselves until Jane and Reuben disappeared up the hill, then the buzz of gossip grew as loud and busy as a hive of bees. It was a scandal that would sustain the village for weeks to come, for not only was Jane marrying way beneath her socially, she was also marrying an outsider and the villagers were extremely suspicious of 'foreigners'.

While Matilda was accosted and questioned, Clare and Christopher walked on. Although Clare was recovering well, the experience had also brought about a change in her. She had learned a little humility, was more sensitive to others' feelings and no longer enjoyed watching Christopher blush.

With the success of the school, Christopher had grown more self-confident too, and he talked about it constantly. It had been running for a month now but on the first Monday he opened, only two pupils turned up, a boy and a girl, both of them the blacksmith's children. After all the effort and expense, that had been a grim day for Christopher and it left him wondering if the whole project was doomed. But the miller and the landlord of the Weavers' Arms weren't going to to be outdone by the blacksmith. Their children would have some learning, too. So reluctant scholars had their hair slicked down and noses wiped, then with feet forced into boots, they were handed over to Christopher for instruction and enlightenment. Gradually, as more villagers began to see the value of education, children appeared and now Christopher had twelve pupils on the register.

"It was my idea to charge a penny a week," he told Clare as they turned into the drive. "If parents have to pay they'll want value for money and are more likely to see that the children turn up every day. Although your aunt has made it clear that she wants no child turned away for want of a penny."

"What do you teach them, Mr Harcourt?"

"Not much more than their letters and numbers at the moment, but some are racing ahead, others lagging. But I've so many ideas and I mean to teach the brighter ones Latin eventually." Christopher's voice rang with an enthusiasm that was catching.

"Perhaps I could help sometimes?" Clare suggested as they reached the steps of the front door.

"Would you? Really?"

"The younger ones, yes, or the laggards. Although I'm not sure I'll be any good."

"Oh, you'll be an excellent teacher, I'm sure of it, Miss Pedley. Come down tomorrow during the morning. Sit for a while to see how you like it and perhaps you could assist with the reading."

Chapter Seventeen

Although, to some degree, Clare was always likely to be haunted by that night in London, Matilda had done everything within her power to stop her brooding. She had arranged outings, games of cards and looked forward to Christmas when Adam would be home and there would be parties and other seasonal distractions.

But by far the biggest and most talked about event in the village was the wedding. Reuben, togged out in a green cutaway coat and snowy white shirt, and minus his usual three day growth of beard, had looked almost unrecognisable. But standing beside his bride, repeating his vows, it was apparent by the way his fingers clenched and unclenched, that he was uneasy in the role that had been foisted on him. As the miller observed knowingly, 'Ye canna make a silk purse out of a pig's ear.' In other words, folks should know their place, and the general opinion was that, no matter how hard Jane strove to make it otherwise, her husband would always be more gipsy than gentleman.

When he came out of church, Reuben still wore a slightly perplexed expression, as if wondering how he came to be there. Jane on the other hand, glowed with happiness. At her age a husband was an unexpected bonus and she clung possessively to Reuben as they walked down the path between the dark yew trees.

Following along behind with the other guests to the

house, Matilda studied her friend's broad backside with more than a passing interest. "I swear Jane is in the family way," she murmured in an aside to her mother.

"Hush," Esther Pedley mouthed, at the same time making frantic eye signals in Clare's direction, for she deemed such talk unsuitable for a young girl's ears.

But Clare had acute hearing and besides, it was too good a tit-bit to miss. "Do you mean she's going to have a baby, Aunty?" she asked brightly.

"Don't tell the whole village, dear," Matilda reprimanded, "they'll work it out for themselves soon enough."

"If she is, it means Jane's been carrying on with Reuben." Mrs Pedley shook her head in disbelief. "I just can't believe it of a vicar's daughter, brought up on the teachings of the Bible."

"Ask yourself these questions, Mama. Does Reuben look the marrying kind to you? And would you have expected Jane to marry the hired hand except out of necessity?"

"Well I suppose you do have a point."

"Do you want to place a bet on it?" her daughter asked.

"You know I don't gamble. Now stop this please, Matilda. And since we are going to be eating Jane's food and drinking her wine, it would do no harm to be a little charitable."

"I won't say another word on the subject, but you wait and see."

As it turned out Matilda had made an accurate diagnosis. By Christmas Jane could no longer disguise her bulk, and when she announced that she and Reuben would be parents by the following April, no one even bothered to express surprise.

"She's too old to be having her first child," Matilda commented.

"Jane was built to have babies, and I don't see any cause for concern. And if we all pray for her, the good Lord will help her through," said Mrs Pedley, who was a firm believer in the power of prayer.

But what Clare was looking forward to more than anything else was Adam's homecoming. The activity it provoked was astonishing. Cook prepared all his favourite dishes, the house was spring-cleaned from top to bottom, then Matilda and Clare went into Leicester to meet him and bear him home like a young prince returning from the glory of battle.

"I swear you've shot up two inches,' Matilda declared when Adam jumped down off the coach. She embraced him fondly then stood back and gazed at her son with pride and love. There was no doubt about it, with his Cambridge education and looks he would be able to make a fine match. Perhaps even with a girl from a titled family.

Clare wasn't slow to notice, either how every woman in the immediate vicinity, passenger and serving-maid alike, was ogling Adam, and their palpable envy when he moved over to kiss her made her want to laugh out loud.

Because they were cousins and had grown up together, Clare had taken Adam's looks for granted. Now, though, after a three month absence, she saw him as an outsider might and was struck, both by how handsome he was and his uncanny resemblance to Harry Bennett. But then, of course, there was the name. Not that this was unusual. In their particular area, a few surnames were shared amongst many families, and they would all probably be able to claim kinship if they went far enough back in church records. Out of curiosity though, and when she had a spare moment, she would have a word with her aunt and find out a bit more about the history of the family.

"So how is Cambridge, Adam?" asked Christopher Harcourt, coming into the drawing room to shake Adam's hand soon after they arrived home.

"Nothing's changed; I still hate it," Adam announced emphatically. He turned to Matilda. "Can't I leave, Mother? I'd much rather be back here, helping you with the estate."

"You'll have the rest of your life to work. Education is important, Adam. I want you to have the best."

Adam said no more, but he was silent and restless about the house for the rest of the day. Clare suggested they go riding, but he shook his head and the following day, announcing he had to buy more books, he took himself off to Leicester.

"If you're not interested in college or studying, what's the hurry to buy more books?" Clare demanded in a hurt tone. She'd so looked forward to having him home, and now he didn't seem to want to spend time with her.

Adam had mounted his horse ready to move off, but Clare could see by the tinge of pink that stained his cheekbones, that he was put out by her question. In an flash, Clare knew it wasn't books, but something else that was pulling him towards Leicester. A girl was her guess. Not Olivia either.

"It's reading I need to do in the vac," he blustered.

"Oh yes." Here, Clare's mind took several imaginative leaps. Bookshops . . . Emily. She eyed him knowingly. "Don't worry, cousin, your secret is safe with me," she called after him. But Adam was already trotting off down the drive, and he gave no indication that he'd heard her.

But Clare wouldn't let herself be hurt by Adam's neglect for long. The school and the children were taking up more and more of her time, and she'd been delighted when Christopher – they were on Christian name terms now – told her she had a natural aptitude for teaching. Of course, he might have been trying to flatter her, but Clare didn't think so, that wasn't Christopher's way. And she did find a tremendous satisfaction in helping to dispel ignorance. The children were like unwatered flowers after a shower and it astonished Clare how quickly their small, untutored minds soaked up knowledge and grasped the basics of reading and writing. All, that is, except ungainly, slow-witted Freddie. Freddie was Clare's one failure and it irked, because in spite of her best endeavours nothing seemed to take root in his sluggish mind. His mother being a widow, Freddie had free schooling, but Clare did wonder if he should be taking up a space that could be given to a more able child. But there was something dogged about his determination to acquire an education, so she didn't have the heart to dismiss him and he often he turned up plastered with mud after a two mile walk over ploughed fields in pouring rain.

As a special treat, Clare and Christopher had planned a small party for the children during the last week of the term. There were to be games like pass the parcel and musical chairs, Cook was providing cakes, sandwiches and lemonade, and each child would take home a small gift.

The night before the party, Christopher and Clare walked down to the cottage to decorate the small classroom with holly, yew, ivy and painted fir-cones. It was a cold, clear night, the sky lit with millions of candles, although underfoot there was a treacherous black ice. Clare, who had a bundle of evergreen clasped in her arms, didn't notice a frozen puddle until she felt her feet slipping from under her. She gave a squeal of surprise, her arms sawed the air, the greenery scattered and she fell with an unpleasant, spine-crunching jolt.

Quickly, Christopher, all concern, knelt down beside her. "Clare, are you all right?"

Clare, whose dignity, along with her bottom, was rather bruised, was quick to reassure him. "I'm fine, but I think you'll have to help me up."

"Of course." Christopher grasped Clare's small, gloved hand in his and pulled her to her feet. They stood silent in the darkness, each acutely aware of the other, their breath mingling, fingers coiled. In the end Clare, in the grip of exciting, unfamiliar emotions, had to force herself to pull her hand away and in a shaky voice she said, "I . . . I think we'd better get this picked up."

"Yes . . . of course." Christopher let go of her hand, and beween them they gathered up most of the greenery. This time as they walked on, though, Clare tucked her arm through his, and for the first time in his life, Christopher tasted true happiness.

The fire in the cottage had burnt low, but it quickly came to life again with fresh logs. Clare lit the candles then they set about decorating the small room, looping ivy across the beams, nailing swags of fir and holly to the ceiling and forming the pine-cones into small pyramids on the windowsills. When they'd finished, Clare regarded their efforts with a quiet satisfaction. "Looks nice, doesn't it?

"Yes, I would say we've done a pretty good job. The only problem is that the children are so excited about the party, it's been hard to get them to concentrate this week"

"You've done wonders with the children, Christopher."

"Not just me, you too."

"Well, I managed to get Freddie to read his first word today. I consider that a real achievement."

"What was it?"

"Cat." Clare laughed.

"Well, it's a start. Great oaks from little acorns grow."

Clare picked up her cloak. "I suppose we ought to make a move. I told my aunt we'd be back by nine o'clock."

"Wait a minute," said Christopher, "let me show you something. I found it growing in the orchard today." From behind his back he produced a sprig of mistletoe and tucked it in Clare's blond curls. "It means I can kiss you now."

Clare stared up into his eyes. "Does it?" she said quietly.

"Yes." Amazed at his own daring, Christopher leaned forward and kissed her lightly on the lips. When Clare didn't respond, he tensed himself for a sound telling off or slap around the face. Instead he felt her arms slide up round his neck and he began to kiss her with a reckless hunger. The unloved childhood years, the months of worshipping her without hope vanished and a pure joy surged through him. "Oh Clare, Clare, my lovely Clare, I do love you so," he murmured into her hair.

But doubts quickly re-surfaced when Clare's arms fell from around his neck and she took a step back. "Go on, say it," Christopher urged. "You don't return my feelings, do you?"

"Yes . . . I . . . think I do," Clare admitted shyly, then laughed out loud as Christopher swept her up and waltzed her round the small room. Finally out of breath, he collapsed onto one of the children's benches and pulled Clare down on his lap, clasping her tight as if fearful he might lose her again. “Shall we tell anyone, my sweet?”

“Can it be our secret for a while?” Clare pleaded, not even sure that their love would meet with the whole-hearted approval of her grandparents and aunt.

Of course he would have preferred the world to know, but Christopher was in that early stage of love, where he could deny his beloved nothing. So, content to fall in with her wishes, he nuzzled her neck and murmured, “It will be our secret darling, I promise.”

After frequent pauses to kiss and reaffirm their love for one another, Christopher and Clare arrived back home to find the Mummers in the kitchen. Old Father Christmas, St George, the Black Knight, Betsy and sundry players and musicians were there with antlers and masks or blackened faces, keeping the household entertained with scurrilous jokes about politicians and the King. It was obvious that this band of strolling players had imbibed liberally at various stops on the way. Now with Cook’s mulled wine being offered in generous quantities, their voices were becoming a touch slurred, their limbs uncoordinated and when the Black Knight engaged St George in a mock sword fight and was slain, he remained on his back snoring loudly.

Christopher and Clare, drawn in by the warmth and goodwill, went to help themselves to a glass of the hot spicy wine.

“My, you’ve got rosy cheeks,” Matilda commented, when she saw her niece, and gave a knowing laugh.

At her aunt’s remark Clare’s cheeks glowed even brighter than the Mummers’ lanterns resting on the large Welsh dresser.

“It’s coming in from the cold air, Aunt Tilda,” Clare

lied, and, to hide her embarrassment, she crammed one of Cook's mince pies into her mouth.

The Mummers sang several carols, finishing with *The Holly and the Ivy*. Matilda rewarded them generously, and after hauling the Black Knight to his feet they made their exit to an enthusiastic round of applause.

"I must confess I haven't laughed so much in a long time," said Matilda, after they'd gone, noticing at the same time how Christopher's gaze followed Clare around the kitchen. So her little plan might be coming to fruition, and earlier than she'd supposed, which was good, for it was important to have her niece married. And over Christmas, with the various parties and balls they'd been invited to around the County, there would be ample opportunity to start looking for a suitable bride for Adam.

Adam's love-life was going nowhere near as satisfactorily as his cousin's. Impatient to see Emily, he'd galloped off to Leicester and sat twiddling his fingers in Lily's parlour for two hours. But she never turned up, neither did she the following day, although this time at least Lily had a message for him.

"I took my books to be changed this morning and I spoke to Emily. She says to tell you she won't get any time off before Christmas, they are too busy. She promises to try and meet you after the holiday, though."

Desolated, Adam rode back home. He couldn't go on like this. People would say he was too young to know his own mind, but he had no doubt about his love for Emily. And she loved him equally. That being the case, why shouldn't they declare it to the world? After all, there was nothing shameful about their feelings, and it was only because of some stupid family row that they were forced into behaving furtively. And why should he stay at university when he detested it so much? His resentment fuelled by frustration, Adam worried away at these questions all the way home. By the time he was riding up the drive to Trent Hall, he had made a decision; he would ask Emily to marry him. Then, and only then, would he seek permission from her parents and his mother. They were under-age, of course, but nothing was going to deter him and if they refused, well . . . then he would have to find another, more drastic way for them to be together.

Chapter Eighteen

"Out again, Jed?"

Jed, shrugging himself into a coat, looked uncomfortable. "Only for an hour, I promise, Rachel."

"More politics, I suppose?" Rachel was mending a tear in the behind of a pair of Simon's breeches, and without looking up, she snapped off the thread with her teeth. "I imagined after the Reform Bill went through you'd finally be happy with the way the country's run."

"Certainly not. That was just one hurdle along the way. I won't be satisfied until we have universal suffrage. The right for men and women of all classes to vote."

"Jed, be realistic. Do you imagine such a thing will ever happen?"

"Yes I do, and we've already drawn up a Charter," Jed looked at the grandfather clock. "I must go." He bent to kiss Rachel but she didn't respond.

"Are you angry with me?"

"Whatever makes you think that?" answered Rachel coolly.

"Kiss me then, properly."

Rachel gave her husband a dutiful peck. "Now, be on your way." She threaded a needle with deep concentration, picked up a shirt and started to sew buttons on to it.

Emily, behind her book, watched this scene with some amusement, heard her father's sigh of resignation then he went, calling as he clattered downstairs, "I won't be long, I promise."

Emily waited until the door slammed, then she lowered her book. "Can I go round to Lily's, please?" As soon as she opened her mouth, she realised her request was probably ill-timed.

"What, on your own and at this time of night? Certainly not!"

"I never go anywhere these days," Emily complained. "It's like being in prison. Septimus is in London again, and Lily's on her own, so why can't I keep her company?"

"It's not safe for a young woman to go abroad on her own at night."

"Oh Mama, it's such a short distance, I couldn't possibly come to any harm." Very soon Adam would be returning to Cambridge, Emily was desperate to see him, and she needed to talk to Lily.

"Well, we were busy over Christmas and we did work you hard," Rachel admitted. She thought for a minute then laid aside her mending. "And why should I sit here on my own, night after night staring at the four walls? Get your bonnet and cloak, we'll both go and call on Lily."

"What about me?" asked Simon, who was busy with his homework at one end of the table.

"Ben's asleep and you're old enough, surely, to be left in charge for an hour without getting into mischief?"

"Course I am."

Rachel patted her son's head. "Good boy. There'll be a penny for you when we get back, but only if there's been no trouble, mind you." As she spoke,

Rachel pushed her feet into strong shoes and buttoned up her cloak, while Emily struggled hard to hide her excitement. Lily was bound of have a message for her from Adam. It wasn't quite the same as seeing him but it was better than nothing.

Outside there'd been a light fall of snow, but thankfully it had stopped, otherwise Emily knew her mother might have had second thoughts. But, there again, she knew her mother well enough to know that this wasn't so much a visit to Lily as an act of defiance against her father.

Although it was no more than a ten minute walk, they were chilled to the marrow by the time they reached the house. Emily pulled the bell then stood stamping her feet as it tinkled far away in the kitchen. After a pause a light appeared in the fanlight, then a maid, wearing a mob cap so large it almost covered her eyes, opened the door. By her anxious expression it was obvious Lily didn't receive too many callers at night.

"Is Mrs Rodway at home, Bertha?" Emily enquired.

Recognising the voice, the girl's face cleared. "Oh yes, Miss Fairfax, and very upset me missus 'as bin all evening."

"Why, what's wrong?"

"I dunno, I'm sure, but she wa' sobbing 'er heart out earlier," Bertha somewhat indiscreetly informed them.

Emily hovered, not wanting to intrude and uncertain what to do for the best. "Perhaps we'd better leave it for another time," she was saying to her mother, when further along the passage a door opened.

"Who is it Bertha?" The voice was husky with tears.

"Miss Fairfax, Madam wi' another lady."

Lily blew her nose, cleared her throat, moved forward saw Rachel and, a child again, threw herself into her arms. "Oh, it's lovely to see you Rachel," she sobbed.

"Well, it doesn't sound like it, dear. But why the tears? Come on, tell me all about it," Rachel said gently and with a comforting arm round the young woman, followed the maid down the hall in to the parlour.

"Can you bring us some tea, Bertha?" Emily asked the maid then quietly closed the door.

Lily's tears were flowing again unchecked. "I'm so miserable," she sobbed.

"But why, Lily? Tell me." Rachel looked around the well-appointed room with some envy. How could anyone be unhappy in a house like this? she wondered thinking of their cramped quarters above the shop. But perhaps it was Septimus, maybe he was being unkind to her, although this struck her as fairly unlikely.

"I get so lonely with Septimus away, and my sisters still refuse to come and visit me." Lily picked up her small cat and buried her face in its soft fur. Of course this was no lie, it just wasn't the true reason of her misery. Lily wished she was a small girl again so that she could curl up on Rachel's lap and pour out all her troubles, except that she couldn't bear the shame of it. How could she confess that her husband found her so utterly repulsive, that two days ago he'd moved into a separate bedroom, with the excuse that he didn't sleep well sharing a bed. She tried to tempt him with her culinary skills, cooked him his favourite dishes: steak and kidney pudding, tripe and onions, plum duff. He enjoyed it all, praised her to the heavens but nothing, seemingly, could arouse his passion, and yesterday Septimus announced he had urgent business in London and would be gone a week. If that wasn't enough, her mother-in-law had started dropping hints that it was about time she became a grandmother. Well that was about as likely as snow in August.

Bertha brought in the tea and Rachel noticed how Lily's hand shook as she poured. She'd felt angry with her for a long time, but could she really be accused of stealing Septimus? After all, men made their choice, women waited. A bit like going to the top of the tree for the most succulent fruit. And the poor girl really was distraught. In the end you had to forgive and forget or the feud could go on forever. "Would you like me to have a word with your sisters? Try and persuade them to come and see you?" Rachel asked as Lily handed her a cup of tea.

Putting a brave face on it, Lily bent and kissed Rachel on the cheek. "Oh, you are a dear. Ask them to come to tea on Sunday. You and Emily too."

"What was that?" asked Emily, Lily's voice cutting across her thoughts as she wondered at the likelihood of getting to talk to her friend on her own.

"Lily's invited us to tea on Sunday." Rachel stood up with the tray. "I'll take this into the kitchen to save Bertha's legs, she must be tired."

"Tell her when she's washed the pots, she can go to bed," Lily called after her.

Hardly waiting for her mother to close the door, Emily swung round to face Lily. "Has Adam been here? Is there a message for me? A letter perhaps?"

Lily laughed and held up her hands. "Hold your horses. He's coming tomorrow afternoon for certain. But he said to tell you it will be the last time, he goes back to Cambridge the following day."

"Oh no, don't say that, I'll absolutely die if I don't see him," Emily wailed in tragic tones, heard her mother wish Bertha goodnight and hissed, "Tell him to wait, I'll get here somehow."

Lily watched Emily, suddenly composed, stroking the cat and for her mother's benefit, a picture of innocence. In comparison to a humdrum walking-out with parents' consent, how much more thrilling an illicit love affair must be, with its trysts and intrigue, she mused. How hasty assignations and long partings must heighten passion. Well, that was something she would only ever read about. For it was apparent she was never going to experience that union of body and mind with Septimus. Twenty-five and her love-life was over before it had even started. Lily gave a desolate sigh. "I do envy you, Emily. Being loved the way Adam loves you."

The younger girl looked slightly perplexed. "But Septimus loves you, doesn't he?"

Lily gave what she hoped was a carefree laugh. "Of course he does, the dear man absolutely dotes on me."

Lily went with mother and daughter to the door to see them off. "Look, it's snowing!" She held out her hand and the flakes dissolved on her warm palm.

"Not too hard, and fortunately we haven't got far." Rachel hugged Lily, remembering the sisters as small girls. Lord, how they'd squabbled, so fiercely sometimes, blood would be drawn. But they would always be important to her and she wanted them to be at peace with each other. "I'll go round to Butt Close Lane tomorrow and do my best to get the girls here for tea on Sunday. Of course, I might not succeed but you'll want to know one way or another, so I'll send Emily along to you."

"Come in the afternoon, Emily. I've got an appointment in the morning."

"Early or late?"

Lily gave her a sly wink. "Three o'clock would be fine."

Emily wanted to skip for joy as they walked away

from the house. Tomorrow she would see Adam. She didn't like deceiving her mother and with all the secrecy it reminded her of the Capulets and Montagues. And about as much her and Adam's fault as Romeo's and Juliet's. Was that how it would end? She and Adam separated permanently by warring families? She shivered, it was too unbearable even to think about. Linking her arm through her mother's, she asked, "Do you think Papa will be worried? Us out in this weather?"

"I hope so," Rachel answered bluntly and Emily giggled. "Still, we've done some good, cheered poor Lily up."

And not just Lily, thought Emily, with a small smile, which was quickly whipped off her face when they turned into High Cross Street and the snow caught them full blast.

Almost blinded by it, they bent their heads into the wind. "Come on, let's hurry and get out of this," Rachel urged, felt her shoe come up against something solid and would have gone sprawling in the snow if Emily hadn't grabbed her.

"Whatever is it?" Rachel exclaimed. Peering into the swirling darkness, she saw a bundle of rags already almost covered by snow, then heard a hungry mewling. She touched the bundle gingerly and the feeble cry came again. "Good Lord, it's a baby!" Rachel pulled back a piece of sacking. "And a young woman."

"Is . . . is she dead?" asked Emily. She'd never seen a dead body and was frightened to look.

"I don't know. But the baby's alive. Hurry and fetch your father. If he's not back tell Simon to come. We've got to get them home before they freeze to death."

As quickly as she could in the conditions, Emily hurried off up the street, while Rachel found the girl's skeletal wrist. Her pulse beat faintly, but there was still some life there, enough to give Rachel hope. "It's all right, we'll take care of you, and your baby," she murmured to the unconscious girl and gently lifted the infant from her arms. It was wrapped in a tattered shawl and was almost weightless, yet it still managed a cry of protest at being separated from its mother. "Hush, hush, little one," Rachel crooned, tucking it inside her woollen cloak, close against her breast. The warmth of her body quietened it and a moment later, Jed came panting up followed by Emily and Simon.

"Don't ask any questions, Jed, until we get home. Can you and Simon carry the girl between you? I'll bring the baby."

Jed lifted the girl in his arms. "I can manage on my own, there's nothing of her and she's obviously on the verge of starvation. Run and make the fire up Simon."

As they trooped up the street, Rachel recalled very similar circumstances and weather, when she'd turned up on Jed's doorstep, frozen and terrified. Above all, she remembered his compassion. He was a good man, he cared about the world and wanted to make it a better place so that people like this girl and her baby weren't left to starve to death in the gutter. Politics were like breathing to Jed, and it was small-minded to make him feel guilty every time he went out to a meeting.

Jed carried the girl upstairs and into the small living-room where Simon had already built up the fire and now had the kettle on. Carefully, because she was little more than skin and bone, Jed laid the girl down on the sofa. "Bring blankets," he ordered Emily, and when she came back with a pile, Rachel grabbed one and lay the baby on it in front of the fire. Rachel stared down with pity at the girl as Jed covered her with blankets. Her eyes were sunken with hunger, the bloodless skin was stretched tautly over her cheekbones. Her hair, though, was another matter. Filthy and verminous it might be, but there was still no disguising its colour, which was a rich, vibrant red.

Jed tested her pulse again. "When she comes round we must try and get a little soup down her."

"In the meantime I'll try and feed this little scrap."

"Is it a boy or girl?" asked Emily, as her mother lifted the baby up.

Rachel had a quick look. "A girl, and not more than a month old, by my reckoning." It came so naturally, cradling the infant in her arms, warming some milk and water, then very carefully trickling a few drops on the end of her finger into the baby's mouth. Rachel thought it might be too weak to swallow but in the end she managed to get a couple of teaspoons of milk down. Her efforts were repaid when the baby appeared to revive slightly.

"Go and get that crib from under the stairs, Simon," Rachel said and rocked the small bundle gently. "Poor wee mite." She gazed down at the infant with great tenderness, enjoying its small body against her breast and remembering how much she'd enjoyed feeding her own and that mysterious communion between mother and child. For a second Rachel was overcome with an intense longing to have another child, but she quickly took herself to task. She must stop such nonsense. Three children were quite enough to feed and educate.

Although they were yawning their heads off, Emily and Simon were reluctant to go to bed. In the end Rachel had to insist. Jed she had even more trouble with. "I don't want to leave you on your own. Something might happen."

"I'll wake you if it does and someone has to to be fit to run the shop tomorrow. The girl's breathing is shallow, but she's still alive. If we can get her through the night . . ." Rachel crossed her fingers.

"You promise to call me?"

"Yes, dear," Rachel replied patiently, waited until Jed had gone, gave the baby a little more milk, put her in the crib and rocked it with her foot until she was asleep. Curling herself in a blanket, Rachel stared with pity at the half-dead girl and wondered about her circumstances. There was terrible poverty in Leicester and armies of beggars roamed the streets, but what had brought the girl to this tragic situation? Had she parents? Of course the likelihood was that she'd been abandoned by a callous lover. Or maybe she'd been a maidservant somewhere, seduced by a male member of the household and shown the door once she was with child. It was a familiar enough tragedy, for whatever the circumstances, the woman always took the blame.

The changing face of Leicester was also bringing in foreigners. Where, not long ago, Rachel could remember meadows, orchards and bluebells, now smoking factory chimneys cast their grim shadow over the landscape. These factories attracted Irish immigrants, many of whom lived in squalid shacks down by the canal. And this girl, with her colouring, could be Irish. Perhaps she'd come over on the boat on her own and had no one to turn to. Eventually Rachel's weary mind gave up wondering, her eyes closed and she slept. She was awakened by Jed shaking her. It still wasn't light but the lamp was lit, and Jed had thrown some more coal on the fire.

"I'm afraid there's nothing more we can do for the girl," he said quietly, "she's dead."

"The baby? What about the baby?" Rachel threw off her blanket and knelt down by the crib. Fearful of what she might find, she touched the infant's cheek with her fingers.

"Well?"

"She's still alive, thank God, and she's breathing evenly. I'll feed her as soon as she wakes. But she's got no mother now." Rachel stared in sorrow at the poor, dead girl, and tears ran down her cheeks. She'd so hoped she could save her, but the girl had starved to death. She must have nursed dreams, planned a life for herself and now it was over, cut short by the misfortune of being born a woman.

Jed lifted the dead girl gently and the long red hair swung down. Her light had been put out, but nothing could extinguish that colour and it blazed with a life of its own. "I'd rather the children didn't see her, it might distress them, so if you don't mind I'll take her into our bedroom. And she's going to no pauper's grave. At least we'll give her a decent burial."

Jed was only gone for a few minutes and when he came back, he said, "I'll see the carpenter about a coffin when the boys have gone off to school."

"And the baby?"

The Infant Pauper Asylum, I suppose."

"My conscience wouldn't allow it, Jed. If she went there, she'd be dead within the month from neglect."

"Perhaps we'll find a childless couple to adopt her."

"I feel she's almost a gift. Can't we keep her?" Rachel pleaded, for she was already besotted with the tiny girl.

"We barely manage now, Rachel, and it's an extra mouth to feed."

"Please, Jed. You can't send her away, not a man of your principles."

"The burden would fall on you. Teething, broken nights."

Jed was wavering, so Rachel pressed on. "If we hadn't found her, she'd be dead now. And the little thing deserves a chance, which we can give her."

"All right, Rachel, you win."

"Bless you, Jed, you're a good man." Rachel moved over and kissed her husband, then lifted her new daughter out of the crib and kissed her, too, with a secret and intense joy. "What shall we call her?"

"Christmas isn't long gone, so what about Natalie?"

"Natalie Fairfax? Yes, that sounds like a good name to me."

Chapter Nineteen

"Septimus, I think we should have something done to the garden, it's a mess."

Septimus managed to conceal his irritation at being disturbed while he was catching up on the news, and let the *Leicester Journal* fall to his lap. "What was that, dear?"

The house was wrapped in a Sabbath gloom and Lily, bored out her mind, was standing gazing out at the weeping March sky and the lunar landscape of builders' rubble and potholes that passed for their back garden. "I said, we need someone to come and do the garden, make it really nice so that when I invite people round in the summer, we can take tea on the lawn."

Septimus lifted his paper again and from behind it answered, "Do exactly as you please, Lily my dear."

"I can hire a gardener then?"

"Yes, as long as you deal with it, I'm too busy myself. You'll probably need to put an advertisement in the paper, so I suggest you go down to the *Leicester Journal* offices tomorrow."

"Oh, thank you, Septimus." Lily went over and planted a grateful kiss on his forehead, thinking as she did that there were times when she really felt exceptionally fond of her husband. His business was doing well and he was generous to a fault. Out of guilt, Lily suspected, and took advantage of it, telling herself that, since he gave her no emotional support, she was entitled to some sort of recompense. Anyway, while she was spending, she could forget briefly the disappointment of her loveless marriage.

Now that she had a new project to divert her, Lily's depression lifted and she bounced over to the bureau, sat down and drew out a pen, ink and paper. She thought hard, then having composed the advertisement in her head, she leaned forward and began to write in the neat copperplate hand she was so often complimented on.

"How does this sound Septimus?" Lily swung round in her chair. "'Wanted: Experienced and creative gardener to transform a wilderness into a garden of beauty and tranquillity. Testimonials will be required and only men of the highest calibre need apply to Mr and Mrs S Rodway of 6, Orchard Street.'"

"Excellent."

From never having had the slightest interest in horticulture, Lily now began to picture the garden in her mind's eye. With some squared paper she drew up a rough plan of the garden she envisaged; lilac and laburnum, a small summer house, an arbour of roses and a path winding between drifts of tall summer flowers, their scent so powerful it drugged the senses. And when the garden was completed she would invite all her acquaintances round to enjoy it. In fact she ought to get out more, mix with the ladies of the town, do good works. Help the sick and the poor. She couldn't mope around this house doing nothing but read novels for the rest of her life, she'd go insane.

Lily's moods fluctuated, but the following day she tripped off down to the *Leicester Journal* offices in a positive, cheerful frame of mind. She handed in her advertisement, paid for it and was informed by the office boy that it would be in the paper on Friday. After this, unable to face going back to an empty house, she took her usual aimless walk around the shops and market. It was thirsty work, buying goods she didn't particularly need, so, deciding a cup of tea would be just the ticket, Lily headed for High Cross Street.

Lily was rather in awe of Jed and today he was in the shop on his own, with a look on his face that said: don't disturb. So, with a quiet, "I've just popped in to see Rachel, shall I go up?" she tiptoed past him up the stairs.

"Rachel, it's me, Lily," she called, tapped on the door, then opened it without waiting for an answer.

Rachel had just finished feeding Natalie and now had her over her shoulder winding her. In less than two months the baby's starving monkey features had been transformed. She still weighed less than she should, but her eyes were bright as sapphires, her cheeks pink and she was a cherished member of the family.

"Let me hold her, please." Lily held out hungry arms and Rachel handed her over.

"Be warned, she might bring milk up all over you."

"I don't mind." Natalie's tiny body fitted perfectly into the crook of Lily's arm, and she lay there, flexing her tiny fingers and blowing contented bubbles. At this close physical contact, inhaling the warm, milky, baby smell of her, Lily was consumed by a terrible sense of pain, loss and rejection. She was a woman, God had made her to bear children, and yet she was being deprived of that right by a husband who was obviously repelled by her. Clutching the infant possessively, she thought, I want to keep her. And why shouldn't I, when Rachel already has three of her own? But the family wouldn't part with her, she knew that, and who could say whether Septimus would agree to adopt a child anyway?

"Can I have Natalie back, please, Lily? I'm going to put her down for her morning sleep."

Lily kissed each velvety cheek and handed her over, but with obvious reluctance. "You are lucky to have her, Rachel, she's absolutely gorgeous."

"Yes, I think of her as my little Christmas gift. But you'll have a baby of your own before long." As she spoke Rachel realised this might not be a diplomatic remark, for Lily came now on the slightest pretext, always she wanted to hold Natalie, and it had crossed her mind that Lily could be barren.

Lily, dwelling too on her predicament, knew that if she was going to confess her painful secret to Rachel, there would never be a better time. But she felt such an angry shame, the words stuck in her gullet and the moment passed.

"Look, I do believe she has some red hair coming through." Rachel brushed the soft down up into a quiff. "But then it's to be expected, her mother's hair was a most beautiful colour. I cut off a lock of it to keep for when Natalie's a young woman. She deserves to know the truth."

"I wonder what her mother's story was, poor thing."

"Very similar to my own mother's, I would imagine. There are a lot of us unclaimed orphans wandering around the planet. But you have to draw a line under the past. There's no point in spending your life wallowing in self-pity, that way lies hell."

Lily straightened. "True," she answered, and wondered if that was what she was doing, making a hell for herself. If she were, then what was the remedy?

Since there was a great deal of hardship and unemployment in the town, Lily had imagined that once the *Leicester Journal* came out, there would be a steady trickle of prospective employees at the door. Instead, all her advertisement generated was an elderly man, not up to the heavy digging required, and a inexperienced lad of about sixteen. She was thinking that she'd have to re-advertise when, on the Wednesday afternoon, a young man turned up on her step. Bertha had been instructed to take all applicants through to the kitchen to be interviewed and when Lily walked in, the young man was staring out of the window at the heavy clay soil he might soon have to turn over. What struck Lily immediately was the power in his body, the strong neck, straight spine and muscular shoulders. When he heard the click of Lily's heels on the quarry tiles he turned, assessing her with a practised eye.

"Well it looks like a challenge, Mrs Rodway." He smiled, but without the deference Lily considered was her due. She'd been about to invite him to sit down but changed her mind and kept him standing to show who was in charge.

"You don't think you're up to it then?" she asked, wanting to take him down a peg or two, because it seemed to her that he was far too self-possessed for a mere hired hand.

"Oh yes, I like nothing better than virgin soil." Again he smiled and Lily could have sworn he put an extra emphasis on the word, 'virgin'.

"May I know your name, please?"

"Martin. Pierre Martin."

Pierre? It was such a high-falutin' name, Lily suspected he was making it up. Supposing he was some ne'er-do-well or criminal type, she thought, and grew uneasy when she remembered there was only her and Bertha in the house. "Not an English name by the sound of it."

"No, French, Huguenot actually. But my family settled in England a long time ago."

"Well, about your gardening experience, Mr Martin."

"Plenty of that. I've worked in some of the best houses in the land."

"So why did you leave?"

He shrugged. "Itchy feet. I have the wanderlust. I like to move around the country seeing as much of it as I can."

"You have testimonials?"

"Yes." He produced several documents from his pocket. Glancing over them, Lily noticed that most of the testimonials bore the crests of some very noble families. Furthermore, they were glowing, which only increased her suspicions.

"Where are your lodgings?"

"In Wharf Street, although I intend to move out once I have found employment."

"Can you start tomorrow?" She'd had every intention of turning him down, but somehow the words slipped out of her mouth before she could stop them.

"Yes, I can Mrs Rodway. But what about wages?"

"That is something you will have to discuss with Mr Rodway, my husband. So be here at eight and he'll settle the matter with you. Rest assured, he won't be ungenerous." Maintaining a haughty demeanour, Lily swept from the kitchen, calling as she did, "Bertha, see Martin out please."

Once Pierre started work, Lily frequently found herself drawn to the back bedroom window. Here, well hidden by the heavy curtains, she couldn't help but make comparisons between her husband and their new gardener. She remembered how Septimus's flesh hung loose like a half-set jelly, whereas Pierre's body was taut and strong, enabling him to work at a steady pace, his muscular arms turning over the heavy clay soil with ease. Neither had Lily ever felt the slightest desire to run her fingers through Septimus's pale wisps of hair, whereas they itched to grab a handful of Pierre's dark curls.

At noon each day, Lily would instruct Bertha to take bread, cheese and beer out to Pierre. Leaning on his shovel he would accept the food with a smile and a remark that always sent the maid scuttling back to the kitchen all giggly and with a blush on her plump cheeks. Although she daren't ask, Lily longed to know what it was he said to Bertha. Their easy intimacy irked, too, until she reminded herself that he was a mere hireling, she the lady of the house.

March moved into April and the days grew warmer. Suddenly the temperature soared and a stunted looking tree at the end of the garden burst into miraculous pink bloom. From her look-out upstairs, Lily stood transfixed one afternoon as Pierre paused to discard his coat, roll back his shirt-sleeves and undo the collar. Not a man to waste time, he recommenced the smooth rhythm of his digging, allowing Lily to feast her eyes on his muscular frame straining against the material of his shirt. Her breath grew ragged and fire surged through her, right down to her most private parts. Shamed by the wayward response of her body, and telling herself it was the heat of the day, Lily rushed into her bedroom and drew her newest and prettiest summer gown out of the wardrobe. She tore off her ordinary cotton workaday dress and stood in front of the pier-glass studying her figure. Pretty good, she decided, but was it to Pierre's taste? Maybe he preferred buxom women. Imagining they were Pierre's, she closed her eyes and ran her hands over her breasts and down to her belly in a slow sensual movement. When Lily opened her eyes again, they glittered diamond-bright, her cheeks were flushed and it was the face of a stranger who gazed back at her. Moved by a powerful emotion, she stepped into her gown, loosened her ringlets to give her hair a more tumbled look, then ran downstairs to prepare fresh lemonade.

"My that's a welcome sight," Pierre said, when he saw Lily bringing the drink out. He paused and wiped his forehead with a red spotted handkerchief.

"You looked hot." Lily poured a glass and handed it to him and their fingers briefly touched.

"Thank you, Mam." With a healthy masculinity, Pierre threw back his head and gulped down the drink. As he drank the tendons stood out on his neck and Lily had an intense desire to reach out and run her fingers down the smooth, lightly tanned skin. She wanted, more than anything, to be able to stand and chat to him in a casual manner, like Bertha did, but her throat muscles had constricted with nerves, and when he held out his glass for a refill, she slopped drink into it then turned and rushed back into the house. Engulfed in oceanic waves of bliss and longing, Lily leaned against the kitchen table, closed her eyes and planned her campaign.

The following afternoon Lily sent Bertha to the market with a very long shopping list and invited Pierre into the kitchen.

"I'm none too clean," he apologised, as he stepped across the threshold.

"Never mind."

Although he stayed standing he observed Lily closely, noticing how she made tea and sliced fruit cake, acting extra busy to cover her agitation, all signs he'd become familiar with over the past few years. Pierre had never forced himself upon a woman in his life, and he always left it to them to do the running. He was modest enough about his looks to be sometimes puzzled by his own sexual powers, although it did afford him some secret amusement to know that, scattered about the Shires, were several fledgling cuckoos roosting in some extremely noble nests.

"Please sit down," Lily invited at last and poured the tea. She clutched the handle of the teapot tightly to control her nervousness, then to make it absolutely clear she had only invited him in to discuss the garden, she continued in a businesslike tone, "I see you've almost finished the digging, Martin."

"Yes, Madam. There's the lawn to be laid next and after that I plan to make a footpath with bricks from the builders' rubble. I could also put a seat round the base of the almond tree. A shady place for you to sit and read when it's hot. I'll plant aconites, snowdrops and crocuses under it, and Christmas roses, lily of the valley and violets in a small bed close by."

The words rolled off his tongue in such poetic cadences Lily was entranced. "It sounds lovely. How long will it take?"

"A month, no more."

Lily straightened in alarm. "A month? But there's the summerhouse to build and I want a rose arbour, and . . . and," she thought quickly, "a small fish pond."

"If your husband is agreeable, I could certainly do all that."

"Septimus has given me a free hand and it's what I would like. I intend, with your help, to have one of the prettiest, most admired gardens in Leicester."

Pierre said no more. Instead he drank his tea, ate his cake and stood up. Knowing that these weren't the only labours he'd be called upon to perform in the coming weeks, he paused by the door. "I'll be getting back to work then, but thank you for the refreshments Mrs Rodway."

The following afternoon Emily called round to see if there was a letter from Adam. To her great disappointment, there wasn't but she did stop for a cup of tea. "I don't know how long I can go on being secretive like this and deceiving my parents."

"Tell them, then. They could hardly disapprove of Adam, he's no monster."

"They hate that family. And what about his mother? She obviously thinks we're common as muck, even though Papa told me her grandfather was nothing more than a drunken prison turn-key. And she's got big plans for Adam. A girl of considerable wealth, not a bookseller's daughter."

"Life is complicated, isn't it?" Lily sighed.

"It is," Emily agreed. She was slouched in her chair, sipping her tea disconsolately, when Pierre's muscular frame was suddenly outlined in the window. "Gosh, who's that handsome creature?" Emily placed her cup and saucer on the table and sat up straight.

"My gardener." Lily's tone was proprietorial.

"Is he married?"

"I haven't the slightest idea. Nor do I intend to ask."

"I bet Bertha makes sheep's eyes at him."

"I'd better not catch her, I don't want any hanky-panky between my servants," Lily answered icily and wondered about those conversations they had.

"Pack me an overnight bag, Lily, I have to go to Nottingham today, and I shall be away for the night." As Septimus spoke he foamed his face with a brush, then leaned towards the mirror and began to shave.

"Yes, dear." Fingers trembling with agitation, Lily

packed her husband's bag. When he had finished shaving, she helped him into his coat and brushed the collar with a wifely devotion.

"Will you go straight on to the business tomorrow?"

"We're so busy with orders, I'm afraid I must. But I promise faithfully to be back tomorrow evening at a reasonable time."

"Then I shall cook you your favourite meal; steak and kidney pie," Lily promised even though her mind was racing with other plans. She could barely eat her breakfast and after she'd waved Septimus off, she waited impatiently while Bertha washed the pots, made the beds and dusted the parlour. When she'd finally finished, Lily pressed a coin into her hand. "Here's sixpence. Take the carrier's cart and go and visit your family in Oadby."

Bertha, astonished at her mistress's sudden largesse, stared at the money. "Can I go now, then, missus?"

"Yes." Lily almost pushed her out the door, then to the maid's departing back, she called, "And you needn't hurry back. Stay all night if you like." Once she had the kitchen to herself, Lily set to preparing her specialities; small meat pies, a fruit loaf and a sponge cake that was as light as an angel's kiss. At midday, instead of taking Pierre out his usual fare, she called from the kitchen door, "It looks like rain, would you like to come inside and eat?"

"Thank you, Madam." Pierre cleaned his spade then, guessing this might be the day he would be required to oblige the lady of the house, he stripped to the waist and sluiced his head under the pump in the yard. He gasped from the coldness of the water, then shook his wet hair like a dog, so that droplets of water ran down the smooth, golden plane of his back. Although he accomplished a great deal during his working hours, Pierre always worked with a neat exactitude and never hurried. Now, mesmerised by his grace and beauty, Lily handed him a towel.

"Thank you, Madam," he said, dried himself and put on his shirt. Before entering the kitchen he thoughtfully removed his boots.

Lily poured beer into a tankard and offered Pierre a meat pie which he ate with obvious enjoyment. "This is really tasty, you're an excellent cook, Mrs Rodway."

Yes, and all learnt to impress Septimus. Still no knowledge was ever wasted, thought Lily and pushed a second pie on to his plate.

"Why aren't you eating?" Pierre asked.

"I'm not terribly hungry," Lily replied, fiddling in a distracted way with the lace edging of the tablecloth. She was aware of damp armpits and a dry mouth. What in God's name was she doing behaving like a common whore? And did it look terribly obvious? Her conscience answered both these question for her, which only increased her agitation.

The kitchen door was half open and a sudden gust of wind slammed it hard against the wall. Glad to find occupation, Lily jumped up to close it, making sure to turn the key. "It looks like the good weather is over, it's raining cats and dogs out there." How normal her voice sounded.

"Only an April shower I expect." Pierre was now standing close behind her and her heartbeats thrummed so loudly in her ears, Lily was sure he must hear them.

"Yes, but you can't go outside until it clears."

"That sounds like an order."

Lily turned and faced him. "It is."

"So what do you suggest we do in the meantime?" Pierre gave her a lazy, knowing smile, then, slipping an arm round her waist, he bent and kissed her.

*　*　*

Afterwards Lily could never recall how they made it from the kitchen to the bedroom, but her awakening, the exquisite sensations Pierre aroused in her, would remain branded on her memory until the day she died. His mouth on hers, his exploring tongue then the slow disrobing. He unlaced her stays with skilful hands then, lifting and caressing her breasts, he watched her expression in the pier-glass. "Do you like that?" he murmured in her ear.

Lily, her head thrown back against his shoulder, shuddered with pleasure. "Oh yes."

"What about this?" His hand moved down to the gap in her drawers, exploring with gentle fingers. Abandoning herself to these exquisite pleasures, Lily felt herself being lifted in his arms, carried to the bed. He removed the last of her garments and, although it was the first time she'd lain naked next to a man, she felt no shyness.

"Hold me," Pierre ordered, "down here." He grabbed her hand and guided it to his mysterious 'thing' which was large and hard.

"Do you want me to put it in you?" Pierre liked to tease.

By way of an answer, Lily pulled him on top of her, and as he penetrated her, she felt a tearing sensation and a slight pain.

In his astonishment, Pierre paused and withdrew and saw there was blood on the sheet. "You can't be a virgin, it's impossible!"

Lily buried her head in his chest in shame and didn't answer.

"But you're a married woman."

"You don't have to tell me that, I know." Her voice cracked with misery. "Does it put you off me?"

"On the contrary . . ." Pierre asked no more questions, they could wait while he put matters to right. He entered her again, moving gently and watching her reactions. Untried as she was, Lily began to move with him, and as he thrust more deeply, she gave small moans of pleasure and wrapped her legs round him. He wanted her to remember today, and him, without regret, so he managed to wait until she came, then he let go and his seed gushed into her, potent and strong.

"Did you enjoy that?"

"Oh yes," Lily murmured. "Can we do it again?"

Pierre laughed. "Let me get my energy back first. Come here."

Pierre pulled her into his arms and Lily lay there, utterly content, listening to his steady heartbeat and the rain rattling against the window. "Do you know something? I'm an adultress now." Rather taken with the idea, Lily experimented with a few more words. "And I'm licentious and immoral." She giggled.

"And no longer a virgin."

"No, thank God," said Lily fervently.

"But why were you?"

"Septimus never seemed to want to."

"How strange," Pierre mused, and wondered if her husband was one of those men who preferred his own sex. "Just as well I came along then, isn't it?" he smiled, then kissed her.

"I shall be eternally grateful."

Downstairs a clock chimed three. "I'd better get up," he said, "there's work to be done."

But Lily pressed him down on to the bed with a kiss, murmuring against his lips, "There's even more important work to be done here, so why don't you just get on with it?"

"But your husband?"

"He won't be back until tomorrow night."

Chapter Twenty

"I hear Clare is betrothed." Harry and Judith had taken a stroll down to the small lake to feed the family of ducks that had made a home there and as he spoke he tore off pieces of bread and aimed them at the water.

Unaware of their calamitous effect on his daughter, these words were tossed casually into the conversation. For Judith, though, it was as if someone had committed an act of violence against her person and shock sucked the breath from her lungs. "Betrothed?" she managed to croak.

"Yes, to that young man, Christopher Harcourt. Best thing that could happen after that nasty business with her father."

"No! I don't believe it! It's impossible!" Judith shrieked.

Taken aback by Judith's outburst, Harry gave her a concerned glance. Anguished eyes stared at him from a deathly white face. "Are you all right?" He asked the question out of habit because it was apparent she was anything but.

In reply tears gushed from Judith's eyes, then she turned and fled back to the house.

"What the . . . ? Judith, come back here." Of course she ignored him and, scattering the remaining bread to the ducks, Harry hurried after her, mystified by her extaordinary behaviour.

Keen to avoid Charlotte, questions and explanations, Harry entered the house the back way. "Have you seen Miss Judith?" he called to the cook as he strode through the kitchen.

Cook, whose expression was never anything but sour, looked up from preparing a fruit pie. "No sir," she answered unhelpfully and without any more ado, went back to crimping the pastry edges.

Irritated, and wondering why he had never sacked a woman he disliked so much, Harry pushed open the kitchen door and nearly went flying over a maid, on her hands and knees polishing the hall floor.

Although it wasn't her fault the girl, fearing for her job, apologised profusely.

"Don't worry about it. But tell me, have you seen Miss Judith?"

Glad of a chance to ease her tired back, the girl straightened. "She's just gone up to 'er bedroom, sir. Seemed a bit upset, she did," the girl provided, but Harry was already half-way up the stairs.

He knocked then called through the closed door, "Judith, are you there?" When there was no reply he tried the handle, expecting it to be locked. But the door gave way to his touch. It was like walking into the barn at Christmas when the geese were being plucked and the whole room was blanked out by thousands of swirling feathers.

"What on earth . . . ?" Harry sneezed violently several times, waited for the feathers to settle and was confronted with a sight that turned his stomach cold and filled him with foreboding. Judith was kneeling on the bed, her hair hung loose and her eyes were wild. But far worse, she was clutching a pair of scissors and stabbing viciously at the eiderdown and pillows. And as the feathers spilled out, she grabbed great handfuls and scattered them about the room.

Convinced that his elder daughter had gone truly mad, Harry rushed over, grabbed her hand, and twisted it until the the scissors dropped from her fingers. "Stop it Judith, do you hear me!" Feathers continued to spiral to the ground and every conceivable surface was now covered with them. "What on earth has got into you?"

Judith wrenched her hand from her father's grip, flung herself face down on the bed and burst into heartbreaking sobs.

Still mystified by her behaviour, Harry sat down beside her and stroked her dishevelled locks. "Please tell me what's wrong, little one, then I can help you."

"It's Clare!"

"What about Clare?"

The sobs ceased for a moment. "She's getting married."

"Is that all?" Harry relaxed.

"But she can't, not when I love her more than anyone in the whole wide world!"

"Come, she's a girl." Harry tried to sound jocular, but there was a hard knot of anxiety right at the centre of his being.

Judith lifted her head and stared at him with red, puffy eyes. "I don't care!"

Harry had never been at such a loss in his life. Hell, what did he do now? He knew of mannish women, of course he did, but his own daughter . . . Harry gave a shudder of revulsion, then almost immediately felt ashamed of himself. Judith was his daughter and she was being driven by emotions she probably didn't even fully understand. Perhaps, too, he had to accept some of the responsibility, for he'd always encouraged her in her tomboy ways. What she needed was help, not rejection, and a young man to interest her. Harry sat up straight. Yes that was it. This infatuation for Clare was probably only a passing fad. A husband and babies would soon put paid to these strange notions.

In the meantime, it was important that Charlotte didn't get wind of any of this. Once Judith had calmed down, he'd get the maid who was polishing the hall to come in and clean up this mess, although some financial inducement would probably be necessary to keep her quiet. The next thing to do was to fill the house with eligible young men then sit back and wait for nature to take its course. In the meantime he'd try not to worry about it too much, for, as he'd found over the years, most things tended to come out in the wash.

* * *

Clare was to be a midsummer bride and her wedding dress was being made for her at Mrs Dumelow's shop in Leicester. Although the lady herself had long since passed on, the shop still bore her name and still made the prettiest, and most expensive, gowns in the County.

Bearing in mind what Harry had done for Clare, Matilda was in two minds about whether to add him to the wedding guest list. She wrote his name down then, envisaging complications, scored a line through it. With Jane, now proud mother to lusty, black-haired Gabriel, she had an even bigger problem. Jane was her oldest friend, but she couldn't invite her without the surly Reuben, and to exclude Jane would be so deeply wounding, it was unlikely their friendship would survive. With a sigh, Matilda added Mr & Mrs Reuben Smith to her list. How complicated weddings are! But, while Matilda fretted, she still made sure that any well-connected family with a marriageable daughter was sent a gold-embossed wedding invitation.

On Clare's final fitting but one, Adam drove her into Leicester, dropped her outside the shop in the High

Street and said he would pick her up again in an hour.

"I'm not allowed to invite Jed and Rachel to the wedding but I think while I'm here, I'll pop in and see them. Meet me there," Clare ordered.

Adam was about to protest, but the shop door had swung open and an obsequious assistant was greeting Clare and inviting her to step inside.

Adam turned the trap round and drove back down the High Street and into Gallowtree Gate with a worried frown. In the present circumstances he felt uneasy about meeting Emily's parents, certain that if her father discovered they were seeing each other, Jed would horsewhip him. Then Adam remembered that in a very short while he would be holding his lovely Emily in his arms. Cheered by this thought he was whistling as he turned into Orchard Street. But the notes died on his lips when he saw Lily. It was obvious she'd been waiting for him, because she immediately ran towards him.

"I'm sorry, Adam but I'm expecting guests. Septimus's mother and sister, so you can't come in."

She sounded so agitated, Adam felt obliged to calm her down. "Don't worry, it's a nice day and with the trap I'll be able to take Emily for a drive. Anyway, how's the garden coming along? Nearly finished?"

"Oh no, there's still heaps to do. It will be a month or two yet. Anyway, I must get on."

"What about next week? Clare's having her final fitting then."

"I'll let Emily know. I really am rather busy at the moment . . . now, if you'll excuse me . . ." and with that Lily turned and hurried back to the house.

Adam watched her disappear through the front door with a perplexed frown. How strange. Lily had always been so welcoming in the past, she'd enjoyed the subterfuge and was a more than willing participant in the clandestine meetings. Maybe the novelty had worn off. If that was the case, what would he and Emily do in the winter? To Adam it was all becoming more and more impossible, and through no fault of his or Emily's.

Emily was often delayed, sometimes she didn't turn up at all, so all Adam could do was wait and hope. To relieve the tedium, and stretch his legs, he jumped down from the trap. He was leaning against a wall, wondering if he had time for a cigarette when he noticed Bertha come out of Lily's house. She strolled towards him, wearing a stylish bonnet that was way above what her pocket could afford and looking quite the young lady. When she drew level with Adam she smiled and called, "Afternoon, sir."

"Hello Bertha, off to do the shopping?"

"No, me missus 'as given me the rest of the day off. She give me this bonnet, too." Bertha fiddled proudly with the large velvet bow tied under her chin.

"I must say you look charming in it, Bertha."

"Oh thankee, sir." With a giggle of pleasure, the girl skipped off down the street, so pleased with herself she almost collided with Emily.

They spoke briefly, Adam walked the horse towards Emily and helped her into the trap. "I'm taking you for a short drive, Lily can't have us today."

"Why's that?" asked Emily as they moved off.

"Visitors." Adam thought for a moment. "So why has she given Bertha time off?"

Emily giggled. "You obviously haven't seen her gardener or you wouldn't ask that question."

Adam turned and stared at Emily. "Are you saying . . . ?"

"My lips are sealed," Emily answered primly.

"Come on, you can tell me."

"Well, it's only a suspicion. You don't see Lily as often as I do, but take my word for it, she's a changed woman. I could never understand why, but often in the past she seemed really unhappy. Now she's all smiles and I put that down to love."

"Good heavens! But Septimus . . . ?"

Emily shrugged. "Perhaps there's something missing in the marriage, but Lily's been good to us, kept our secret, so we owe her the same. Pierre will be gone soon, let her have a little happiness while she can."

Adam lifted Emily's hand to his lips and kissed it. "I agree with you, my dearest, and that is why you and I have to talk seriously about our future. Because as soon as Clare is married I shall tell my mother that it is my intention to marry you."

"She won't allow it. Neither will mine."

"We'll see about that. And if they go on being stubborn, we shall just have to think of another way of being together, won't we?"

The world was a high summer green, nectar dripped from the tasselled flowers of lime trees and the sky was as blue as the cornflowers decorating the trap carrying Clare and her grandfather to church. Bells jingled on the harness and the horse's mane and tail were plaited with white ribbon. Everyone in the village had turned out to wish the bride good luck and cast critical eyes over Clare's dress. They weren't inclined to keep their voices down and as the bridal party passed the cost of the dress was hotly debated. Two years' wages, the more numerate reckoned. They all agreed on one point, though. The bride looked exquisite. Although the dress, of ivory silk, was deceptively simple in its cut, it was embroidered with tiny flowers and the neck and wrists were lavishly trimmed with seed pearls. To signify purity, Clare wore a crown of orange blossom and she looked composed and happy.

Outside St Philip's the children from the school were assembled in two orderly lines and as the bride walked up the path on her grandfather's arm, they burst into well-rehearsed song. "*There was a lover and his lass, with a hey and a ho . . .*" their young voices trilled, which brought a blush, pink as the rosebuds in her posy, to Clare's cheeks.

Concealed behind a gravestone, Judith watched this charming scene, all her defences peeled away, her throat aching with misery and loss. Why did Clare have to go and do it? Tie herself to a man and servitude, when she could give her a love that was unconditional. Judith heard the children shout, "Good luck miss," saw Clare bend and kiss each child in turn, then glide, ethereal and lovely into the church to make that final commitment to Christopher.

Throughout the service the church doors remained open and, torturing herself, Judith stood listening to them make their solemn vows. She managed to keep her emotions under control until the vicar came to the most powerful words in the marriage service: "Those whom God hath joined together let no man put asunder." Sounding like Jehovah, his voice thundered its terrible warning. The words bounced round the small churchyard and resounded in Judith's ears with such finality, she fell against the gravestone and her nails dug into the mossy surface. She knew she was torturing herself, remaining there but she had to have one last glimpse of Clare to carry away with her.

Psalm one hundred was sung, the bells began their triumphant pealing, then the bride and groom, with eyes only for each other, stepped out into the sunshine. Soon they were at the centre of a crowd of family and friends and being kissed, embraced and congratulated. Then with Clare's aunt organising them, three small girls skipped on ahead, strewing rose petals under the feet of the newly-weds as they walked down the path and through the lychgate to start a life together.

"No, no, no!" Judith shook her head in denial then, unable to endure a moment longer, Clare's luminous happiness, she fled, mounted Star and galloped the mare home. "Take her," she ordered Ned, handed him the reins, then fled. She wanted oblivion from the dead weight of her misery and giving no thought to where she was going, she ran sobbing down to the lake.

Judith paused, but only for a fraction of a second, then she flung herself, head first, into the water. She surfaced spluttering, but her heavy clothes began to drag her down again and she let go, abandoning herself to her fate. Her eyes were open, she saw floating reeds and there was a tremendous pressure in her ears. But the water was green, cool and peaceful. In a moment she would die and there would be no jealousy, no more pain . . . nothing . . .

Judith was drifting away, when she felt her hair being roughly grabbed. She was pulled to the surface, dragged to the shore, turned face down and thumped on the back. Water and snot spewed from her mouth and nose and she lay coughing, retching and sobbing.

Agitated voices came and went, Judith heard the piercing sound of bird-song and the earth against her cheek vibrated with running feet. Then her father was shouting in an unsteady frightened voice, "What's happened, Ned? Tell me, for God's sake!"

"Miss Judith seemed a bit upset, like, when she came into the yard, and I don't rightly know why, but I followed 'er. She ran straight for the lake. Lucky I wa' around," Ned added modestly.

"It was, you probably saved Miss Judith's life. I'll see you generously rewarded for this, Ned, but I'd rather you kept the incident to yourself. I don't want the other servants finding out."

Ned nodded. "I won't breathe a word, sir."

"Now I'm going to take Miss Judith up to the house." Harry lifted his daughter in his arms. "She might need the apothecary."

"Why didn't you just let me die?" Judith wailed into her father's shoulder.

"Hush baby, here's your mama and Olivia. We don't want them to hear you say such a silly thing, now do we?" her father murmured and Judith was aware of her mother and Olivia fussing around.

"Whatever's happened? She's soaking wet," Charlotte exclaimed.

"She's had an accident, she fell in the lake," said Harry.

"Fell in?" Charlotte repeated with an expression of disbelief.

Thinking quickly, Harry went on, "She was overcome with the heat and had a dizzy spell. It's thanks to Ned she's still alive." When it looked as if Charlotte might be satisfied with the explanation, he turned to Olivia. "I want you to run and fetch the apothecary in the village. And be quick please."

"Yes, Papa."

They'd now reached the house and Harry carried his daughter straight up to her bedroom and laid her on the bed while Charlotte went to find a maid to take off her soaking garments and fill a bath.

Judith's hair was a tangle of slimy green weed, her face was streaked with mud and vomit. She lay on her back, staring at the ceiling, tears rolling down her cheeks onto the pillow. "I'm so unhappy."

Harry's heart ached for his daughter. "It's Clare, isn't it?" Harry knew this was the day of the wedding.

Judith nodded dumbly and Harry took her small, cold hand and tried to rub some warmth and his love into it. It was incomprehensible to him that one person could love another with such passion they were prepared to die for it. There were always more fish in the sea, was his motto, and even when Matilda rejected him he'd quickly found consolation elsewhere. But Judith's sad, desperate love for Clare had driven her to the edge of insanity, and the ultimate act of violence against her own person. But for Ned's quick actions they might now be dragging a corpse from the lake. Harry shuddered. He had to face an unpalatable truth. Judith was never going to be interested in men. There was only one solution. He had to get her away from here and the object of her desire. A long way away. Paris, Harry decided, where she could pursue her unnatural sexual tastes away from prying eyes.

Chapter Twenty-one

The day after the wedding, Clare and Christopher left for the Lake District on a tour which would take in Mr Wordsworth's home in Grasmere, a poet Christopher greatly admired. Without company of his own age, Adam grew increasingly bored and his trips to Leicester so frequent his mother was moved to comment on it. "You spend an awful lot of time in Leicester these days, what's the attraction, my dear?"

"Nothing in particular," Adam answered evasively, but for a week or so following this conversation, he was careful to act with a little more circumspection, although part of him would have almost welcomed his mother finding out. As far as he was concerned, there'd been enough shilly-shallying and he was ready to take the bull by the horns and have everything in the open. Unfortunately he couldn't convince Emily, who somehow imagined that if their parents found out they would be separated forever.

Riding back from Leicester late one afternoon, Adam heard wheels behind him and his name being called. Recognising the voice, Adam slowed his horse and waited for Olivia and her father to catch up with him.

"Hello, Adam, you're a stranger these days." Olivia smiled but there was an implied criticism in her tone.

"Well, I am away at Cambridge during term."

"It's not term-time now," Olivia twinkled.

"No, it isn't," Adam agreed lamely.

Harry, observing his daughter's flirtatious manner towards Adam thanked heaven that Adam was in love with another young lady, otherwise the complications would have been too horrendous to contemplate. He'd come across the lovers quite by chance when he'd been leaving the house of a friend up in the Newarke. Harry, who was well-schooled in the art of clandestine meetings knew immediately he saw them that this was a secret tryst, and ducked out of sight behind a tree. He'd felt a bit of a voyeur hidden there, but there was no mistaking their desire for each other and Adam's wooing of her was passionate and intense. A chip off the old block, Harry thought proudly, although the girl couldn't stay long, in spite of Adam's entreaties and having to drag herself from his arms. But she was anxious; frightened she'd be missed and she flew down the street with Adam calling after her, "I'll be here same time Wednesday, Emily."

So that was her name, Emily. Suddenly Harry was back in the Assembly Rooms and Adam was dancing too often with one girl. A girl Matilda disapproved of, Rachel's daughter. The irony of the situation wasn't lost on Harry and he smiled to himself. To think he'd tried, and almost succeeded once, in seducing the lovely Rachel. She'd been one of his rare failures so he wished his son better luck with her daughter, it would be a sort of poetic justice. Adam was to be congratulated on his good taste, too, for she was almost as beautiful as her mother.

Of course, Adam could be like him in other respects, maybe one woman would never be enough to satisfy his sexual needs. If that was the case, he was glad he was taking both his daughters out of the country, that would nip in the bud any growing attraction on Olivia's part. Harry shuddered. Imagine having to explain why her and Adam's relationship could never go beyond friendship. He was handsome, though, this son of his, much like he had been at that age. But taller, and Harry recognised in Adam's jawline a determination that he was realistic enough to know he lacked. There was none of that indolence in his features, no looking for the easy way out as he was inclined to and it struck Harry that Adam would have made a fine soldier. Not that Matilda would ever consider such a career. And why should she? Only second, penniless sons, like himself joined the army.

"But then we're off soon, aren't we, Papa?" Olivia's voice interrupted Harry's reverie.

"Indeed we are."

"Where's that? London?" asked Adam.

"Oh no, somewhere far more exciting. Papa's taking Judith and me to Paris."

Adam had to admit to being impressed. "Gosh, how long for?"

"A month at least. I'll write and tell you about it if you like."

"That would be nice."

"You'll be far too busy to write any letters, Olivia," her father interjected. "Now if you don't mind, Adam, we'll wish you good day. We're catching the packet-boat from Dover on Thursday but in the meantime there are a lot of details to be settled."

With a flick of the reins, Harry drove on. Olivia turned waving and smiling and, watching them become mere dots on the landscape, Adam felt more abandoned than ever. Clare and Christopher gone, now Judith and Olivia.

It was with dread rather than joy that Lily watched her garden take shape that summer. By the end of July Pierre had dug out a small pond and stocked it with fish, trained pink-scented roses over an arbour and made her a small bench round the base of the tree, like he had promised. When there were no further tasks left to detain Pierre, Septimus thanked him for his work and paid him off. Lily pleaded a headache that day, and the next, and lay in a darkened room sobbing broken-heartedly. But she did have one tiny morsel of hope to sustain her and two weeks after her lover's departure, she invited her immediate family, plus Rachel and Emily, round for Sunday tea. To be served in her new garden if the weather was fine, she informed them.

As it turned out, it was a perfect day. Warm enough to sit outside, but not hot enough to scorch the skin or turn it an unbecoming brown. Lily had baked until she was exhausted, and although Bertha was a bit cack-handed, she had managed to knock it into her head that cucumber had to be cut paper thin for sandwiches and not in thick wedges.

Once everyone had arrived they moved out into the garden. Lily poured tea and Bertha handed round plates of cake while the guests, knowing what was expected of them, exclaimed over the abundant display of flowers, the cleverly twisting path, the small statues and many other imaginative touches. It was particularly gratifying for Lily to hear these compliments from her sisters' lips, although she refused to accept all the credit.

"Well, it wasn't just me, I had this marvellous gardener, Pierre. He did whatever I asked. Nothing was too much trouble."

Perhaps we should get him in to do our garden, Mama," suggested Septimus's sister, Agatha.

"He's gone," said Lily hastily. "He's gets itchy feet and never stays in one place long."

"What a pity."

"Anyway it wasn't only to show you the garden that I invited the family here today. There is another reason." Septimus was polishing off the last of the gingerbread, but Lily took his hand and drew him to her side. "Septimus and I have some news for you all, haven't we, dear?" Lily smiled coyly at her husband.

Although Septimus looked a trifle perplexed, he knew what was expected of him. "Yes, Lily."

Fearful he might bolt, Lily gripped his hand tightly. "Septimus and I are . . ." she paused for effect ". . . expecting a happy event sometime in the spring." Naturally enough, the effect of this astounding news on Septimus was cataclysmic. Through her fingertips, Lily felt currents of shock and astonishment. Under the circumstances, it was understandable, for Septimus could never have expected to find himself about to become a father. But he'd get over it, Lily decided. Once the initial shock subsided, he might even become quite taken with the idea. Even so, Lily carefully avoided any eye contact with her husband. Instead she stood bright-eyed and triumphant and waiting with queenly dignity for the congratulations that were her due.

"I'm so pleased for you," said Rachel, coming up and wrapping her arms round Lily and kissing her. "I know it's what you've wanted for a long time."

While everyone gathered round to congratulate the mother-to-be, Emily watched Septimus closely, a huge question mark in her mind. His face wore the bemused expression of a man totally out of his depth. It required tremendous effort but he did manage to collect himself sufficiently to respond to Jack Brewin when he strolled over, slapped him on the back and remarked in a jocular tone, "So you've done yer duty by my daughter at last, eh Septimus, old chap."

Septimus dabbed his sweating forehead with a handkerchief. "Ah . . . eh . . . yes."

Jack Brewin laughed. "You don't sound very certain. Anyway let's hope it's a boy. Personally I've had enough of girls. And you'll want a lad I'm sure, to carry on the business."

Septimus nodded, sat down and, to comfort himself, stuffed six scones with strawberry jam and cream into his mouth, one after the other.

Emily waited until the excitement had died down, then she went over to speak to Lily. After offering her own good wishes, she went on, "Pierre gone, has he?"

Lily's eyes didn't waver from hers. "Do you mean the gardener? Oh yes, he went ages ago." Lily lowered her voice. "I don't see much of you and Adam these days. Remember, it is still open house. Come any time. Natalie must be growing, too, bring her up to see me. When my baby comes, they'll be able to play together." Lily gave Emily's hand an excited squeeze. "Oh I'm so looking forward to being a mother."

"I'm sure you are, and you'll be a wonderful one."

Recently Lily had been disinclined to offer them hospitality, but now, with the gardener gone, they were back in favour again. Out of gratitude, Emily kissed her friend and thought: well, whatever there was between Lily and Pierre, it's over now. The rest is between Septimus and his wife. Everyone, including his mother, is delighted about the coming event and she had no real proof of Pierre's part in it. It was all conjecture and as long as she kept her opinions to herself, all would be well.

Although Natalie was now crawling and as lively as a cricket, in Jed's opinion what this new daughter of his needed was plenty of fresh air. So he spent several evenings banging together a long handled box on wheels as a means of transport for the baby girl. It became Emily's task to take her out, which she did gladly, pushing her small sister up the London Road in the little cart to Lily's house. There, lying on a blanket in the garden, Natalie would kick her plump little legs in the air and try and clutch at passing butterflies and bees.

A short while later Adam would arrive and watching them from the kitchen window playing with the baby, Lily would think what a cosy domestic scene it made and how Emily and Adam were so obviously made for each other. She could watch them now without being tormented with envy. She'd chosen her own lover well and the summer months had passed in a haze of lust which had left her completely satiated, for the time being at least. Lily smiled. Young Bertha must have thought it was Christmas every day, being sent off with threepence and told not to come back until tea-time. Damp, crumpled sheets, their sweating, grinding bodies, the murmur of summer through the open window, as later they lay drowsing in each other's arms. Those were memories that could never be taken away from her. She had been heartbroken when Pierre left, but she was slowly putting the pieces back together again. And, realistically, Lily knew what she'd had with Pierre was special because of its brevity. Poverty and habit would soon dull their passion. Now she only had happy memories and his special gift to her. Looking at it practically, she was far better off with Septimus, he would provide generously for the child, and she could depend on his discretion, there was no question about that.

It was so unusual to hear raised voices in her home, Emily paused on the stairs.

"With this new Act we've got rid of the old corrupt

Corporation, electors can't be bought by candidates with the deepest pockets any longer and I intend to stand for the new Council," she heard her father say.

"I will not spend night after night here on my own, while you pursue your politics," her mother answered in an unusually angry tone. Acutely embarrassed at overhearing this altercation between her parents, Emily rattled the door handle loudly before opening the door. "Hello," she said, glancing from one angry face to the other.

"Nice walk, dear?" asked Rachel automatically.

"Yes, thank you. What's wrong?"

"Politics. Whatever else is it? Your father's obsessed with it. You might as well know, Emily, I've had enough. He can choose, politics or me." Rachel took Natalie from her daughter and laid her in her crib.

"I'm not standing listening to this, if you want me I'll be in the shop," answered Jed and thumped off downstairs as angry as Emily had ever seen him.

Rachel sighed. "Would you like some tea?"

"Yes please." When the tea was made and poured, Emily sipped hers thoughtfully for some moments. "Mama, what did you mean when you said Papa had to choose?"

Rachel stroked her forehead wearily. "Oh, I don't know."

"But you know how much politics mean to Papa, it's his whole life."

"Exactly. To the exclusion of everything else. I've been tolerant long enough."

But Jed wasn't the man to be deterred by threats, he went on with his electioneering and the atmosphere at home became more chilly by the day. It affected everyone, but Emily loved both her parents equally, saw both points of view and refused to take sides. Instead, she used it as an excuse to spend as much time out of the house as possible. One afternoon, telling to her mother that she and Lily were going blackberrying, she slipped out of the shop with her basket to where Adam was waiting by a stile in Evington Lane.

Adam never failed to be entranced by the sight of Emily and he watched her now, walking towards him in a simple blue cotton dress, swinging her basket. She was his sun, moon and stars, his whole universe and love surged through him and when she reached him, he lifted her up, swung her round and kissed her. "I love you totally, absolutely."

Emily laid her head against Adam's chest. "I know, and I love you too."

"Sometimes I feel ripped apart by it."

"Come on, let's go and pick blackberries," said Emily, sensing where the conversation might be heading, and climbed over the stile into a field of stubble. Adam followed her and they cut a path through the middle of it, making for a thick hedge where they knew blackberries grew in abundance. It didn't take long to fill the basket, then they sat down under a tree to share the refreshment Adam had brought: ginger beer, a hunk of bread and some cheese.

Slicing the cheese exactly in half with his penknife, Adam handed her a piece. "I'll be going back to college soon."

Emily had been feeling quite hungry, but at this reminder her appetite went and she flung the cheese aside. "Don't talk about it, it makes me unhappy."

Adam eased Emily gently down on the ground, and kissed her. Suddenly his young desire got the better of him and he began pushing up her dress and trying to find the string on her drawers. "Please let me, Emily. Please let me," he murmured hotly in her ear.

"No! Stop it, Adam, please!" Flustered, angry, Emily pushed him away, sat up and adjusted her clothes.

Adam ran his fingers through his hair in a distracted manner. "I can't go on like this, it's driving me mad."

"If I let you do *that* you wouldn't respect me any more."

"Oh I would, I would," Adam declared passionately. "I don't think you truly love me. If you did, you would want us to be one, united body and soul." Adam's blue eyes grew sulky, and he sucked on the end of a piece of straw.

Emily stood up. "How could you belittle my love by saying such a thing, Adam Bennett! It's you who doesn't love me!" Her expression thunderous, Emily picked up the basket of blackberries and strode off. Behind her she heard Adam call, "Wait, please, Emily," and deliberately broke into a trot, leaving a trail of squashed blackberries behind her. She could hear Adam gaining ground but she'd scrambled over the stile into Evington Lane before he reached her.

Grabbing her arm, he swung her round. "Don't fall out with me Emily, not when I'm going away so soon."

"Sometimes you ask too much of me, Adam."

"I know." All contrite Adam pulled her to him and stared deep into her eyes. "Can I help it that I love you so much?"

They were so enthralled with each other, neither of them heard the brake until it drew level and a man's voice, harsh and accusing, cut through their self-absorption. "What the devil is going on?"

Adam and Emily leapt apart. "Papa . . . wh-what are you do-doing here?" Emily stuttered.

"Well, it's obvious what you're up to. Something I'd thought I'd never see, my daughter acting fast and loose with a man in public. Get in this brake, I'm taking you home. And I'd better not see you around again, young man, or I'll horsewhip you."

"Sir," said Adam bravely. "My name is Adam Bennett, I am a gentleman and my intentions towards your daughter are entirely honourable."

"Your name is Bennett you say? With a name like that, I doubt if you'd know what an honourable intention was if it leapt up and hit you in the eye." Jed raised his whip threateningly. "Now go."

"Papa, stop it!" Emily sobbed and grabbed her father's arm. "I love Adam."

"Good God Almighty." To relieve his feelings Jed brought the whip down on the unfortunate horse's back. "I'm not listening to any more of this rubbish."

"And I want to marry your daughter," Adam shouted as the brake moved off.

"Over my dead body."

Great waves of desolation swept over Adam, tears coursed unchecked down his cheeks and Emily's wan features beseeching him to understand wavered in front of his eyes. Passers-by eyed him with curiosity, but Adam's pain was so intense it was like a bereavement and he was unaware of anyone, or even the passing of time. He didn't move for over an hour then, gradually, a resentment began to stir. Was he going to sit back and let this be the end? Adam asked himself. His jaw set in a stubborn line, he straightened his shoulders and wiped his eyes. No, by God, he wasn't. He and Emily had done nothing wrong, so why should their lives be blighted in this way? If Emily's father wouldn't let them marry openly, then he would live up to his expectations and do it dishonourably, although if his scheme was to succeed he was going to need Lily's help.

Chapter Twenty-two

Jed didn't utter one word all the way home, but even sunk as she was in a state of complete wretchedness, Emily was aware of his scorching anger and sat as far apart from him as possible in the brake. When they reached the shop, still without speaking, he grabbed her arm, hauled her from the brake and pushed her in front of him into the shop. Having never been treated with such contempt in her life before by her father, Emily was mortified. She wouldn't give him the satisfaction of seeing her cry, though, but when she stumbled over the threshold, followed by a grim-faced Jed, her mother's face moved from a welcoming smile to a look of alarm.

"What on earth has happened?" asked Rachel, her mind racing towards some awful tragedy. Her sons dead perhaps.

"I found this daughter of yours with a man. In the fields." Jed uttered the words in cold disgust.

"I might remind you she's your daughter as well," Rachel snapped back.

"I feel like disowning her. Do you know who it was, of all people? Adam Bennett, son of Matilda Pedley and God knows who, nephew of George Pedley, grandson of Joseph Pedley. I loathe and detest that whole bunch. Apart from her deceit, do you want her mixing with a man who has tainted blood running through his veins?

A family, I might add, we both have good reason to hate."

"Is this true, Emily?"

Emily didn't feel inclined to justify herself and her expression grew sullen. "Yes. But what's so wrong about it? Adam has never done you any harm and he loves me," she threw back defiantly.

"Yes, no doubt he tells you that for his own evil end. Then he forces you into lies and deceit so that you can go cavorting over the fields with him. What sort of man does that? Tell me Emily, and I want the truth, did he do anything wrong to you?"

Emily's head jolted up, but she disdained to answer.

"Jed! Really!" Rachel exclaimed on her behalf. "How could you think such a thing of Emily? You shame me." Rachel put a comforting arm round her daughter's shoulders. "How long have you been seeing this young man, Emily?" she asked, in an attempt to diffuse the situation.

Although Emily's emotions were being assaulted on all sides, a warning signal flickered in her brain. She must be careful not to drag Lily into this. "A few weeks," she lied, amazed at her own brazenness.

"You'll see him no more. Is that understood?" her father barked.

"There's not much chance, he's going back to Cambridge soon. I'll probably kill myself anyway, then all your problems will be solved." Her voice was high, on the edge of hysteria and having delivered this threat, she pushed past her mother and ran up the stairs to her small room under the eaves. Turning the key in the lock, she fell on the bed. "Oh Adam! Adam! what's to become of us?" she sobbed into her pillow, and eventually fell sleep without finding an answer to this question.

"Satisfied?" asked Rachel, grieving in her own way for her unhappy daughter. "What do you suggest we do now? Lock her in her room for the rest of her life?"

"I hadn't planned on anything quite so drastic," Jed answered icily.

"You used to complain about her spending all her time with books and never getting out, now you're forbidding her to see a young man."

"But not any young man."

Remembering the hateful George, his attempted rape of her and Matilda's spitefulness, Rachel knew in her heart it wasn't a match she could bless. All she could do was pray that it was a girlish infatuation that would cool while he was away, for they had no future together. Nevertheless, Rachel needed someone to blame for the mess that had landed in her lap, and she instinctively lashed out at Jed. "Perhaps if you put your family first, instead of politics, this sorry mess might have been prevented."

Jed stared at her, cold-eyed and tight-lipped. "I wondered how long it would be before the problem was turned around and it became my fault," he flung back at his wife, then turned and slammed out of the shop.

Having made his decision about their future, Adam didn't waste any more time and set off in the direction of Lily's house. As he walked, he brooded over Jed Fairfax's remarks. Adam had never been treated with such contempt in his life before, and it had severely dented his pride. But Fairfax would live to regret it, and he'd show him who had the strongest hold over Emily.

Even though she wasn't expecting him, Lily made Adam very welcome and she listened with a sympathetic ear to his troubles. Having known the pain of being parted from a lover she could share his anguish, understanding the heartache of loss.

"What does Emily's father know about love?" Adam asked with a young man's disdain. "How can he understand our feelings for each other? I bet he's never wanted to die for love. And why should Emily and I be punished because of something that happened between the two families before we were even born?" Adam had been nursing his head in his hands but now he looked up. "It isn't fair, is it, Lily?"

Lily shook her head. "No, it isn't."

"But I don't intend to let him stand in our way. I have a plan, but I need your help and absolute secrecy."

Lily leaned forward, an eager participant. "You can depend on me, Adam."

"Do you think you could get word to Emily? Go in the shop, without them suspecting anything?"

"Easily. They know I dote on little Natalie and I'm in and out all the time."

"This is my plan. I shall pretend to go back to Cambridge on Friday, but instead of catching the coach I'll put up at the Swan with Two Necks. I have money enough. Emily will come to me there and we will run away."

Lily turned a trifle pale. "Where to?"

"North of the border, where no parent can reach us."

Do you mean . . . you are not thinking of Gretna Green?" Lily stuttered.

"Yes, where we shall be become man and wife." Adam's voice rang with certitude.

Lily's stomach curdled with a mixture of fear and excitement. "Rachel has been very good to me over the years, so it must never come to light that I was in any way involved in this."

"You've been an absolute brick and I swear I would never implicate you, Lily. All I'm asking you to do is pass on a message to Emily. Nothing will be written down."

Lily rubbed her hands together. "All right, then, when do we start putting these plans into operation, captain?"

* * *

Harry's trip to Paris lasted a lot longer than he intended, mainly due to his daughters who, whenever he mentioned returning home, pleaded with him to stay for just a few more days. And it wasn't hard to be swayed to linger on, tasting the delights of the city. But the most powerful reason for remaining was the dramatic change in Judith, so that in the end he didn't arrive back in England until September, accompanied only by Olivia. Judith he left behind, ostensibly to improve her French under the tutelage of Madame Gérin. Solange Gérin, whom Harry had been introduced to by a mutual friend, was a worldly Parisienne with Sapphic tendencies who strutted around Paris in men's clothes and who was rich enough to not give a fig for anyone's opinion. She had also quite fallen for Judith's hoydenish charm. Her salon was famous throughout France for the writers, intellectuals and free thinkers it attracted, and Harry was confident that under Solange's guidance Judith would truly come into her own. Harry was man of the world enough to realise there was no future for his daughter in Leicestershire where, if her predilections were discovered, she would end up a social pariah, her life stunted by convention. In Paris she could be her true self. It had been hard for him to accept, initially, that he had a daughter who would only ever love other women, but he considered himself a tolerant man and in his opinion everyone was entitled to enjoy a fulfilling sexual life. When she reached twenty-one, Judith would have the money left by her grandfather, enabling to lead an independent and, he hoped, a happy life away from prurient eyes.

When Harry arrived back at Fern Hill minus one daughter, at least Charlotte wasn't hypocritical enough to pretend that she might miss Judith. He was aware that Judith's presence irritated his wife and his explanation that their elder daughter wished to improve her French, seemed to satisfy her. Of course he would miss Judith, but Harry consoled himself with the thought that while she was resident in France he had ample excuse to cross the channel whenever he pleased.

A day or two after his return, discovering his horse needed shoeing, Harry rode his horse over to Halby. Told by the farrier he would have to wait for an hour, he decided to have a drink at the Weavers' Arms. He was making his way across the Green when he caught up with Clare, trying to keep a troop of children in an orderly line. Her class was obviously on its way back from a botany lesson, for every child clasped a specimen of some sort: seed heads, leaves, sprays of ivy and branches of red berries.

"Hello, Clare," he called, when she stopped to wipe a small boy's nose.

"Mr Bennett, how are you? And Judith and Olivia?"

"Judith stayed on in Paris, but Olivia is back home."

"Tell her to come over and see us. Christopher and I have our own cottage now, almost next door to the school."

"How is the school going?"

"Very well. Show Mr Bennett how you can do your five times table, children," she instructed her pupils.

"One five is five, two fives are ten," they chanted

happily. "Shall we do our six times table now, Miss?" a small boy asked when they'd finished.

"No that will do for the time being, thank you, Tommy. But perhaps Mr Bennett would like to come and see our small school?"

"I'd love to," answered Harry, and as soon as he walked into the cottage it became apparent, by the way the children responded to him, that Christopher Harcourt was a natural teacher who made learning a pleasure. Their primers were dog-eared, equipment was minimal and space was at a premium, with the children squeezed up tight together on wooden benches. But there was no doubt in Harry's mind that these children would leave school knowing more than the basic three R's.

It was just coming up to twelve and dinner-time and the children were growing hungry and restless. Christopher clapped his hands to get their attention, then said, "Right, stand up and move out in an orderly fashion, please."

"Good morning, Miss, good morning, Sir," each child recited in turn, their small faces studies of angelic virtue, until they were outside the door, that is. Here, freed from the restrictions of education, the boys proceeded to wrestle and joust, the girls to skip and leap-frog. Watching them from the window, Christopher smiled indulgently. "They're letting off steam."

"We eat our main meal of the day later, when we have time to relax, but you're welcome to come next door and have a glass of beer and some bread and cheese with us," Clare offered. "Then you can tell me about Paris."

"If I'm not intruding. I do have an hour to kill."

Harry was surprised that the young couple should be living in such humble surroundings as a labourer's cottage a few yards from the school, although looking around he could see that it had been made extremely comfortable. The roof had been re-thatched, carpets covered the stone floor, heavy curtains hung at the doors to exclude winter draughts and the furniture was hardly the type normally found in a cottage.

Noticing his eyes wandering round the room and obviously reading his thoughts, Clare said, "We could have stayed with Aunt Tilda at Trent Hall, but we wanted to be on our own." She turned to her husband and clasped his hand. "Didn't we, Christopher?"

Christopher gazed at Clare with adoring eyes. "Yes, my darling."

Love's young dream, how nice – but it won't last, Harry thought cynically. Christopher poured beer into a tankard for him, and Harry was settling himself in a wingback chair by the fire when the knocker went and he heard Clare greeting her aunt. Harry smiled to himself. How fortuitous. He had his back to the door and he knew Matilda wasn't aware that he was there when she accepted a cup of tea from her niece and sat down as well.

Harry swung round in his chair. "Hello, Matilda."

"What are you doing here?" she asked, and it passed through Harry's mind that her tone could have been a touch more welcoming.

"Clare and Christopher invited me over. My horse is at the smithy, I'm waiting for it."

"Oh." Apparently satisfied with his answer, Matilda went on, "I hear you've recently returned from Paris. How was it?"

"Marvellous."

"Don't they keep having revolutions and things?"

Harry laughed. "Occasionally. But in between the French do know how to live."

"You'd like that. You were never one for the quiet life, were you, Harry?" It was a reprimand.

Harry gave her an indolent smile. "Life's short, enjoy it while you can is my motto."

"Even at the price of other people's happiness?" The words came out unbidden and Matilda was aware that Christopher and Clare had both gone quiet and were listening to their exchange with some interest.

Harry shifted uncomfortably. "Not these days."

Matilda lifted her eyebrows in mock surprise. "Reformed character, eh? I find that hard to believe, Harry." Aware that a bitterness was creeping into her tone, Matilda finished her tea and stood up. "I must get back."

"Did you come for any particular reason, Aunt Tilda?"

"No, just for some company. Adam going back to college on Friday left me feeling a bit low. Mind you, he did seem happier this time. Usually he complains bitterly, so perhaps he's at last accepted the benefits of education."

Harry finished his beer and stood up too. "My horse should be ready now. If I may be permitted, I'll walk a little way with you, Tilda."

"If you like," Matilda answered with feigned indifference and kissed her niece. "Come up for a game of cards one evening if you've nothing better to do," she said and her invitation made Harry wonder if she was lonely. Perhaps she was without a lover at the moment. If that was the case, now was the time to make a move. With caution, though. As he cast his mind back to past pleasures, his body began to stir. She must want it still, he thought with a sideways glance. A woman with Matilda's passions couldn't go off it.

"The young couple seem well content with each

other," Harry remarked as he and Matilda walked up the hill together. "And Clare appears to have recovered well from that other unpleasant business." He knew Matilda wouldn't welcome being reminded of George, that blot on their escutcheon, but it did no harm to jolt her into remembering his own part in Clare's rescue. And there was the small question of an undischarged debt.

"Yes, Christopher is a fine young man and, of course, they share a common interest in the school, which is going extremely well. I even have a waiting list."

They'd now turned into the drive of Trent Hall, and Harry waited for Matilda to dismiss him from her presence. He knew he might be pushing his luck when he followed her up the steps, through the half open door and into the drawing room, but when she didn't object, he allowed himself to feel hopeful.

"It's changed since my uncle's time. Hardly the same house," Harry observed, gazing around him at the fine furnishings and remembering the squalor he'd found on the first occasion he'd visited his uncle.

"Yes, in spite of everything my life has worked out quite well."

"You're happy then?"

"Perfectly."

"And fulfilled?" Harry smiled, and when Matilda didn't answer he moved nearer. Instead of moving away she stood quite still and ran the tip of her tongue around her lips in a small, nervous movement. Harry was about to reach out and take her hand when the front door bell was tugged with such unwarranted force, Matilda jumped back in alarm.

"Who can that be?" she asked.

Harry had no idea, but he was cursing them for their ill-timed arrival when an elderly Hodge came shuffling into the room. "A Mr Jedidiah Fairfax wishing to speak with you, Madam."

"Jed Fairfax? What on earth does he want with me?"

Hodge swung his head from side to side. "Dunno, Madam, but 'e ses it's most urgent and won't move from the steps until 'e 'as spoken with you."

"Oh, all right, show him in. But stay with me please, Harry," Matilda said and stood hands clasped in front of her, shoulders back, very much the lady of the manor.

But if she imagined Jed would be intimidated by her haughty manner, she was mistaken, for he strode into the room beetle-browed and with a face like thunder.

"What can I do for you, Mr Fairfax?" enquired Matilda. In spite of Jed's manner, her voice remained well-bred and cool.

"That's for you to decide. You see that son of yours has run off with my daughter."

Matilda's composure slipped a fraction and she took a step backwards. "Bu-but that's impossible! Adam's in Cambridge."

"No he isn't. He's abducted Emily and is on his way north with her."

Matilda's legs buckled under her and she would have collapsed if Harry hadn't grabbed her. "What are you talking about, Fairfax?" Harry demanded, then remembered with an unpleasant jolt how he seen them together in the Newarke.

Jed thrust a note into Matilda's hand. "Read that."

Peering over Matilda's shoulder, Harry's eyes quickly skimmed the page. "Dear Mama & Papa, Everyone wants to keep me and Adam apart, just because our families hate each other. But we've done nothing wrong and we love each other. We are going to be married.

Please don't follow us. If you try and stop us we will kill ourselves. We have decided that we either live together or die together. In spite of everything I do love you both. Your loving daughter, Emily."

Matilda turned deathly pale and put her hand to her heart. "Good God in Heaven," she murmured and sat down heavily in a chair. "I had no idea they were even seeing each other."

"Neither did I until last week. I caught them together in Evington Lane. I forbade Emily to see Adam again so how they planned the ridiculous escapade, I don't know."

"Do you think they mean it . . . about killing themselves?"

Jed's features were grim. "We can only pray not and we must find them quickly. Emily has always been a quiet, bookish girl. She would never deliberately set out to cause her parents this anguish, she's been pushed into it. I place the blame entirely on that son of yours, and if anything should happen to my daughter . . ." Jed didn't finish.

Harry could see that Matilda's carefully constructed world was tumbling around her ears and she was past defending either herself or Adam. "Come on now, Fairfax, aren't you being a little unreasonable? What your daughter has done is of her own free will is evident from her letter. There is no point in apportioning blame, instead we need to find them quickly before they do anything stupid. It's a fair bet they are making for Gretna Green."

"I had managed to work that out," answered Jed dryly. "I'm catching the six o'clock coach to Manchester this evening."

Matilda bit the inside of her lip very hard. The self-induced pain concentrated her mind and stopped her from collapsing into a snivelling, undignified heap. "I'll pack and come with you."

She stood up but Harry pressed her back in the chair. "No, you stay here, I'll go with Fairfax. It will be a long, hard journey."

"I won't waste any more time then." Half-way out of the door, Jed stopped and turned. "I'll meet you at the Swan with Two Necks at five-thirty, Bennett," he said, and then was gone.

"I must get my horse from the smithy, go home and pack a few things and be on my way. I'll bring Adam back to you, Matilda, I promise."

"Thank you, Harry."

"But there is a condition."

Matilda eyed him warily. "Oh?"

"You must tell me honestly, is Adam my son?"

Matilda nodded. "I swore I'd never tell you but now you know."

Harry gave a deep sigh of satisfaction, then leaned forward and kissed her. "Thank you for telling me, Matilda. Now I can say with truth that it's our son I shall be bringing home."

Chapter Twenty-three

Emily tried to sleep, resting her head on Adam's shoulder, but as the coach swayed through the night she began to feel sick and, although she hardly dared admit it, frightened too. Initially, spurred on by her parents' unreasonable attitude and intoxicated by her own defiance, running away had seemed both daring and right. But during the long journey, doubts wormed their way into her mind. With each fall of the horses' hooves, her worries grew until they'd reached monstrous proportions, all of it made worse by the lack of opportunity to confide her fears to Adam.

And yet how different her mood had been when when Lily came into the shop, ostensibly to change a library book. But her friend had a great sense of the dramatic, and Emily knew by the way her eyes darted hither and thither, as if her parents might leap out of the woodwork at any second, that she had a message from Adam.

"Well?" Emily had asked eagerly.

But this was a role to be played for maximum effect and Lily would tell her in her own good time. Pressing her index finger warningly to her lips she moved over to the bookshelves.

Curbing her impatience, Emily waited. Her friend chose a book, the latest Maria Edgeworth novel, placed it on the counter, then leaning towards Emily, she put her lips close to her ear. "Adam says you are to meet him at the Swan with Two Necks at eleven-thirty this evening."

Although it was the message she'd been half expecting, Emily's body went rigid, her heart began to race and two bright red spots appeared on her cheeks. "Thi-this evening?"

"Hush," Lily exclaimed and cast a panicky glance round the shop. "And go prepared for a long journey, he said. To Gretna Green. To be married."

Emily's eyes grew wide. "Married?"

Lily's features wore a look of edgy excitement and forgetting to keep her voice down, she exclaimed "Oh yes. Isn't it thrilling? You must go. Love is the most important thing in the world and worth any sacrifice." Lily spoke with the assurance of one who knows about such matters then, imperceptibly her manner changed. As cool as cucumber she picked up her book. "I'm going to have a word with your mama now," she announced and she trotted off up the stairs, calling as she went, "Coooeee, it's me, Rachel." There was a second of silence, the kitchen door opened then before it closed again, Emily heard her friend trill, "Why I do believe Natalie's got some teeth coming through."

Lily's chameleon-like qualities quite took Emily's breath away at times and, although she knew that it wasn't a good trait in a woman, she couldn't help but admire the brazen way in which Lily set about getting what she wanted: first Septimus, then Pierre and now a baby. And Lily wouldn't think twice about running away to Gretna Green, if it was with the man she loved. Emily stared down at her hands and thought: soon I could have Adam's wedding ring on my finger. Winded by the enormity of what Adam was asking of her, Emily collapsed into a chair. Almost immediately she stood up again, her chin thrust forward at a determined angle. I will go, I will marry Adam. That way no parent will ever separate us again.

Although her mother tried her best, the atmosphere in the home remained chilly, her father distant. But whereas yesterday, Emily had hated it, today it suited her. If she could set herself against her father, think: it's his fault, he's making me do this with his unreasonable attitude, it helped deal with any residual guilt. By the end of the day, however, Emily was taut with nerves and terrified she would let slip some some injudicious remark and give herself away. She almost gagged on her supper and had to force herself to eat and it was a relief to be able to escape finally to her bedroom. She lay in the dark, not daring to close her eyes and waiting for her mother and father to retire for the night. She gave them half an hour, then slipped out of bed, lit the candle, dressed, packed, sat on the bed again and waited. When the clock struck eleven she wrapped a dark cloak around her, placed the note she'd written to her parents under the chamberstick, then crept from her room and down the stairs. Every creaking floorboard sounded as loud as a pistol shot in Emily's ears and her heart drummed violently against chest. In spite of her terror, she managed to make it to the back door, ease the bolts, slip down the side entrance and into the street.

There was just the possibility she might bump into a neighbour on his way home from a tavern so Emily didn't dare pause or look round. Instead, with her face well hidden under the hood of her cloak, she tucked herself in amongst the shadows of the buildings, and moved with the stealth of a cat down High Cross Street. In the High Street, exposed by the gas lighting and the lateness of the hour, Emily felt much more vulnerable. Only women of ill repute wandered about the town alone at this time of night, there was no constable to offer her protection and a heavy man was swaying towards her. He stopped when he reached Emily, and peered at her with unfocused eyes.

Emily went to pass but he blocked her path. "Let me by," she demanded in a haughty tone. Ignoring her request, the man made a lunge at her. But Emily had the advantage of being sober, and she struck out hard with her carpet bag. Already unsteady on his feet, the man yelled, "Bitch!" and fell backwards into the gutter. He made to grab her ankles but Emily was quicker and, kicking away from him, she picked up her skirts and ran, not daring to look round until she arrived panting and hot at the Swan with Two Necks.

Here Emily felt even more conspicuous and she searched amongst the crowds with anxious eyes. Coaches were arriving and departing, ostlers shouted, dogs barked, and all was confusion. What she needed most was the assurance of Adam's presence, but there was no sign of him. Already in a state of great agitation, Emily began to imagine the worst. He'd had a change of heart, that was it. Or maybe it was Lily's fault, perhaps she'd given her the wrong time, even the wrong day.

"Emily!" She turned when she heard her name called then, her skin rosy with love, she ran towards Adam and was enveloped in an embrace. "I'm so glad to see you. For a moment I thought you hadn't come," she murmured into his heavy coat.

Adam rested his chin on the top of her head. "I was even less sure you would come. But we're together now, for good. See, I've got the tickets, so let's get in the coach, if we stand around we might be seen."

The coach had galloped off into the night with the two runaways, while Emily clutched Adam's hand and tried to push aside a rising sense of doubt. For it had hit her that there could be no changing her mind now, no going back to how things were. By eloping, her reputation was in tatters, her life as she'd known it, finished. She dozed, her head on Adam's shoulder half aware of a man marking the passing of each town. "Just going through Loughborough," he would announce, or Derby or wherever. At intervals the driver would stop at the turnpike gates to pay his toll, or a new passenger would take the seat of a departing one and the blast of cold air would set everyone shivering resentfully. But they settled again quickly enough and in the enclosed airless space, heads were soon nodding on chests. Finally they drove into Ashbourne. "Breakfast and a change of horses here," said the knowledgeable fellow and the sleeping stirred themselves, while the insomniacs groaned with relief.

But as his stiff and weary passengers staggered down from the coach and into the steamy warmth of the coffee-room, the coachman put matters back into perspective. "Twenny minute stop only," he shouted.

Emily's eyes were grainy with fatigue and she shivered in spite of a large fire. About now, too, her mama would be going into her room and discovering an empty bed and the note she'd left. Emily saw the scene with a guilt-ridden clarity; her mother's initial horrified reaction, then, half out of her mind, collapsing into a chair with a scream loud enough to bring her father running.

"Happy?" asked Adam, breaking into her troubled thoughts.

Although it was a struggle, Emily smiled for his benefit. "Oh yes."

But she was in a pensive mood, Adam could see that and it worried him. "You're not regretting coming away, are you?"

"Oh no," Emily hastened to reassure him. "I'm just a little tired, that's all."

"Things always look grim in the early hours but you'll feel better as the day goes on. I know you're sacrificing a lot coming away with me like this, but you'll never regret it, Emily. I will love you until my dying breath. I swear it, and this time next week we'll be man and wife."

Adam's reassuring words, the love blazing from his eyes, vanquished Emily's doubts and she smiled back at him. "Yes, we will, won't we?"

Adam fumbled in his waistcoat pocket. "And I've got the ring, look." He held up the gold band for her inspection and Emily took it from him. She went to slide it on her finger, but Adam snatched it back. "No, don't do that, it's bad luck."

Emily laughed. "Now who's the doubting Thomas?"

"Having got this far, I'm taking no chances."

Coffee came and Emily drank this with gratitude but when a rather greasy fried egg and a slice of toast were banged down in front of her, her stomach immediately revolted and she pushed the food away. "I'm sorry, Adam, but I can't eat it."

Adam, who was tucking in to kidneys and mutton chops, pushed the plate back at her. "You must," he insisted, "we have a long journey in front of us."

"Further than we've already come?" asked Emily who, never having travelled more then a few miles in any direction from Leicester, was a little hazy about distances.

"Twice as far. But we've got to get right away, where our families can't find us."

"Osses is changed and rarin' to go," the coachman hollered across the coffee room, forcing Emily to make the decision to stuff the congealing egg into her mouth and wash it down with the rest of the coffee.

It was starting to rain as they all piled back into the coach and it didn't let up for the rest of that day. Emily noticed too that the terrain was becoming more and more hilly, the roads a quagmire. On a particularly steep slope with the rain streaming down it the horses slowed, then came to a stop. A moment later the driver opened the door and ordered them all out.

"Sorry, we're stuck in a rut. You'll all 'ave ter get out. And the 'osses ain't gonna get the coach moving on their own, so I'll have to ask some o' you gents to put yer shoulders to the wheel."

With a great deal of grumbling everyone disembarked. Glad of her warm cloak, Emily wrapped it tightly round her and pulled up the hood. However, when she stepped down from the coach, she found herself almost up to her ankles in mud. But with everyone in the same boat, it was pointless complaining. With the rain hissing in her face, she struggled dejectedly up the steep incline, the mud sucking at her shoes, her dress and cloak trailing behind her.

The coachman tugged at the horses' reins, the poor beasts struggled but couldn't budge the coach and the men shouted "Heave." The wheels moved a fraction of an inch to a small cheer and slowly, painfully, the coach reached the top of the hill. The ground levelled out and everyone was allowed back inside. Throughly disgruntled, teeth chattering, drawn together by adversity, the passengers threatened to report the coachman and demand their money back. But by now, Emily was so cold and tired she couldn't muster up any emotion. Her mind was entirely focused on sleep and a deep feather mattress to sink into.

Adam, aware that she was exhausted, wiped the steamed-up windows and pointed to some factory chimneys. "Look, Manchester. Not long now. We'll stay here for the night and move on to Carlisle tomorrow."

Manchester, built on cotton, was supposed to be one of the great manufacturing cities, but to Emily it was a depressing sight. A thick pall of smoke hung over the town, the brickwork on buildings was blackened and she could even taste soot in her mouth. Even the rain surging down open gutters was inky black. Suddenly Emily was overcome with a wave of homesickness for Leicester.

Finally, two hours late, the coach reached the Star Hotel. Stiff, chilled and exhausted, Emily refused all food, followed the chambermaid to her room, removed her cape, dress, dirty boots and stockings, fell on the bed and was asleep almost before her head hit the pillow.

At half-past-four the next morning, Emily was awakened by the chambermaid banging on the door then coming into the room with a jug of hot water. "No time to waste, Miss, yer coach leaves at quarter-past-five," she advised.

Emily groaned, even though she'd slept for twelve hours. "Thank you." Her voice sounded husky and she was aware of a soreness in her throat. Nevertheless, she knew she daren't lie there in case she drifted off again. Rolling out of bed, she washed, brushed her hair, put on a clean dress and stockings and felt a good deal better. Emily also realised, by the way her stomach reacted to the smell of frying bacon drifting up from the kitchens, that she was extremely hungry. Lured by these aromas she found the coffee room and Adam already eating.

"How are you this morning?"

"Fine," Emily answered brightly, deciding not to mention her sore throat. Adam was concerned about her anyway, and she didn't want to heap more problems on his shoulders. Besides, it would probably clear during the day.

"It's stopped raining, so with a bit of luck we'll be in Carlisle tonight."

"What time?"

"About midnight. Then the following day we'll go by chaise to Gretna. To become man and wife at last," he murmured close to her ear then kissed her.

Chapter Twenty-four

With each passing mile the scenery grew more mountainous and spectacular: leaves turning to gold against a cobalt sky, glimpses of lakes and tarns. Emily was so awestruck by the beauty of the area that for a while she was able to disregard her pounding temples and a throat that now felt as if someone had taken a nutmeg grater to it.

But a bout of sneezing caused a woman enveloped in widow's weeds to pucker her lips in disapproval, draw out a black bordered handkerchief and flap it around the coach to shoo away the germs. "You, young lady, are obviously ailing and should be in bed," she accused. "I just trust it's not infectious, or we shall all succumb."

"I have a chill, not smallpox," Emily responded bravely. "One doesn't die from a cold." For the woman's benefit she sneezed again.

Adam glared at the widow and put an arm around Emily to protect her from the woman's hostility. "Do you feel ill, dearest?"

"No, I'm fine," Emily lied.

"It was that wretched coachman hauling us out into the pouring rain. When we reach Carlisle you must have a hot toddy, that will put you right."

Emily's ungloved left hand lay in Adam's and the widow studied it with inquisitive eyes. Ah, no wedding ring and making for Carlisle. Not difficult to calculate the next stop. Gretna Green she would guess, and about to break a mother's heart no doubt. What were the young coming to? They showed no regard for their elders these days and did exactly as they pleased. Of course it was probably the girl leading the young man astray, she looked a bit of a hussy, and cheeky with it. The widow gazed at Emily with thorough disapproval and wondered if there was anything she could do to put a spoke in her wheels. Report her suspicions to the police, perhaps, when they reached Carlisle. That is, if they reached their destination without expiring from some fatal disease. Pulling out her handkerchief again, she very pointedly held it against her face like a mask for the rest of the journey.

But Emily was past caring what the woman's opinion was of her. The day seemed interminable, she shivered and sweated by turns, her head throbbed and her nose was red as a clown's from continual blowing. Some bride she'd make tomorrow, she thought.

Emily tried to hide her deteriorating condition from Adam, but by evening there was no question of it, she was developing a fever. She drifted in and out of an uneasy sleep and was roused some time in the night by Adam shaking her. "Emily, we're here at last. Carlisle and the Bush Inn."

Her head felt as if it was stuffed with wool and Emily found it difficult to focus her thoughts, but while Adam gathered their belongings together, she made an effort to rise. As she did, faces became blurred and the coach tipped alarmingly. With a small cry she clutched the air, lost her balance and fell back on the dusty upholstery.

The widow, just stepping down from the coach, turned and eyed the prone form with an air of triumph. "What did I tell you? The fev—"

But her comments were wasted on Emily, who was

fighting not to succumb to the grey fog rapidly enveloping her.

"Oh, my God, she's fainted," Adam exclaimed, grabbing Emily's hand and rubbing it frantically.

"Inflammation of the brain, I shouldn't wonder," the widow diagnosed. "Usually fatal," she added mighty cheerfully.

"If you can't help, I'd be obliged if you'd keep your opinions to yourself, Madam," Adam snapped, but the woman's words terrified him. So far his life had been smooth sailing, the most tragic incident the death of a beloved horse. But supposing Emily did die? Then it would be the result of his selfishness, his demands. Gripped by an almost paralysing guilt, Adam tried to imagine a world without her, thought of her mother, father and brothers, their grief and the unforgiving hate that would pour from them. It would set in stone the animosity they felt towards his family and Adam decided that if Emily did pass on, he would have no choice but to end his own life too.

Strangely comforted by the idea, he gathered Emily up in his arms and hurried into the inn. Standing in the hall he called out, "Please, I need a doctor, quickly, this young lady is seriously ill."

His fraught tone brought the landlord running. The man saw Emily lying insensible in Adam's arms, realised the situation was grave and beckoned him through. "Come this way, sir, we must put the young lady to bed straight away." Then to an ostler he instructed, "Bob, go and wake Dr Jenkins out of his bed this minute. Explain that there's a young lady very ill and there's not a moment to be lost."

"And tell him I'll pay double, treble as long as he comes," Adam added recklessly, forgetting how light his purse had grown over the past few days.

Hoping amongst all this munificence there might be something for him, the ostler touched his forelock. "Right you are, sir."

"Is the young lady your wife, sir?" asked the landlord as Adam laid Emily on the bed.

Adam shook his head.

Another pair of runaways, I'll be bound, thought the innkeeper. The girl's good name already in ruins. Oh the folly of the young! Going to the door, he beckoned to a chambermaid. Then he took Adam's arm. "The maid will get her undressed. In the meantime we'll go downstairs and wait for the doctor. You'll need to explain to him how she came to be so ill."

Mr Brown, the innkeeper, was a hospitable gentleman and seeing the state Adam was in he drew him into his own private parlour and offered him a tankard of ale. But Adam refused. Instead he paced the small room with growing agitation and continuously checked the time on the grandfather clock. "When will he come, this doctor?"

Mr Brown took a sup of his ale. "Soon. That's if he's at home."

Adam swung round. "Are you saying he might not be there?"

"There is always a possibility. Dr Jenkins is a very sociable gentleman, he attends numerous functions in the town."

Adam slumped down in a chair in defeat and buried his head in his hands. "I can't bear this. If Emily should die . . ." He choked back a sob.

"Listen." The innkeeper stood up, there was the sound of hooves on cobbles, cold air shot in under the door, then a hearty voice boomed, "Where's the patient then?"

Adam tore out into the hall, almost colliding with a

large, barrel-chested gentleman in evening clothes, who Adam judged to be a little the worse for drink. However, now wasn't the time to question his competence. "This way," he answered and led the doctor up to Emily's room. It was lit by a single candle, but the fire had been kept going and the room was warm. Even across the room, Adam could hear Emily's laboured breathing, and as they entered, the young chambermaid rose and wiped the sweat from her forehead. Fearful of what he would find, Adam crept to the bed. Emily's eyes were closed and she looked so small and frail in the large bed, Adam felt ashamed of his own robust health.

"What have we here, then?" enquired the doctor, standing over the patient. He placed his hand on her forehead then, pulling out his watch, he took her pulse. "Mmm."

"What?" Adam was too young to hide his emotions and he stared at the doctor with stark terror.

"The young lady's temperature is sky-high. All we can do is wait and hope the crisis passes."

"And . . . and if it doesn't?"

"Then you'll have to send for the parson and a carpenter," the doctor answered brutally.

"No," Adam shouted out in denial, the tears welling up in his eyes. "You're a doctor, do something, please."

The doctor patted him on the back. "Stay with her, keep sponging her down with vinegar and water, and pray, that's my advice young man. Oh, and that will be one guinea please." He held out his hand, pocketed the money, then called over his shoulder as he stomped out, "I'll be back about nine tomorrow morning."

Aware of the chambermaid hovering in the background, Adam blew his nose and struggled to compose himself. "Bring me a bowl of water and vinegar and a sponge," he ordered. "Then you can go to bed."

"Yessir." The girl gave a quick bob, left the room and returned five minutes later with a jug and bowl. "The master ses, if you be wanting more, jes' help yourself in the kitchen."

"Thank you." The door clicked shut and, left to himself, Adam sat down by the bed and took Emily's hand, stroking it gently and calling her name. She continued to breath with difficulty and she twisted her head from side to side on the pillow with a jerky, feverish movement. Occasionally she would mutter a few disconnnected words, but nothing that Adam could make any sense of, not even when he pressed his ear close to her mouth. As the doctor recommended he sponged her hot skin and petitioned God with every single prayer he could remember. Adam heard the rustle of mice in the wainscotting, the clock downstairs striking two then three, and struggled to keep his eyes open. But he couldn't fight off his exhaustion, and in the end his head slumped forward on the bed and he slept.

Wrathful voices and heavy footsteps woke him. Befuddled with sleep and half-remembered dreams, and for a second not even sure where he was, Adam wrestled with his aching limbs. By gripping the back of the chair he managed to ease himself up and he was facing the door when it was flung open and Emily's father burst in the room.

"Out!" Jed thundered like Jehovah.

Adam was quailing, but he hid his fear and bravely confronted Jed. "No. Emily is ill and I'm staying with her."

Jed advanced on Adam with his clenched fist raised and a murderous expression. Just in time another figure intervened. Taking Adam's arm in a firm grip, Harry guided him to the door. "I think it might be a good idea if we went downstairs, young man, and had a serious talk."

In the coffee room Harry pushed Adam down into a chair with an angry movement and ordered breakfast. Adam looked tired, frightened and sullen, but he had no intention of sparing him. "Have you the slightest idea of the agony you've caused, with this damn-fool exploit of yours? Two mothers, both ill with worry, plus Emily's good name in tatters. If word gets out it will cause the most tremendous scandal in Leicester and do you imagine any man would consider marrying her then?"

Adam lifted his head proudly. "Emily will marry me, no one else."

Harry gave an exasperated sigh. "I doubt if you'd say that with such confidence if you knew what Jed Fairfax threatened to do to you on the way here."

"How did you find out where we were anyway?"

"Emily's note pretty well gave the game away."

"Oh. I didn't even know she'd left one, she never said."

"At least it's saved you from an even greater folly."

"No it hasn't. Once we were married no one would be able to do a thing about it," Adam shot back.

"Her father might have tried to get it annulled. He's a determined man, and you are both underage."

"Why does he hate me so? What harm have I ever done him?"

"It's not you, it's your family. Skeletons can rattle in cupboards for a long time. Joseph Pedley, your grandfather, ruined Jed's father. Your late uncle, George, tried to rape Rachel and as if that wasn't enough, he also used his cousin's simple daughter for sex. She died having Clare. Need I go on?"

"Oh God," Adam groaned. "I'd no idea."

"There is also your mother's opposition to the match. Rachel was once a serving girl in the Pedley household, a beautiful girl too," Harry reminisced. "There is no love lost between them and your mother has her heart set on you marrying into one of the grand County families."

"If I can't marry Emily then I shall remain a bachelor. But you think it's hopeless, don't you?"

It went against the grain to deprive Adam of all hope, but Harry knew he had to be honest. "Pretty hopeless, I would say."

Defeated, Adam's head dropped forward onto his hands. He could feel the tears welling up and, ashamed of revealing such an unmanly weakness, he tried valiantly to stem the flow. But for the life of him he couldn't, and they slid down his cheeks and onto the tablecloth. Had he spoilt everything? Was it really all up for Emily and him?

Watching his son, Harry felt helpless but he had to admit to a certain envy as well. There was a nobility in loving with such intensity. It was no passing fancy either, and it struck him as ludicrous that they were being punished for other people's crimes, crimes committed before they were even thought of. He would speak to Matilda when they got back, try and talk some sense into her, Harry decided. Surely she wouldn't want to see her beloved son in such a state of misery? On the journey up he'd had a taste of Fairfax's implacable nature, so he was likely to be a harder nut to crack. Pretty Rachel was much more malleable, though, and if he exerted his charm, he could probably talk her round.

A hearty tone Adam recognised as the doctor's made him look up. Pulling out a handkerchief, he blew his nose, scraped back his chair, and stood up. "That's Dr Jenkins come to see Emily. I must go to her."

"Sit down," Harry ordered, "unless you want her father to break your jaw. I'll go and find out how she is. But whatever happens, we can't stay here. I'm booking tickets for us both on the next coach out."

Harry hovered outside the bedroom door until the doctor emerged again. Jed was close behind him and Dr Jenkins turned, held out his hand for his fee and announced, "The crisis is over, your daughter will pull through, Mr Fairfax, but she must remain in bed for the next week."

"No thanks to that boy," muttered Jed grimly. "If my daughter had died . . ."

"Well she didn't." Dr Jenkins slapped Jed on the back. "Don't be too harsh on the young man. Your daughter is a lovely young woman and the boy is deeply attached to her. For love, people do wild things. They are both young and their blood is hot. Try and remember your own youth, be understanding."

"I've paid you for your medical skills, not your advice. Good day to you, Doctor." Jed turned and went back into the bedroom, and through the open door, Harry had a glimpse of Emily sitting up with a pillow behind her head. At least he had one piece of good news for Adam, thought Harry with profound relief, but as for their chances of a future together, they looked pretty bleak.

Chapter Twenty-five

Three days later Harry and Adam were back at Trent Hall. "Thank you, Harry," Matilda murmured, as her son swung down from the chaise, because from his sullen expression it looked likely Harry had put a stop to the lawless marriage. But Matilda knew it didn't do to count one's chickens, so she was already fielding questions at Harry as she ran down the steps to greet them. "Are they . . . has he . . . ?" Matilda paused, her fingers crossed behind her back.

Harry shook his head. "No."

Relief flooded through Matilda. "Thank you, Harry, I shan't forget this," she promised, then turned and embraced her son. "Oh Adam, why did you do it? Why did you try and break my heart?"

Adam's skin was pale as candlewax, the long dark lashes hiding the mutinous expression in his eyes and he stood stiff and unyielding as a toy soldier. "I still intend to marry Emily, Mother. When we are twenty-one no one can stop us."

Matilda took a step back and stamped her foot in frustrated anger at her stubborn son. "You'll live to regret it, for I shall disinherit you if you persist in this folly. That girl only wants your money."

Adam bowed insolently. "Thank you for telling me Mother. At least I know where I stand now. I'd better start thinking seriously about my future, and a career that will enable me to support a wife." He made a move towards the house. "In the meantime it will probably cause less trouble if I return to Cambridge."

Matilda watched her beloved son disappear indoors then turned to Harry. "What am I to do?" she entreated and burst into tears.

Matilda vulnerable, pleading for his help – it was a gift. Harry, ever the opportunist, tucked his arm through hers and patted her hand in an avuncular manner. "Try not to upset yourself, dear, but I do think you've got to face facts. And Adam is a determined young man." As he spoke, he drew her towards the house. "Let's talk about this inside."

In her drawing-room, Matilda, ashamed that Harry had caught her behaving like some feeble woman, wiped her eyes and poured them both a brandy. She handed Harry his and sat down on a sofa where he immediately joined her.

"You said I had to face facts. What do you mean, Harry?"

"I mean that you won't part them. I've seen the strength of Adam's love."

"Are you saying I should agree to the union?"

"If only it were that simple. But Fairfax wouldn't countenance it. I've never met such a pig-headed man in my life."

"So he thinks my son isn't good enough for his daughter?" Matilda snapped back irrationally.

"I think you must accept that it's rather more than that, Matilda. His hatred runs deep, with good cause, I think you'll have to admit. And finding Emily ill when we reached Carlisle didn't help matters."

"Why, what was wrong with her?" Matilda gazed at him in alarm, the unthinkable running through her mind. Dear Lord in heaven, she couldn't be in the family way?

Harry, who could read Matilda like a book, laughed. "Don't worry, she's not about to make you a grandmama. Our son's behaviour was beyond reproach. If he hadn't behaved like a gentleman, I can only guess what Fairfax would have done to him, deprived him of his manhood most likely. No, Emily developed a severe chill but she was on the mend by the time we left Carlisle. She's a splendid girl, you know, and it's Adam she loves, not his inheritance. She would make him an excellent wife and how many marriages do you know that are based on love?"

Matilda thought hard. "None," she admitted.

"But you would still prefer Adam to have a marriage of convenience?"

Matilda gave him a sharp look. "It's what I had, remember?"

Harry didn't respond to the remark, but he did have the grace to look uncomfortable. "Do you really intend to cut him out of your will?"

Matilda shrugged. "Maybe I spoke hastily."

"And alienated him further. Please, Matilda, don't let him go back to Cambridge with this animosity between you." While he'd been speaking Harry had edged closer to Matilda, but as soon as their thighs touched, she jumped up and went to the window. "Thank you for going all that way and bringing Adam back, I shall be eternally grateful to you."

Now's your chance to show it, he thought. "Would you like me to return tomorrow . . . perhaps in the evening? You might be in need of company."

Matilda had her back to him but Harry knew by the set of her shoulders that she was doing battle with conflicting emotions, and he willed her to say yes. But finally she turned, hands clasped nun-like in front of her. "Thank you, Harry, but I don't think that will be necessary."

Olivia had been sitting on a window seat reading and when she saw her father ride up, she threw down her book and rushed out to greet him. "Oh, Papa, where have you been?" she wailed, flinging her arms round his neck and kissing him soundly. "With Judith in Paris and Mama perpetually ailing I get so bored I could die."

Harry returned Olivia's kiss then, draping an arm round her shoulders, he pulled her away from the house. "We don't want that happening, do we?" he smiled. "Come, let's walk round the garden."

"Well, where have you been?"

"If I tell you a great secret you must promise never to breathe a word of it to a living soul, not even Judith, for it would ruin several reputations."

Olivia wriggled with excitement. "I promise, but do tell me quickly, Papa."

"I've been to Carlisle, to fetch Adam back."

Olivia paused and stared at her father. "What was he doing there?"

"He ran away with a young lady, Emily Fairfax. They planned to marry at Gretna Green. Fortunately her father and I reached them in time and prevented them from doing something they might both live to regret."

"I had no idea." Olivia found a seat and sat down heavily.

Harry standing over her, was concerned at her pallor, then, with an unpleasant jolt he saw what he had suspected: Olivia nursed a secret affection for her half-brother. Harry began to sweat, imagining the complications if the attraction had been mutual. Supposing, instead of Emily, it had been Olivia he'd had to pursue to Gretna Green? Supposing they'd made it over the border, married, consummated their union? Gazing at his daughter's pretty face, saddened by disappointment, he thought, Oh God, the sins of the fathers. One way and another, they were certainly being visited upon the next generation. There was also the possibility that Adam, frustrated in his love for Emily, might still turn to Olivia for consolation and that would be a disaster of monumental proportions, even Matilda would accept that.

Although Olivia still didn't show much interest in him, Max, Sylvia's boy, was his one hope and the hunting season started soon. Next time he was in London he would pay a call on Sylvia and try and wangle an invitation to their place in Derbyshire. If not, it looked as if another trip to Paris to visit Judith, might be on the cards.

Although she wrote to him frequently, Matilda only received one letter from Adam after he went back to Cambridge, and that was just before Christmas. "A letter at last." Matilda smiled happily at Clare, who'd called for some reading books, sent out on the carrier's cart, and broke the seal with eager fingers.

Clare watched her aunt's face as she read the letter, saw it darken, then to her astonishment she screwed it up and flung it across the room.

"What's wrong, Aunty?" asked Clare.

Matilda's lips pursed with anger. "Read it."

Clare bent to retrieve the note, smoothed it out and read the curt missive. In it Adam informed his mother that he would be spending the whole vacation in Scotland with a friend, James McBride, and therefore not to expect him home until Easter at the earliest.

"Shall I write to him?" Clare offered. "Try and make him see sense."

Matilda's expression hardened. "No, let him be. If my son chooses not to come home, so be it. He thinks he's punishing me. But I will not be browbeaten. Two years from now, he'll be thanking me for saving him from this marriage, you'll see."

Clare, who only wanted her cousin to be as happy as she was with Christopher, was puzzled by the whole business. She longed for a confidante and it would be so lovely if Emily, a kinswoman after all, could come and live in Halby. But both families were absolutely set against a marriage, although she couldn't really understand why. "Apparently Emily has never recovered fully from her illness, and the doctor treating her is quite worried," Clare informed her aunt, gathered up the books and went back to the less complicated atmosphere of school life.

But Rachel knew all right what the trouble was with her daughter, knew that she was pining for Adam, knew that her heart was slowly breaking. When she said as much to Jed, however, he dismissed it as feminine nonsense. In his opinion, Emily should buck her ideas up and get back behind the counter where she was needed.

But Emily continued to languish. She and her father were barely on speaking terms, she never went out and her mother despaired of her ever returning to full health again.

"What would be the harm in their marrying?" she asked Jed one evening when Emily was in bed. "She's a shadow of her former self. I think you'd rather see her die."

"People only die of love in novels. She's not marrying into that family. I don't want our good blood mixing with their bad blood and I can't understand why you should want it either, not after what they did to you," Jed accused.

"You've got to forgive and forget and get on with life, otherwise bitterness just rots your soul. And why should they be punished for other people's sins? It's your pride, really isn't it Jed? Stupid pride."

"It is nothing of the sort." Jed stood up. "I'm going out."

"That's right, walk away from your responsibilities," Rachel shouted after him and in a rush of fury, picked up a plate and aimed it at her husband. But it hit the wall, smashed into a hundred pieces and woke Natalie, who began to cry and had to be lifted out of her crib and comforted.

Although no one, as far as she was aware, knew about her part in the elopement, Lily had some anxious moments after the runaways' return. Deciding it would be best to keep away from the shop and its complications, she feigned sickness, although in fact she was bursting with health. Then her belly began to swell and it would have been improper to go out in society, anyway. Confined most of the time to the house, with visits only from her sisters, she knitted, sewed and pondered on why the elopement had failed and wondered if she'd ever hear the full story. But there was no one she could question. Her sisters knew nothing of the affair and she could understand Jed and Rachel keeping quiet; for certainly if word got out, it would cause a scandal of such gigantic proportions Emily's good name would be compromised and she would never be able to hold her head up again in the town. She knew Emily was unwell though, had even suggested to Marigold that next time she called she should bring the younger girl with her. However, Emily never took up the invitation and slowly the affair faded from her mind and as her pregnancy progressed, Lily's thoughts closed in on her own preoccupations and approaching motherhood.

The pains started on the third day of April and when her waters broke Lily calmly told Septimus to go and fetch her stepmother. She'd brought her, and her three sisters, into the world, and her faith in her abilities as a midwife was absolute. The labour was long, Lily had never known such excruciating pain was possible, swore she'd never have another, and she moaned and sweated through a never-ending night. But at ten past five the following morning, with a final exhausted push, her son slithered head first into the world. Her stepmother immediately placed the slippery little creature in her arms, and any memory of the pain vanished in a great tidal wave of love.

Septimus, who'd sat up all night was, to Lily's amazement, ecstatic. He gazed at the baby in wonder, touched his tiny fingers, stroked his cheek and asked, "What shall we call him dear?"

Lily gazed down at her son with a sense of pride and achievement, pretended to think about it, then said innocently, "What about Peter?"

"Master Peter Rodway, Rodway and Son." Septimus rolled the words round on his tongue. "Yes, that sounds all right." He looped his own work-calloused index finger through the baby's again. "Those are real craftsman's hands, I can tell. I bet he can't wait to get hold of a chisel."

Lily laughed, completely happy and strangely, she felt closer to Septimus that day than in all their previous months of marriage. Motherhood brought a constant stream of callers, she wallowed in the attention and the gifts she received and at the same time, marvelled at a small baby's ability to mend fences.

"Thank God it's a boy, Another girl and I'd have shot myself," her father informed her brutally, but he did slip a bag of sovereigns into his grandson's shawl. Septimus's mother was reviewing her opinion of her daughter-in-law now that she'd produced an heir and her crabby features melted into tenderness as she gazed down at Peter. Even Marigold, who although not actually being courted, was receiving some attention from a widower across the aisle in church, was less hostile towards her and positively drooled over the baby. Finally Rachel called with Emily.

Lily was dying to have a word with Emily on her own and she did finally manage a few words when Rachel took Peter outside to admire the golden drifts of daffodils Pierre had planted. "How are you? You don't look well." Lily gazed at her friend with concern.

"I'm all right, I suppose. I just feel that my life is over," Emily answered listlessly.

"Do you hear from Adam?"

Emily shook her head. "How could I? Clare told me he didn't even come home for Christmas. They are expecting him this week, though."

"Perhaps he'll come and visit me. Maybe I could arrange a meeting."

"My father acts like he's my gaoler and never lets me out of his sight. But if he does come, tell him I still love him and always will, won't you?" Emily pleaded.

Lily squeezed her friend's hand. "Of course, my dear, it's the least I can do. But don't give up hope, Adam is a determined young man and I'm sure you and he will marry one day and live happily ever after."

Adam's letter informing her that he was coming home,

provoked in Matilda a flurry of joyous activity. Their alienation had darkened her life these past few months and sent her spinning into a deep depression. But now she'd convinced herself that his return was a signal that he'd finally seen the light as far as Emily was concerned, and all would be well between them again. Although she idolized her son, Matilda had always been terrified of turning him into a Mummy's boy so she had never mollycoddled him, and their relationship had always been one of close but easy affection. She wanted that relationship back, and she was prepared to make any sacrifice to regain it.

It was almost midnight when Adam arrived. His kiss was perfunctory and he looked exhausted, although when she rang for sandwiches and coffee, he bucked up at bit and ate fairly heartily.

Matilda was careful to avoid any mention of Emily, and kept to non-controversial subjects; the estate, Cambridge and this new friend of his, James McBride, who Adam seemed happy to talk about.

"James lives in a castle and his family are enormously wealthy. The land they own would practically cover Leicestershire, but there's nothing on it but sheep."

"Has he sisters?" Matilda couldn't resist asking.

Adam gave her an exasperated look. "No, Mother, five brothers." He bit into a ham sandwich, chewed it reflectively, swallowed, then said, "Actually that's what I want to talk about. This is something of a farewell visit. I've come to say goodbye, Mother. James and I are off to America. The ship leaves from Liverpool in five days' time."

Matilda thought she might faint with shock. "But . . . but you can't."

"Oh yes I can."

"What will you do for money?" Matilda blustered.

"James has an uncle in Louisiana who owns a cotton plantation, and he's invited him out there to learn something of the business. James's father wanted him to have a travelling companion, so he has kindly paid for my ticket and we will also receive a wage for any work we do. I need to earn my living. You also said I should see the world and that's my intention, for certainly there is nothing to keep me in this country any longer."

"Oh Adam, please, please reconsider, I beg of you." Matilda was openly weeping.

"It's too late, I'm committed to going now."

"How long will you be away?"

"Two years, maybe three. America is a big country, there's money to be made out there."

"I blame that girl!" Matilda spat out.

"Please, don't bring Emily into this. Blame instead your own family for making her father hate us so." Adam stood up. "I'm going to bed now." He bent and kissed his mother on the forehead. Her eyes were puffy with weeping, middle-age was creeping into her face, and his heart lurched with pity for her. He was all she had, so was he being terribly cruel? Punishing her beyond what was justifiable? No, he wasn't, he told himself, because the only way he would maintain his own sanity was by putting an ocean between himself and Emily.

Matilda hadn't expected to sleep that night and she didn't. However she had a practical mind and by dawn she had formulated a plan. As soon as it was light enough to see, she rose, went to her writing desk, drew out paper and pen and started to write. "Dear Mr and Mrs Fairfax, after giving it considerable thought over the past few months, I have come to the conclusion that we should be considering Adam and Emily's happiness rather than old family feuds. I am prepared, therefore, to allow them to marry and I assure you I will be most happy to welcome Emily into the household as my daughter-in-law. Perhaps we could meet to discuss this. Either I could come into Leicester or you can visit me here. Please let me know by return if possible. Yours truly, Matilda Bennett."

Matilda sealed the letter, addressed it then gave it to Hodge to be delivered by hand. "And see you wait for an answer," she ordered as he drove off.

Chapter Twenty-six

Jed broke the seal on the letter, read it then handed to Rachel. "What do you make of that? Something's made madam change her tune."

"Oh Jed, let's talk about it at least. We're losing Emily and I can't stand it. If she were to . . ." Rachel didn't finish.

Jed knew in his heart that things couldn't continue as they were, his daughter alienated, his wife downright miserable. However, he did have his pride and he wouldn't be seen to be giving in easily, particularly not to someone in *that* family. "All right, we'll drive out to Halby and discuss the matter, but I'm not making any promises. And not a word of this to Emily, is that clearly understood?"

Rachel kissed her husband spontaneously for the first time in months. She smiled at him, too, and that hadn't happened in a long while. "Bless you, Jed. I'll go and tell the driver. When shall I say we're coming? This afternoon?"

Jed gave a defeated shrug. "Why not? Emily can keep an eye on the shop."

It felt strange driving along Main Street in Halby. There were so many memories; Woodbine Cottage where she'd met Jed for the first time, the horse-chestnut tree under which she'd been discovered weeping by

Harry, the church where Polly, Susan and Robert had been laid to rest. Driving up to Trent Hall, Rachel nervously adjusted the bow on her bonnet, smoothed her gloves over her fingers and tried to remember she was no longer Matilda's maidservant. Her instinct was to go round to the back of the house, like in the old days, but Jed was more confident by nature and he ran up the front steps and rang the bell. A servant showed them into the drawing-room and a moment later Matilda appeared

"Thank you for coming. Sit down," she invited and rang for tea.

Rachel tried hard to appear relaxed, as if every day she took tea with the gentry, but she just couldn't manage it, so in the end she left it to Jed to do the talking, to find out the real motive for Matilda asking them here. Her own faltering questions, she knew, would just bring that old condescending sneer to Matilda's face.

"So you've had a change of heart and now think my Emily's a suitable match for your son." Jed stirred his tea slowly. "What brought this about, if you don't mind my asking?"

"I'll be truthful with you. Adam is leaving for America in a few days' time. He'll be gone for two years, at least. In fact if he goes, I fear I might never see him again."

"I ought to have guessed it wasn't altruism that made you change your mind. This isn't for the children's sake but your own, Matilda. With my daughter as the bait." Jed slipped into using her Christian name with ease.

"I admit to self-interest, to wanting to keep him here, but it's more than that. Adam has become a stranger to me and I can't stand it."

His own relationship with Emily was in such tatters,

Jed could sympathise with her over that, but his hatred of Matilda's family still ate into him and he had no intention of letting her have her own way, just because it now suited her. Crossing his legs, Jed gazed at the far wall. "Personally I think your son should go to America. It will be the making of him and they are both far too young to be considering marriage."

Matilda's lips tightened. "I might have guessed I'd never get you to change that inflexible mind of yours, Jed Fairfax."

Rachel gazed at the pair of them in alarm and thought: Lord, that's fixed it. Daggers drawn now.

Jed raised his hand magisterially. "Before you lose your temper and say more than you should, I haven't quite finished. I'll make a bargain with you, Matilda. This separation will test the strength of their love. Adam's a handsome young man and possibly he'll be meeting other young women who will be attracted to him, he to them. However, if after two years, Adam comes back and still feels the same way about Emily, Rachel and I will be prepared to let bygones be bygones. I promise you we won't stand in the way of them marrying, will we Rachel?"

Hiding her astonishment, Rachel cleared her throat. "No, we won't." After months of bluntly refusing to even consider Adam as a suitor for Emily, then suddenly he capitulates, just like that. What an unpredictable man. "Can they see each other before Adam leaves? Will they be allowed to correspond?" asked Rachel, feeling she might as well pitch in with her own bit of bargaining while she had the opportunity.

Matilda, who realised she'd been out-manoeuvred, stared distractedly at Rachel. Her scheme had served no purpose, she was about to lose her son and on top of that, most probably she was going to find herself linked by marriage to a woman who'd once been her servant. "I suppose so. Bring your daughter over tomorrow, Mrs Fairfax, they can say their farewells then."

Adam and Emily walked through the garden hand in hand and quietly and profoundly happy.

Adam paused, kissed her then ran his fingers over the soft contours of her face. "I love you so much, little one, and I want to store every dear, sweet feature in my memory." His voice husky with emotion he held her hard against his breast. "These past months have been hell on earth for me, Emily. Even so, I never dreamed we'd be together like this, and with the blessing of our parents."

"And now you're going away." Emily gave a deep, sad sigh.

"But the two years will speed by, you'll see, then we'll have the rest of our lives together."

"Will you write to me?"

"Of course, every day, once I get to America."

"They will have a long way to come, your letters, all the way from Louisiana."

"These new railroads they're building will speed things up. And you're to answer immediately. I'll want all your news."

"I never go anywhere, whereas you'll have heaps of new experiences to write about, and you'll be meeting all those beautiful southern belles," Emily added jealously.

"I won't look at another woman, I swear it."

Emily wondered but said nothing. He would be invited to balls and parties and how could anyone as handsome as Adam not attract the attention of some rich young woman. How could he resist? At the very least there would be flirting. "When do you leave?"

"I'm catching the coach for Liverpool tomorrow. Mother is coming to see me off and to cast an eye over James to see if he's a suitable companion."

"I'll miss you so much." There was a small sob in Emily's voice.

"I know, dearest, and I'll miss you, desperately. But at least me going has brought matters to a head. Since we were forbidden to meet anyway, we'll be seeing no less of each other. It's just that there will be more miles between us." Adam looked back at the house then drew her into the walled kitchen garden. "Look, I have something for you." He took a small box from his pocket and handed it to her.

Emily opened the box and inside was a heavy gold locket engraved with her initials.

"It's lovely, thank you." She reached up and kissed Adam. "I shall wear it always. Put it on for me." She lifted her hair from the nape of her neck and Adam clipped it on. Then he bent and kissed her gently.

"There is a likeness of me inside. Look at it every day, then you'll never forget me, will you?"

Emily turned to face him, her eyes shining with love and tears. "I will never forget you, Adam, not until my dying breath."

Harry bathed, changed into fresh linen and a blue coat, newly made by his tailor, then stood back from the looking glass and studied himself with a dispassionate eye. Not bad, all things considered, not much in the way of a paunch and . . . he turned his head sideways . . . only the merest suggestion of a double chin. On the whole he felt pretty pleased with life. The affair between Adam and Emily, while not fully resolved, allowed him to feel optimistic, as long as the boy's eyes didn't wander in America, of course. From her letters it appeared that Judith was continuing to enjoy her life in France, and appeared to have no wish to return home. Sylvia and Basil's invitation had arrived, and next weekend he, Olivia and Charlotte would be going to stay at their place in Derbyshire. As well as a promise of several days good hunting, there was to be a ball for which Olivia had insisted on a new gown, and that was a good sign. Whether it was to impress Max he wasn't sure. But even if nothing came of that relationship, there would be other young men there, and Olivia had grown into a quite outstanding beauty. He'd watched her flirt, too, and suspected that his daughter, given half a chance, might be sexually wayward. There would be ample time for that sort of carry on when she was safely married, but she had to go to the altar a virgin, so he would need to keep a very close eye on her.

Harry brushed his collar, tapped his pockets to check he had everything then, humming to himself, he ran downstairs and out into the stableyard. He jumped into the trap waiting for him, ordered the horse to walk on, and was soon on the open road. Because what completed his happiness that day was the brief note in his pocket from Matilda which he could recite by heart.

"Dearest Harry," it said, "I have just arrived back from Liverpool after seeing Adam and his friend off to America. I feel desolate and lonely, so please come and keep me company this evening and stay to dinner. Yours always, Matilda."

It was an order, but one with which Harry was very happy to comply, for reading between the lines, it was more than company she was seeking. Tickling the horse's back with the whip, and whistling happily, Harry trotted off in the direction of Halby and, he sincerely hoped, a delightful night of pleasure in Matilda's arms.